MYSTERY OF THE CHARRED BONES

THE DAISY DAY MYSTERIES
BOOK TWO

K.D. UPTON

IM²

ISBN e-book: 978-1-956954-91-3

ISBN print: 978-1-956954-02-9

❀ Created with Vellum

For the mystery lover... Thanks for reading.

CHAPTER 1

The cases brought nothing but misery and pain. Worse? They were connected. They had to be. What with the flurry of intercepted encrypted messages, the bones in Boston now topped the list of items to steal, and from Anice's movements, they held significance to the ones uncovered in Scotland. But how? Worst of all, Didi was caught in the middle yet again. That woman had unknowingly gotten herself into a world of danger, but hopefully she was safe for now.

The blast of air that broke through the blazer made me wish I was back on a tropical island, sipping Mai Tais and taking beachside naps, but alas, that wasn't on the menu. Nope, my hunch was Anice was preparing to attack stateside, but how was I to warn Didi? She'd barely made it back, and from her sleepless nights and constant lock checking, she wasn't up for yet another note from me. But how long could I keep her out of it? Probably two days max, but maybe that was enough time to glean more information before I left yet another message on her doorstep.

The honk of the horn jolted me out of my thoughts just in time for a wave of muddy water that sprang forth and drenched my trousers and loafers. Ah… Boston. Nothing quite like it. The people, the food, the weather…but reminiscing must wait. The redhead hurried into a rundown pawn shop with a white linen bag in tow, and that meant one thing. She was low on cash, or she was using a stooge for something distasteful. Either way, she was getting sloppy. Luckily, a big city meant it was easy to tail, and before the next wave of blaring car horns, I'd crossed the street and hid from behind dark sunglasses and a Boston Red Sox cap, blending in like another part of the whirling city streets, nose deep in my cell phone. I'd snuck a few photos, acting the tourist, and zoomed in. The redheaded woman who'd entered the pawnshop a minute ago had wrangled a cartouche out of the sack, revealing a tattoo on her inside wrist.

Wait.

I zoomed in further, studying the design. A serpent practically swallowed up by a bunch of purple flowers. That wasn't all. A knot of fear lodged somewhere between alarm and all out panic. I snapped a few more shots. The woman raised her hands and shook the cartouche, but the salesman failed to express any fear or worry. His expression remained fixed and calm. I failed to get a frontal shot, and without one, I couldn't be sure if it was truly Anice or not. The red hair was definitely a wig. A few strands of dark brown or black stuck against the nape of her neck when she'd bowed her head to inspect something else the salesman had brought out. She'd picked up a magnifying glass. But it was the next picture that nearly stopped my heart.

I flattened like a pancake against the brick wall beside the store window, the color drained from my face. How could this be? When did she get those?

I rushed into the road, slamming my fists against the car hood that almost smashed into me. Epithets flew out of the pepper-haired driver along with a few hand gestures, but I was off, running down the bustling sidewalks, past store fronts unlocking their doors and raising their gates for customers to flow in. On I pushed, winding through this street and that until I'd zigzagged back to the cockroach-infested room I'd rented for the next week. I bolted up the stairs until reaching the sixth floor, and upon nearing my door, I plucked out the key when I froze. Broken glass crunched under my boot.

They had found me. It was a trap.

CHAPTER 2

I stepped in front of Christof, blocking him from entering the apartment. He reached for my face, but stopped cold when I flinched, dropping his hand beside him.

"I don't want to argue."

"Daisy..."

I noticed the stubble around his jawline, the pinched lines on his forehead and the corners of his eyes. He hadn't slept. The strain of the past couple of days showed. On the long flight home from Scotland, the trip from Hades, I'd listened to his stern warnings about this being the last time. I'd worried him enough. Didn't the near-death experience, leaving me laid up in a hospital bed, convince me to give it up? He'd been desperate. Afraid.

However, the scene that kept flashing before me wasn't the charismatic, successful lawyer act he wore like a trophy. Hair gelled and sculpted into the latest fashion, face smooth-shaven, gold cuff links sparkling in the light, wearing his navy suit—he was fresh for another day at the office. Never mind it was a Sunday. He looked marvelous. Too much so. Even my noisy neighbor across the hall had cracked her door open to get a full view of him. He radiated confidence. What male or female could resist him?

I folded my arms around my waist and gripped my t-shirt with both hands. The shattered vase he'd thrown across the hospital room was all too vivid. He'd never expressed anger this way before. Rage shone in his eyes that night.

I peered down at my painted pink toenails. My older sister Laura had left a half hour before, and I couldn't wait to take off my shoes and feel the carpet scrunch between my toes. I'd intended on a hot shower and some food, then I'd gotten Christof's call and everything was postponed. Like usual.

"Now's not a good time, Chris. I haven't even unpacked."

Christof tugged his collar. I reached behind me for the door handle, ready to slam it in his face if need be. The last several days were enough to turn my hair white, and while I yearned for sleep, my mind refused to shut down. It was as if a vat of espresso had been hooked up to my veins and constantly refilled. I was jittery and distrustful, but almost dying did that to a person. Or so I imagined. First, there was Dr. Pinnick's murder, then the discovery of a millennium—a shield maiden's tomb—which, on any other occasion would be cause for celebration. Excitement warped into horror when my nephew Nick was kidnapped. Add on the other deaths, plus the visions I kept having, and it was all simply too much.

"I'm sorry." His voice cracked. He clenched his fists. "Didi, I'm sorry. Please..." He stepped backward, his mouth pinched. "Can we try again?"

He wrapped his fingers around a lock of my hair. When I flinched, he dropped his arms by his sides. "I can't take back what I said or how I acted, but please... please don't do this. Let's start over. Remember what it was like in college? That first time I saw you, ugh... I haven't spoken about this before, but I was a mess that day, Didi. My heart was in tatters. For all intents and purposes, I was dead inside. Then... then I saw you. You were with a group of girls walking into the cafe." He closed his eyes for a second. Opening them, he stepped forward in earnest. "It had been raining. Do you remember?" A million miles away, he grinned as his eyes glazed over. "A downpour. We got soaked and Brady raided the cafeteria napkins trying to get us dry. But the second I set eyes on you..." He refocused on me and grasped my arms. "... the gloom departed. It was like someone had poured a bucket of ice-cold water over my head, and everything wrong seemed right again."

Chris drew me closer. Around his mouth danced a lighthearted smile.

I, too, was transported to those very first days. The wonder. The lust. The scene played itself out in my mind's eye. Brady was Christof's best friend in those days, and they were practically glued at the hip. That should have been a clue for me to tuck tail and run for the hills, but I was too broken to notice. Though my parents' deaths had happened years before, the void they left swallowed up any light that entered my stratosphere. But that day, the day I met Christof, changed everything. For better or worse, he'd awakened something in me. A brightness. The stench of death slid away, and life had been restored.

I snorted. "And you call *me* dramatic."

"You kind of are, but it's endearing."

He rubbed his thumbs against my arms. In the end, I gave in and rested my cheek against his chest. A whiff of brandy clung to his clothes, and the scene from the plane resurfaced. I tensed. He'd upgraded us to first class on the flight from Scotland to Boston, and the perky attendant hovered nearby, refilling his glass the second the last drop hit his tongue. I noticed the lingering looks, the quick brushes against him. Sure, they blamed the turbulence, but we'd flown through clear skies, and not once did the plane waver.

I stiffened and stepped backward. "We do need to talk, but I'm not in the right headspace for it now. With Dr. Pinnick's antiquities find in Scotland, my nephew's abduction because of it, and some lunatic woman that tried to kill me, I'm spent."

He placed his finger on my lips. "I respect that. I'll leave, but first, would you accompany me to Derrick's party?"

I sighed, turned, and stomped off toward my wine refrigerator.

"It's tomorrow night," he continued. "He's passed his boards. We're throwing him a party and everyone will be there. We can talk after if you'd like."

"Chris... gosh, I don't know." His doe-like eyes pleaded and cajoled from across the room while I went about pouring a glass of red. Not wine, just cranberry juice. While I sipped wine occasionally, it fuddled my brain, and I liked control of my faculties. Needed it, in fact. Especially these days. Where wine bottles once sat in my special refrigerator, I'd stocked it full of fresh juices. "I need to get settled here and then there's work. Who knows how long I'll be there tomorrow. Besides, there's next semester's classes to prepare for, books to review, and lots of meetings at the university. On top of that, this whole Scotland thing is hanging over my head and—"

The buzz in my pocket rescued me from blathering on with excuse after excuse.

"Um, I've got to take this." I pressed the cell to my ear, though not before I caught the flash of anger on Christof's handsome face.

"What's up?" I answered.

"*Nothing like a warm welcome.*" Mose's silky-smooth voice reached across the void of jet lag, tension, and uneasiness I was currently swimming in. "*Let me guess... Chris is there.*"

"Don't."

"*What? You're about as warm as an arctic night without thermal underwear. The only time you act this way is when that behemoth is around.*"

"Not funny," I warned, keeping my voice low.

"*But I'm right, yes?*"

"Mose, the days are blending. I'm still on Scotland time, my eyes feel like sandpaper, and I'm craving my bed. Can we skip the bashing for once?"

"Hold on..." Chris's voice was icy. "Mose is on the phone?"

Chris and I met in college when Mose was a teacher's assistant in one of my intro anthropology courses. He was tall then, lanky, with long, shaggy black hair, large-rimmed glasses, and a pen protector. Chris never wasted a chance at taunting him, making "fun" as he'd say. Mose never fled from such taunts though. He'd answer the incessant challenges head-on from religion, politics, and even history, which

Mose excelled at. But it never failed. When Chris tired of harassing him, Mose eventually left, head slumped, a crestfallen shadow on his otherwise smooth complexion. These days, barely a trace existed of the awkward young man trying to prove himself. Gone were the ugly glasses, replaced with contacts, and his shaggy hair was now trimmed and slicked back, much to his students' delight. He'd grown tired of Christof's superior attitude and had matured into a confident, intelligent, handsome man, which bugged Chris to no end.

I whirled around and saw Chris head for the door.

"Wait!" I hustled around the couch, avoiding a small table, and cut him off, splaying my arms wide just before he reached the door handle. "What is it with you two, anyway? Why are you both gunning for the other?"

When Chris failed to reply, I held the phone back up to my ear. "What's your excuse, Mose? Why all the hostility?" Nothing but silence. "Jeez, the testosterone in here is enough to choke anyone. Goodbye, Mose. We'll talk tomorrow."

I hung up and stared at Chris. These two men, by my side for the last ten years, had never seen eye to eye. I was done with their petty battles. But Chris's smirk dared me to speak. I inhaled and blew out a breath, ready for the onslaught, when a soft rap on the door halted the confrontation.

When I cracked the door open, I dropped my head and cursed.

"What?" Chris asked, inching to see around me. "Who is it?"

Mose pushed the door open and stepped inside.

"Surprise!" He folded his arms around me and picked me off the ground, swinging me in a circle. When he placed me down, I adjusted my top and grinned. I couldn't stay angry with him, and with the murders and discoveries in Scotland, he was the first person I'd longed to see even if I'd just hung up on him.

"Why are you here?" I heartily punched his arm, and like always, he feigned distress. "Funny, Mosewan, but I'm not buying it."

"No?" His eyes sparkled mischief. "Then would you buy... let's say, a box of charred bones? From Denmark?"

I noted Christof's stiff frown. Mose continued ignoring Christof's presence, and to his credit, Chris remained quiet, which was a good sign.

"Era?"

Mose hesitated. A broad grin fixed his sun-kissed complexion. "Viking."

I rubbed my brow, my heart fluttering a million beats per minute. "Are...Are you sure?"

Perspiration broke out on my forehead, bile rose into my mouth, and I gagged. The room suddenly tilted. Knees rubbery, I reached for the first thing to steady me, the couch, but fell into Christof's arms.

"What's wrong?" Mose bounded forward but halted when he caught sight of Christof's venomous glare. "I thought you'd be excited."

"Yes, I am, but—"

A man with a long, groomed beard dressed in antiquated clothing materialized beside Mose and boldly stared back at me. He was not see through either; a solid form standing an inch taller than Mose. I waggled a finger in his direction but failed to utter anything coherent.

"Didi, are you unwell?" Christof's voice sounded muddled, like it was coming through a wind tunnel. He wrapped his arms around my waist and pressed me to him, all the while repeating questions I failed to comprehend. Mose loped off to get something, maybe water, but it was all gibberish except for the man who'd locked his gaze onto mine.

I feebly pushed against Christof's chest, pointing a shaky finger at the man, wondering why they had not acknowledged him. Those piercing blue eyes drank me in, and his hard countenance softened. Toned arms fit into white linen sleeves while he held a hand aloft a richly decorated sword hilt. With one step toward him, my mouth dropped open, but I remained speechless. Young and warriorlike from head to toes, he was an anachronism. He wore a bright blue tunic decorated with silver and gold threads in various patterns and white linen sleeves. He kept a curious focus on me, almost as if deciphering a friend from a foe. What was I?

Mose returned with a glass of water, blocking my view, but I waved him off, craning my neck to see the man.

"Who are you?" I blurted, subsequently recovering my voice.

The twenty-something warrior remained mute. His gaze dropped to my neck. Instinctively, I laid my fingertips against the pendant resting there, but within a blink of an eye, he vanished.

"What just happened?" I reached an unsteady hand toward Mose. Stepping forward, my fingers rifled through thick air where moments before the man had stood. "Who was he? Didn't you see him?"

"Didi? Are you alright?" Mose's golden-brown forehead pinched together in concern. He took my arm, flopping through the air beside him, and placed my hand between his two warm palms. I fleetingly looked at him, a protest on my lips.

"She's tired, Mosewan. She'll be fine. Probably jetlag." Christof draped his hand around my waist and tugged me free, guiding me toward the bedroom before I snapped back to reality.

"No." I shook free of his grasp and folded my arms. "I'm fine. Honest." How could they have missed him? First Hulda, and now this...

"Yeah, well," Mose countered, "a moment ago, you asked me who I was. Why don't you sit and sip some water?"

"I'm fine, Mose. It's nothing. I just... well..." I had to think of something and fast, but what? "It's that I remembered something... um, uh, you know... about the shield I inspected in Scotland."

"Right." Mose handed me the water glass. Like most people, he had a tell. He never challenged me. He stuffed his hands into his pockets. "Why don't we leave you alone so you can rest? Chris?"

Mose walked toward the door but Christof's snort had Mosewan spinning in his tracks. I didn't have the energy to stop them from hashing it out in my tiny apartment. From the hours on the plane to the harrowing escapes in Scotland, I'd had all I could handle. I placed a clammy hand against my forehead and sighed, bracing for the worst and half wishing the mystery man would appear and stop all this nonsense.

"She's my girlfriend, Mosewan. I have no intention of leaving. Clearly, she needs someone to look after her, or are you blinded by your unsung love for my girlfriend?"

"Now's not the time," I half-heartedly interjected, but a dark cloud of anger swirled about Mose's head, pitting his black eyebrows together.

"Again with this nonsense," spat Mose. "Take the highroad, my friend. She doesn't need this. Not now."

Christof wagged a finger at Mose. "Let's get something straight, Mosewan. I assume from your Egyptian lineage that angles and measurements won't be too hard of a stretch. I'm not your friend. Never have been, never will be."

"Whoa." I stepped between Mose's advancing form and held up my palms in surrender toward Chris. "That's uncalled for. Since when do you attack someone's ancestry?"

"Since always," Mose barked.

"This ends." I pointedly stared at Christof, hoping for a shred of the person I'd met all those years ago. The man I'd fallen in love with. "Now, Christof"

Chris pinched the bridge of his nose and exhaled measuredly. "Didi, you've got too many men in your life. It's time to clean house."

A hot flush spread across my face and neck. "What the hell are you implying?"

Chris, voice devoid of emotion, continued. "As if you don't know. That man," he jabbed a finger at Mose still standing behind me, "has been pining after you since day one. It's all anyone ever talked about at school. Geez, Didi, it's all anyone at the firm talks about. It's a freaking joke. Why can't you see it?"

"That's not true." Mose's voice was steady but low.

I swallowed back the dry lump of dread forming in my throat and felt the burning hot liquid swelling within my eyes, clouding my vision.

How did we get here? Why was this happening now, of all times? I dropped my hands to my sides and headed for the kitchen, turning my back on them both. Maybe it was Christof's tone, or the way he'd shown up on my doorstep after we'd left the airport on uneasy terms, or maybe it was the way he'd always "handled" the situations of my life. Whatever it was, I chose to walk away.

"Go ahead, you two. Get it out. Whatever this is between you both needs to end here."

I hopped onto the barstool at the kitchen counter and swiveled on my backside to face them. They each regarded me curiously. I wasn't mediating between them anymore. This time I was staying out of their macho crap fest.

Chris crossed his arms, chin thrust forward, ready and determined. He never lost an argument. A smirk marred his otherwise handsome features. It was almost like he was enjoying this.

"Chris let's get something straight. I don't have feelings for your woman. I'm dating someone and have been for some time. Why must you always bring this up every chance you get? It's a button you press too often with Didi. Yes, she caves. It's obvious what you're doing."

"What's that?"

"Control, counselor."

Chris rolled his eyes. "Funny. Who's been controlling the narrative since Daisy and I first started dating, huh? All those times you poisoned her with lies about me seeing other women or flirting with my female colleagues? What was that if not to undermine our relationship? You're just jealous that a better man won."

"Hold up," I interjected, raising a finger, ignoring the "won" part of the argument. "Did you read my texts? Are you kidding me?"

Chris glanced at me and then looked away. His ears glowed red.

"Answer me, Christof. Did you or did you not read my text messages?" It was the only conclusion. The women, the affairs... he'd done it all. But in my need to keep the fairytale afloat, I ignored them. Mose refused to let me bury my head in the sand and confronted me each time he'd witnessed Chris with another woman. He'd sent the evidence by text.

"What? Lost your tongue, counselor?" spouted Mose.

I glared at my best friend. "Enough, Mosewan. Chris, please tell me you haven't been reading my texts."

Christof stood straight, tugging at his cuffs. He tilted his head to the right and then the left. A series of audible cracks from his neck stood my hairs on end.

"Why?" I searched his face in vain.

"He's nothing but a control freak, bordering on obsessive," Mose mumbled.

"I'll splatter your brains all over the street!" spewed Christof. "But I bet I won't have to. No, I think you're all talk and no action. If I were you I'd keep it shut and stay the hell out of my way. Oh, and Didi?" He jabbed a finger in my direction. "If I ever see you near her again I'll kill you. Painfully."

"Wait." I hopped off the stool, marched forward, and held up a hand for each man. Chris stepped into it, and his heart thumped against my palm. "This has gotten out of control. Mose, I'll call you later."

"But—" he protested.

"No buts. Later."

I refused to look at Mosewan. Keeping glued to Christof's twitching jaw muscles, I heard the door softly close behind Mose's padded footsteps. Even in anger and defeat, he walked lighter than a cat hunting its prey. "Chris, Mose is a friend. A great friend. My best friend. No matter how insecure you are, that will never change. You can't tell me who I can and cannot see. As for reading my *private* messages, that stops now."

"Daisy, that man—"

"Is my best friend, Christof, and the sooner you realize that the better off we'll be. Don't go around threatening people."

The inferno within Chris' eyes cooled. "So we're not over? You're not leaving me?"

He laid his warm hand over mine still resting on his chest and peered down at me. He traced a finger from my jaw down to my pendant, fondling it.

My back stiffened. "I never said we were definitively over, Chris."

"It sounded like it in Scotland. That Scottish brute refused me entry into your hospital room, Didi. I can only assume you approved that."

"That Scottish brute is a police detective." I shut my eyes and inhaled before continuing. "Why shouldn't I? I've never seen you so...

so… uncontrolled. When you smashed that glass against the wall, that was it, Chris."

He grunted and dropped his hands from my body, stepping back. He ran his hands over his face, holding them against his mouth while he searched me for… what?

"Right," he said after a while, striding toward the door. "Let me know if you want to come to Derrick's party, Didi, but don't take too long." He stopped and turned at the last second. An icy coldness darkened his otherwise milky brown eyes. "I won't wait around forever."

My eyebrows arched upwards. "Chris… I… you're overreacting."

"Am I? I don't think so. Text my assistant your answer. If I don't hear from you in the next few hours, I'll find myself another date."

With that, he stormed out, not even stopping to shut the door.

CHAPTER 3

A hot, ashy smell smacked me in the face when I plodded over
to shut the door. The lingering scent of garlic and tomato
sauce made my stomach growl in protest.

How long had it been since I'd eaten?

Twenty-four? Ugh, my sister would flatten me if she'd found out,
though I wasn't about to tell her. Being a grumpy new mom thanks to
a precious bundle of joy, she snapped everyone's head off these days,
regardless of the request. Ever since she and her husband brought
home their adopted infant, neither had gotten much sleep. Although,
from what my nephew Nick had mentioned, Laura's husband hadn't
been home most nights. He'd slept over at his office claiming a heavy
workload, but a part of me wondered if it wasn't all roses and
lollipops between them. For her part, Laura hadn't complained about
it, but the dark circles under her eyes, the stained shirts she wore
around, plus the lack of showers, spoke of a woman teetering on a
serious breakdown. Yet the baby was a gift, and she treasured her.

Laura had tried for years to have another baby after Nick, and at
first, she and her husband wrote it off to stress. After a few years, it
became, "It's not the right time." That attitude faded into the background while Laura kept working her surgical shifts, burying herself

in work. Soon, the cracks in her marriage were too obvious to ignore, and her relationship with her sixteen (almost seventeen) year old son, Nick, was gone.

That's why I'd offered to take Nick with me to Scotland for the summer. He'd tag along to a dig site and spend some time with his favorite aunt. His only aunt. Plus, he was on the brink of manhood, and he hungered to break free of his mother's yoke, especially since they'd gotten the call Laura had been waiting for since Nick had turned two. I guess it didn't help that I'd nearly gotten Nick killed. Although it wasn't my fault, it would take some time to truly convince myself of that.

I rubbed my eyes and stifled a yawn. Grabbing the foot-high stack of takeout menus sitting on the counter beside the refrigerator, I trudged to the couch and turned on the television. Rifling through the stack, I settled on pizza and ordered. Since it would take an hour, I opened a bottle of the rare red wine I saved for just such an occasion, poured a generous helping in a wine glass, and sat down again, turning up the TV volume. Blue lights flashed across the screen, highlighting the fresh face of the newest journalist reporting on the latest scoop:

"...ports of shots fired in front of Harvard Peabody Museum of Archaeology and Ethnology in Cambridge today. A few witnesses reported a black SUV leaving the scene of the crime, hitting a pedestrian. That individual is in critical but stable condition, but few other details have been offered. The police chief states it's a fluid situation, and we'll report as soon as we hear anything. In other news, rare jewelry was stolen from..."

I tossed the remote onto the couch, dug out my cell phone from my pocket, and dialed.

"I assume you've heard the news reports, my dear." Dr. Gates' usual jolly voice was somber and guarded. *"Why not get some rest? We can discuss this tomorrow at work."*

I plowed ahead, my thoughts all jumbled together. "Isn't that where your friend works?"

The audible sigh told me everything I needed to know. "Tell me."

"Didi, we don't even know if it's connected."

With a calmness that surprised me I said, "Spill it."

"At around noon, three people walked into Roger's office. One demanded the contents of a certain box. At first he was confused, because they specialize in Native American and Mesoamerican collections. When he tried to tell them that they had the wrong place, two men dressed in black suits and sunglasses brandished guns."

I gasped, not wanting him to finish. "Oh, Dr. Gates..."

"His wife phoned a while ago. He's on life support with a poor prognosis."

"How did you get all this information?"

"Roger's notorious for taping all his meetings. Don't mention this to anyone, but his memory isn't the same as it used to be. Anyway, his wife, Moira, remembered this, and the police found the recording. It's awful, Didi."

"Is someone with Moira?"

"Yes, her eldest son is staying with her for the time being, and the police have a security detail outside her home just in case, but again, we don't know if this is connected."

"You keep saying that. Wait." I fingered the pendant that had brought so much attention from the warrior ghost's vision I'd seen earlier. It had been a gift from my mom on my twelfth birthday. Someone had broken it because the clasp wouldn't open. Still, it was a beautiful pendant and one that I never took off. It was like my parents were still with me, and I needed all the comfort I could get right now. "Is Roger the one who analyzed the shield of the suspected shield maiden?"

A long pause followed. *"The very one. What's even stranger is that he'd drawn a letter in his own blood on the office floor. It was an "s.""*

Goosebumps dimpled my skin. "But they're not connected?" I hmphed. "Until otherwise, we'll assume they are. First Dr. Pinnick, and now Dr. Phillips. Besides, J mentioned Anice escaping on some boat headed for Spain. It gives her plenty of time to travel here."

I sank into the couch, resting my head against the cushion, and closed my eyes.

"Didi, my dear, I assume by your statement that you mean the mystery man leaving you notes and packages, and while he may be correct, we must

wait until the police say otherwise and consider this to be a coincidence. Borrowing trouble is not worth wasting energy on."

I sat up straight. "But the police don't know about Scotland. They aren't aware of the shield... that it holds the key to turn the anthropological world on its proverbial head, nor do they probably care. Dr. Gates, did Moira mention if one perpetrator was a female?"

My pulse slammed like a bongo within my ears. "There was, wasn't there?" I whispered.

"Didi—"

"That means she's here. She's in Boston." I drew my legs up to my chest and rested my chin upon my knees. The room was suddenly chilly in the dead of summer. "What does she want? How did she get out of the psychiatric hospital?"

"No idea. But have you considered that perhaps it's not her? Maybe this J person isn't the man you think he is. Have you considered that he's in on it too? Why didn't he rescue you in Scotland, and for heaven's sake, why hasn't he shown himself?" Dr. Gates huffed. *"Anyway, it's only a thought. The best thing you can do is rest and stop investigating this. You'll do no one any good dead. Get some rest, and I'll see you tomorrow. First thing, young lady. We've got those runes to discuss. Roger... let's talk about it in the morning. Good night, Didi."*

"'Night."

When the phone went silent, I kept it to my ear for several more minutes. The thought of Anice running around Boston toting a gun, let alone with two henchmen in tow, left little doubt how much sleep I'd get. No, rest would have to wait. The people I loved were now in the sight line of a crazy woman or someone linked to her. But how did she get out of the psychiatric ward? Why was she still hunting down information on the shield? It wasn't like Roger Phillips had it.

I checked my watch, imagining the auburn-haired man sitting in his unbuttoned white shirt, tie askew, drinking his evening cup of coffee. And then I was dialing.

CHAPTER 4

"*I*'d say I'm flattered, but somehow I don't think this is a personal call."

His thick Scottish brogue calmed my racing pulse and was a distraction from the image of Dr. Roger Phillips clinging to life and unconscious in a Boston hospital. I shook off the dark boding. No need to alarm Callum. Not yet.

"Good evening, Detective. I'm calling to check in on how Anice Foster is doing. I suspect she's been a handful."

If what the mystery man J said was true, Callum would know, and it would put some of my fears to rest.

"*Ah, Mrs. Anice Foster. Of course... she's safely tucked away in her wee corner somewhere, sleeping with the fairies, I suppose. But the bigger question is why you're asking. You, lassie, don't strike me as someone who wastes words or thoughts on trivial matters.*"

"It's not *not* trivial, is it? I'm merely asking about her welfare."

I took a sip of the wine, blinking back tears from the unexpected burn of the alcohol down my throat.

"*Alright, I'll play. As we speak, Mrs. Foster is tranquilized in an Edinburgh psychiatric ward, likely dreaming of haggis and scotch.*"

"You're sure?"

"Quite sure. Now why don't you tell me what's got your knickers in a bunch?"

Huh. Was Dr. Gates ultimately right? Was this J person sent to throw me off? According to Callum, Anice was safely locked away, but the uneasy feeling stuck, refusing to budge. I likened it to electricity. A warming hum always present underneath my skin. It was a warning system of sorts built in from birth, and it was presently flowing like lava. So much so that if I were to come close to a metal object, a lightning bolt would surely arc from me to it. However, if Callum was certain she was locked up, then I needed to leave it alone for the time being.

I swirled the red wine in the glass. The waves lingered on the part near the rim. For a moment, some molecules of it stuck near the top. I studied the rings forming and then slipping down, only to reappear with the next swirl. It was like an illusion or lingering past that kept returning. An imprint.

"Callum… do you believe in ghosts?"

"I do. We've discussed this before."

I stopped swirling. "When?"

"In the hospital. You mentioned something about seeing one."

"That's all kind of blurry. Anyway, what can you tell me about them? Have you experienced any?"

"Nae, I don't have second-sight like Bonnie-Jean, lassie, but I have seen… things."

I held the wine glass up to the light and swirled, focused on the lines left on the glass after each twirl. Bonnie-Jean. The sweetest, white-haired Scottish woman I'd met. She had second sight. She'd warned me when I arrived in Kirkwall, and again in the nave of St. Magnus Cathedral where Nick was held hostage and I'd nearly lost my life if not for a warrior ghost woman named Hulda.

"What about imprints?"

"Imprints? As in fingerprints?"

"No." I shook my head and grasped for a better way of explaining it. "Okay, let's say someone was attached to an object during their lifetime. Like really, *really* attached. It brought some meaning to them. So much so that when they died a part of them stayed with it."

"*Ah, yes, imprinting of the soul, right?*"

"Yes." I licked my lips and felt the heat rise in my face.

"*Uh... I suppose it could happen, but why are you asking? Have you had another vision?*"

"Yes... no... I don't know." I sounded nuts. "Earlier, when Mose and Christof were over, I saw this, um... image, no, it was more like a vision. To be honest, it was probably a ghost. Yep. It was definitely a ghost."

An audible intake of breath crackled on the line. "*Did they speak to you?*"

I thought back to that unreal moment, how shocked and shaken I'd been. "No, he didn't say a word."

"*He? A man or boy?*"

"A grown man. He had a long, groomed beard, and he was wearing this anachronistic clothing."

"*So not from modern time?*"

"Definitely not."

"*What else? Describe his clothing.*"

Luckily, he wasn't ridiculing me or insisting I have a psychiatric evaluation like most people in my life would have. Trauma did funny things to people, but I was certain of my sanity. I was seeing things. People. But their significance was still murky.

"He wore a blue tunic with holes cut through for his white linen sleeves. On the tunic were patterns made from what appeared to be gold and silver threading. His pants, uh, they were linen, but they didn't go past his knees. So, I'd say he was from..."

I hesitated. On the one hand, I knew what' I'd seen, and being a doctor of anthropology, the facts lined up. On the other hand, I'd witnessed a ghost, an apparition of sorts, which didn't fall into the category of rational with some people. I was unsure if he'd believe it or if he was humoring me, which made it even more confusing.

"*Where?*" prompted Callum.

"Oh, uh, he was old Norse."

Silence. *"Are you sure he was real?"*

"Of course he was real. Anyway, it was odd. It felt like I'd known him for years. Like I'd seen him before, but that's crazy."

However I tried explaining it, it sounded insane. I didn't want Callum thinking I'd lost my marbles.

"Okay, even to me this sounds bizarre," I rambled on, "but I know what I saw. There was a Viking man in my apartment, standing next to Mose. It was clear as day, and *no*, he wasn't transparent. That man was as real as you or me."

"Was he menacing?"

"Ugh, I don't know. Definitely intense, but he wasn't talkative."

"How long was he visible?"

"A few seconds. Long enough to look at my pendant, and then poof, he was gone."

"Your pendant? Describe it, lass."

I held it away from my chest and looked down at it. It was given to me a long time ago by my parents. The thought of losing it was too much to bear. It was the only thing I had left of them.

"Nothing extraordinary. Not to other people. To me, it's priceless. It's got eight tridents pointed outward. An old Norse symbol meant to guide people so they wouldn't get lost. My parents gave it to me shortly before they died." I remembered that special day. "They said that no matter what happened we'd always be together. I suppose my father got it from some shop on one of his many travels with Mom."

"When the man saw it, he vanished?"

"Yes, but not before he stared at it for a while. Why?"

"I don't understand its significance, but that ghost appeared for a reason. That pendant holds some importance. Until you find out, keep it close."

I rubbed the familiar object between my fingers. "Don't worry, this thing never leaves my neck."

"Well, it's late, lassie. Sleep calls."

"Oh, sorry. Have a good night, and Callum?"

"Yes?"

"Thanks."

When I hung up, I clutched the pendant in my palm before taking it off and replacing it in the tiny locked safe on my nightstand. Disguised as a book of Shakespeare, it even had pages in it. Any would-be robber would likely overlook it.

Bright sun rays shone through the bedroom blinds, and the shadows crept toward me for hours until the last peep of light flickered out. Darkness had come, and I was alone for the first time in ages, save for the blackness swirled images of Hulda and the Danish charred bones. Were the bones related to the robbery at the museum? And was Anice truly locked away in a psychiatric hold in Edinburgh, Scotland, or was she haunting the streets I called home?

The Viking man's appearance left me stumped. What was his purpose?

Eventually, sleep overcame my befuddled mind, and once again I was frolicking by the bluest of lakes hemmed in by the most magnificent mountains. My very blood called to this place; the place I'd first seen Hulda traipsing through the green grass. A ghost in her own right. The very one who'd saved me from certain death by Anice in the underground tunnels of St. Magnus Cathedral in Kirkwall, Scotland. As I ran my fingers through the greenest patches of grass and dipped my toes in the coolest of water, the faintest of sounds called from behind.

I whipped around, searching. Nothing except for the awe-inspiring fjords. I was entirely alone.

The salty air delighted my exposed skin, and I relaxed, breathing in the ocean, wet earth, and sweet summer, when upon the wings of the wind a haunting male voice faintly called out a familiar name.

"Hulda. Find me."

CHAPTER 5

*W*hen the alarm went off, I blindly slapped at the nightstand until I hit the off button. Rolling over, I stretched against the soft pillows, extending my arms way overhead, when something crinkly brushed against my skin. I twisted around like a beached whale to stare down at a handwritten note neatly folded and lying next to me on the white pillow.

"What the...?"

I warily scanned the room, half expecting someone to bolt out from behind the curtains, but nothing was amiss. No sign of human, feline, or canine. Besides the cracked door, all appeared as it had prior to me falling asleep.

I rubbed my bleary eyes and stared at the note. How did it get there? After a second fleeting sweep of the room, I picked it up with an unsteady hand and ripped it open. The unfamiliar script leapt up from the page. After the first few words, I slumped against my pillows and placed a hand over my thudding heart.

Mystery guy was at it again. But why was his handwriting so different?

I scratched my forehead and kept reading.

She's secure. For how long is anyone's guess. Others are involved, but I can't tell you more right now because the walls have eyes. She's highly connected, but you already know that. Be careful. Stay close to your friends and family. By the way, you're not fooling anyone. Those dark circles under your eyes are a dead giveaway. Sorry we can't meet. Not yet. But soon. Until next time, stay safe and trust no one.

P.S. I injured my hand. Sorry about the writing.

Ever yours,

J

I let the note flutter to the bed. So, the mystery man was still around. Watching me in my sleep? A little creepy, sure, but in a way, it was comforting.

"Trust no one," he'd written. Goosebumps broke out like a bad road rash. As much as I hated to admit it, that included him. While he'd helped Nick get away from the kidnapper at the church cemetery in Scotland, until I met him, stood face to face and found out more about him, there was no way of telling if "J" was a friend or foe. I'd be a fool to think otherwise. Though, he *was* the one who'd left a manila envelope on my doorstep the day I'd gotten the assignment in Scotland. It was full of information on suspected black-market dealers and warned that Dr. Pinnick, the dig's former anthropologist, and Dr. Gates' best friend, had been murdered. Mystery Man J had guided me ever since through texts, notes, and emails.

I threw my hair up into a makeshift bun on the top of my head and went over the note again.

"She's secure." That was surely about Anice Foster. Callum had assured the same, but if true, and that was a big if, then who attacked Roger at the museum? Maybe Dr. Gates was right. The two weren't connected. Yet the gnawing ache at the pit of my stomach told me otherwise. As for the sleepless nights spent tossing and turning, my dreams had been invaded by a ghost. Waking hours were spent combating the assaults of everyday life, not to mention my best friend and boyfriend were at each other's throats, and it all was enough to create dark circles, bags, and gray hair to boot.

My phone beeped, saving me from more troubling notions. The clock showed 6:15 A.M. If I didn't get up now I'd be late for work, and to run into the dean even a minute late on my first day back at the university was enough to make me forget about the letter and everything it implied, along with all the questions it stirred up.

I threw off the comforter and dressed quickly, casting a sideways glance at the refrigerator and making a mental note to buy groceries later. I hurried to my car and raced through the jammed streets like a Formula 1 driver, zigging and zagging amid constant honks and foul gestures, which only made me grin wider. Raised among these city streets, there wasn't anything better than to be home.

After a quick stop to grab an egg white breakfast burrito and black coffee at the school cafeteria, I zoomed to the university parking lot reserved for staff members, and smiled at Harvey, the officer standing watch over our cars. He smiled back and waved me in. As luck would have it, I pulled into one of the last spaces. Maybe my luck was turning for the better?

The clock struck 7:00 AM. *Shoot!* Cramming the burrito in my mouth, I washed it down with a swig of coffee. The scalding liquid scorched the lining of my esophagus and I sputtered and choked, flapping my arms around like a fledging duck. To add to insult to injury, I had christened the steering wheel and dash with a spray of coffee mixed with chunks of egg white. Flipping open the glove box, I swiped a few napkins across the mess and took a moment to breathe. The warm sunrays kissed my skin and the honks and screeches, squealing rubber on the road, along with the occasional curse word, tugged at the corners of my mouth.

"Ah... home."

I straightened my blouse, grimacing at the dark brown coffee stain growing darker by the minute on my white linen button-down shirt. Setting foot to pavement, I raced to the shared archaeology and anthropology building of the university and hiked up the steps, carrying my two-ton backpack laden with my latest research on Viking heritage. The rush of cool air mixed with scents of coffee, tobacco smoke, and dusty artifacts. I hooked a right down the first hallway and checked my watch, swearing under my breath. I was a few minutes late, but when I neared the dean's office, I slowed. On tiptoes, I took a quick peek inside and grinned. An empty chair. Today must be my lucky day. I rushed on and around the corner.

"Whoa!"

My papers went flying and the backpack slid, throwing me off balance. I pitched forward, slamming my knees on the hard tiled floor, the flurry of papers eventually coming to a rest at the base of the wall. Pain shot through my knees as I stared at the research, scattered and wrinkled, around me on the scuffed tiles darkened by years of misuse.

"Watch out for that one. She's like a fungus you can't get rid of."

I hardened my expression and collected the papers in the file folder, ignoring the sarcastic chuckles. I shoved the folder into the backpack and slung it over my shoulder still kneeling on the floor. Tears stung my eyes, but I blinked them back, refusing to acknowledge the pain, especially in front of him.

"Hello, I'm Brian Smith. Are you okay?" The man stuck out his hand but I ignored it. I hastily nodded before glancing at the man standing beside him. My arch nemesis. The one who'd compared me to fungus. Anyone associated with him was already at the bottom of my list of acquaintances.

"Would you like some help with your bag? That fall wasn't pretty." He again extended a helpful hand. His nondescript brown eyes radiated confidence and a dash of irritation. He stood between 5'9" and 5'11", and was wearing a mixture of cream and taupe colored dress shirt and pants with a basic men's shoe to round out the ensemble. In a nutshell, he was everyone and nobody. Nothing stuck out, which was strange considering the company he kept.

I jutted out my chin and muttered, "I'm fine."

Gingerly rising, I stepped to the side of them and tried passing.

"Don't let your pride get in the way, Didi. Let the man help you. Isn't that what the female species is supposed to do?"

I glared at the man who'd cost me a full-ride scholarship and had poisoned my name with the staff for the last couple of years. He'd made it his singular mission to make my work life miserable. If it hadn't been for Dr. Gates and Dr. Pinnick—may he rest in peace—I'd have been out on my butt long ago.

"Shane Bernard," I said, straining to keep my voice even, "mind your words. This is a higher learning institution that doesn't think kindly of anyone in their employment using sexist remarks."

Shane's eyes flashed. "Oh, I think you've been gone too long. Scotland's mangled your brain." He snorted. "Haven't you heard? You're to report to me now. If I were you—"

"You're not."

"—I wouldn't anger the boss. Doesn't work out for you in the end, I'm afraid. As for the university, my father just donated over two million dollars to the department. You'll find them turning a blind eye to any of your... complaints. Daisy Day, your days here are numbered."

CHAPTER 6

I stomped down the hallway, burying my pride, and rounded the last corner to my office. I was fumbling for the keys in the outside pocket of my backpack when I felt a gentle tap on my arm. Brian Smith stood beside me, an apologetic smile at the ready. He had hair the color of straw, and a smooth complexion. Those nondescript eyes held me in place. If he hadn't been with Shane, I wouldn't have paid him any attention.

"Hi." He flashed his even white teeth. "Sorry about that back there. Shane can be…"

"A jerk?"

I unlocked the door and stepped inside the converted janitor's closet, my home away from home, and rolled my eyes. Not enough money to expand our department, we made do with what we had. But I loved it. My own little slice of heaven even with the dust bunnies, faulty wiring, and the occasional scurry of mouse claws coming from behind the walls.

I'd left a week ago on my first assignment. It had been a grand time! I'd been sent to Scotland. It was a dream dig site, and the archaeological community had found it in the most unexpected of ways. Some maintenance workers had uncovered a set of bones in St.

Magnus cemetery with no headstone. Dr. Pinnick had initially been asked to work the site, but when he died unexpectedly, a victim of black-market antiquities we found out later, the job fell into my lap. Dr. Pinnick was the lead forensic anthropologist. Well, he was until Anice Foster, the head of the black-market antiquities ring, murdered him. She knocked him off and replaced him with someone she believed to be more malleable. Someone like me—a post-graduate student turned assistant professor who was all too eager to make a name for herself. But she was mistaken. Hulda, my guardian ghost, appeared in time to rescue Nick and me from certain death at Anice Foster's hands. Sadly, I feared she wouldn't give up on her black-market business. From the brief time I'd known her, I knew she loved the thrill of the hunt. I was certain she'd soon escape her Scottish psychiatric hospital and track the relics again. It meant too much money for her and whoever this Boss Man was.

Piles of papers were spread haphazardly on my 1940s industrial desk, and the mug I'd last used prior to getting that fateful assignment sat in the same place. A dark ring circled the inside uppermost area of the mug that read "Digging for bones."

Had it only been a little over a week since that cataclysmic day?

I set my bag on the floor, pulled the decrepit swivel chair back, and winced at the high-pitched squeal of the wheels against the yellowed tiles. When I plopped down, the man had unfortunately not budged. He was blocking out any semblance of light provided by the antiquated sconces that had graced these halls for over seventy years.

"What can I help you with, Mr. uh…?" I glanced up at him while ruffling through the stacks of congratulatory cards, last semester graded papers, and faculty notices.

"Smith. Brian Smith? I'm a—"

"Friend of Shane's, yes. Why are you here?" Any person in Shane's sphere was not to be trusted.

"Not exactly."

I stopped rifling through the dean's dozen "requests," which were more like demands. He wanted me to spread the good word about how the university had allowed one of their esteemed professors to traipse across the globe at the end of a semester. It was all for the good of the university, you see. I snorted. "Uh, sorry. That wasn't intended for you." I laid my palms on the messy desk and stared at him. "What do you mean, not exactly? Either you're a friend of Shane's or not."

"I've only just met Mr. Bernard."

"Oh? Are you into anthropology, Mr. Smith?"

"No." He leaned against the doorframe. "My apologies, no disrespect for your profession."

I shrugged. "None taken."

"It's a fine degree, and one I've dabbled in myself over the years."

He stepped into the room and since it was the size of a janitor's closet, he now hovered over the desk. Fingering a few errant papers, he smiled. The manicured nails and smooth skin put questions marks all over his last statement. Dirt was inherent in our line of work, and from the look of things, he paid for manicures on the regular.

"How so?"

"Oh, I've toured many a site all over the world on my travels. But that's not why I'm here." He'd been wearing a nondescript hat until this point, which he now took off and held close to his chest, perusing the room with an inspectorial curiosity. He homed in on something on the metal file cabinet. It was a picture of my parents, sister, and I taken about a week before my parents' death, and the last time everything had been right in the world where sadness didn't monopolize every beat of the day.

He motioned to the photo. "Where was that taken?"

We were standing in front of a bench. The sun shone down on us, haloing our heads in an ethereal light. Like a kiss from the cherubs, we appeared happy. Content. I rubbed my neck and fought the sinking feeling that always started at the mention of my deceased parents. "Uh, that was in front of the Harvard Museum of Natural History."

"Right," he mumbled before refocusing on me. "Anyway, my company wishes to support research in the area, and I thought, why not here?" He smiled, but it failed to reach his eyes.

I tilted my head, examining him in a new light. "How do you know Shane Bernard? Is he a former playmate?"

"No, I've only recently met Mr. Bernard, at a conference. His father is a formidable force with his son's welfare and advancement opportunities."

There it was. Laid out for me to either squawk at or not. Yet why reveal this to me, of all people? He didn't strike me as someone who overlooked the obvious. This was intentional.

"Okay, I'll bite. Is this a warning visit? One where you tell me not to make waves for Shane or you'll sick his daddy on me?"

"On the contrary, Ms. Day. I'm here to offer you an opportunity of a lifetime."

He pulled out a business card from his lapel pocket and tossed it onto the overflowing papers on my desk. "While Shane is capable, I'm interested in someone with actual field experience."

I picked up the card and inspected it, noticing the business address. I jerked my head back and gaped at him. "You're a lawyer."

"I am, yes."

"No." I shook my head to dislodge the shock. "You work at the same firm as my... uh, my, um, friend."

I winced, because I'd never spoken as Christof as just my friend. Why had I not said boyfriend? Why was Brian Smith here in my office offering an opportunity to... what exactly?

"Who is your friend?"

"Christof Raphael."

"Ah, yes. He's an excellent lawyer. A recent junior partner too. He'll go a long way."

"What kind of opportunity, Mr. Smith? You didn't say."

He smiled faintly. "We need a speaker at our next philanthropy event. If you're interested, call me. I promise it'll be worth your time. Lots of high-dollar investors. Good day, Ms. Day."

CHAPTER 7

I flipped the business cared over multiple times before noticing a large envelope underneath my hand with black writing, and my pulse quickened. I stuffed the business card in my pocket, ripped open the envelope, and read the note.

Professor Dahl,

Congratulations on your return. We are serving coffee and pastries in the conference room outside my office at 3:00 P.M. this afternoon. Be there. Oh, and terrible thing about Dr. Pinnick.

The Dean

I hung my head and rubbed the back of my neck, noting the bunched-up tension knots returning. Was it too late to return to Scotland? Anywhere but that conference room, because I had the sneaking sensation that it wasn't to do with my return. Shane Bernard would see to that.

I sighed. Mose came to mind. He'd surprised me yesterday by showing up at my apartment, but what was most startling was him mentioning that he'd been dating someone for a while. Mosewan and I had a long history together. First as student to teacher, which he was perfect at, by the way. He'd spun intricate tales of faraway worlds, and I, along with the entire class, listened, spellbound. We ached to change

33

our majors and follow him to those magical places covered in dust, sand, dirt, and all the red tape a life in the field entailed. Plus, if his talks weren't mesmerizing enough, his good looks were the ultimate persuasion. At least for the others. One time a woman fainted when he accidentally touched her hand passing out our midterm exams. While I usually wanted to punch him, many others had more intimate ideas.

If I'm being honest, Mosewan *was* good-looking. Born in Egypt to renowned Egyptian archaeologists, he'd had big shoes to fill. For the most part, he had done just that. His teaching career was stellar, and he was the go-to person for anything related to Egyptian anthropology and archaeology. He'd achieved tenure in record time, despite all the naysayers that assumed it was because of who his parents were. He'd never admitted it out loud, but I suspected he figured his parents bought his tenure, perhaps even bribed someone. Because of those rumors, he'd gotten it in his thick skull that it wasn't because of his work ethic and smarts. Time and time again, I tried to convince him otherwise, but he never saw what I and so many others could see.

Mosewan was the leading expert in all things Egyptian. Not because of his parents, who were ever so supporting and thrilled for his own successes, but for the sheer grit and determination to put in the long hours to be the best in the field. Hopefully, one day he'd believe it.

I stood at the desk, palms pressed down on the dinged desktop, and arched my back, breathing in the scents of mold and stale coffee. I could feel my spine popping and locking into place, pulling me upright.

The clock showed 7:30 AM. Now was the best time to reach Mose. Before the hustle and bustle of dry staff meetings and an arch nemesis waiting to get me fired at the slightest grievance. I stepped out of my tiny nook of an office and locked the door before ambling down the hall toward Mosewan's office. Fortunately, he'd hit the jackpot in that department. The coveted corner office fit ten of mine, and the only reason Mose had gotten it was because the previous professor retired on short notice, and the dean didn't have anywhere to put Mose.

What would the university administration think if the dean had placed Mose in a dingy, cramped space no bigger than mine? Not kindly, which was directly related to his status in the anthropological world.

I walked, keeping my head down, and slammed into a hard body. I was so startled I stumbled backward. My face flushed bright red, beyond embarrassed.

"I'm so sorry!" I blurted. The janitor's mop head hit the floor with a splat. "Oh, Freddie. Are you okay?" I stepped forward to retrieve the mop, but he beat me to it. Picking it up, he placed it into the murky, sudsy, yellow bucket.

"Fine, Profesora. It is I who should watch out. Many apologies."

He dipped his head, his curly black mop of hair falling forward, covering his bushy brows. Most students and faculty alike ignored him, dashing past while he cleaned soda spills, swept up errant crumbs or crumpled papers, or worse yet, mopped up vomit from the occasional hungover student. Freddie was the rare bird that treated everyone with a smile and word of encouragement, even to those who treated him poorly.

Freddie was a great janitor who took pride in his work. He was clean cut, a man of few words, and he never complained. He had told me once that Freddie was his nickname. His real name was Francisco Ramirez Garcia. He couldn't have been over twenty-eight, though his leathered tawny-brown skin spoke of the life experiences of a much older man. Despite people treating him badly—unruly students pranking him, staff members telling him to do his job "more quickly," or even the dean looking down his nose at him for simply existing— he never got upset. I had known Freddie for a long time and saw him for who he really was, a sweet man who always smiled whenever I greeted him, and one who loved his wife and children dearly.

"How is Lola?" I asked. "Is her lupus fully controlled?"

He nodded. "She is getting better. Slowly. Thank you for asking."

"How are your children?"

"Energetic! Just like their papa." He beamed and patted his chest.

"Next time you see them, tell them Didi says hi. Here..." I

unzipped the outer pocket of the backpack and pulled out two large rainbow-colored lollipops I'd kept especially for him. I'd found out it was their favorite treat one time when his wife had brought the children to visit Freddie at work. Her arms had been bandaged, but shadows of blue and purple bruising had formed outside the wraps. She'd gone through some intravenous infusions earlier in the day, and was at her wits' end with her feisty children, oblivious to their mother's sufferings. The only thing I had at the time was a lollipop Mose had given me to cheer me up one day. I pulled it out when I noticed her distress, and their faces lit up. They each got half if they promised to be quiet and listen to their mama.

Lola's response was forever burned into my memory. She wiped her eyes with her fingertips, a healthy pink glow flushed across her cheeks, and for a split second, the drawn lines etched around her eyes and mouth had disappeared.

I readjusted the sliding backpack. "Are the immunosuppressants working for her?"

Freddie scrubbed his dirty hands. There was a sadness that enveloped him every time I spoke of his wife. "She's good. Some days are... um, hard, but my Lola is a fighter." He rubbed at a spot on his palm until it was bright red. "This lupus won't get her."

I reached for his hand and gently squeezed. His weary eyes looked upon mine, and I gave him the most reassuring smile I could muster. "Don't give up, Freddie. They develop new treatments all the time. She's strong, your Lola."

He nodded, and I dropped my hand. "Call me if ever you need anything."

"Ms. Day, I—"

I held up my hand to quiet him. "I mean it. Anything, Freddie. Got it?"

"Yes, Ms. Daisy."

"Hug those kiddos for me, Freddie."

I stepped around him to continue to Mose's office. "Ms. Day, please thank Señor Christof for me."

I turned and cocked my head to the side. "Christof? Why?"

Freddie beamed. "He got me a second job at his firm. It helps with the bills."

"Right. I'll tell him, Freddie. Make sure you get some rest too. Take care of yourself."

"Oh, no worries about that, Ms. Day. I'm from strong stock." He fist pumped his chest for added emphasis.

Confused, I waved farewell. Why would Christof offer him a job? The few times Chris had visited me at the university, he'd never given Freddie so much as a glance.

When I strode into Mose's office, I stopped at the threshold, surprised to see a frenzied young man bustle back and forth with dental tools, boxes, and photographs, putting them in various places. After several more minutes of watching the bespectacled, mousy-brown haired man whiz between the examination table and the shelves of books and artifacts, I cleared my throat. He froze. Eyes bulging behind his bottle-thick glasses, he pushed them up the bridge of his nose.

"Hello." I fought a giggle at the young man's surprise and figured it would have to be me to break the awkward silence. "Who are you?"

"Oh, uh, um... I'm, you see, I..." He scratched behind his ear and peered around the room, anywhere but at me, waving a hand as he did so like it would somehow convey what he lacked in words.

"Your name would suffice." I couldn't help but smirk.

"Oh, right. Yes, I'm Landon Fisher. I have a good reason for being here, Ms. Day."

He knew who I was. I studied him for a moment, noticing the ketchup stain on the cuff of his sleeve, the wrinkled shirt and pants, and the baseball-sized sweat stains underneath his arms.

"I'm sure you do, Landon. What's this?"

I strode over to the box full of blackened bones on the table. Laid out in neat rows to the right and left of the box were dental tools, pens, and paper all lined up. Even now he was readjusting the items, making sure they were in perfect alignment.

"Oh, uh, it's Dr. Aten's latest delivery."

I tapped my finger on the tabletop, remembering Mose's surprise the night before. Bending over the box, I inspected each charred remain with a laser-like focus. "When did he get these?"

"The last couple of days." Landon rubbed his palms together and then against his pants. "Aren't they beautiful? It's my first time inspecting something on my own."

I looked at him with renewed interest. "What year are you in school?"

"I'm in graduate school. But my undergraduate professors never let me handle anything. They said I'd break something." His face flooded with color. "I promise you I won't break a thing. I promise."

"Breathe, Landon. You're fine."

"It was only that one time, and Vaughan intentionally tripped me. The box flew out of my hands, but I saved most everything else."

He pushed his spectacles up his nose and then rested his hands on his hips, which sported dress pants two sizes too big. They were held up by old-fashioned suspenders.

"Most everything?"

"Yes, well… okay, maybe one femur fractured, but it's not as bad as you think. They were chicken bones."

"Chicken bones?" My eyebrows arched toward my hairline. "Ancient chicken bones?"

He shook his head, his stringy hair and his bangs dipping into his brown eyes. He stared at me, waiting for the dreaded judgement. "No, they were from a roast I'd brought from home. We were supposed to treat them as finds. It was something the professor wanted us to try before touching the real deal."

I threw my head back and laughed, almost immediately regretting it. Almost. It was too cute. The poor young man. Someone had done a job on his self-esteem.

"Sorry. I don't mean to demean you. It's just that it was modern-day chicken remains. Surely the professor wasn't upset over that?"

Landon snorted. "Geez, was she ever. I got yelled at by the teaching fellow *and* the professor." He closed his eyes and visibly shook himself before looking at me again. "They even threatened to throw me out of school."

My eyes widened at such a response to something so simple as chicken bones. But maybe there was more to the story than he mentioned. "Okay, you obviously passed, or you wouldn't be here."

He nodded. "Dr. Aten was kind enough to take me as his teaching assistant, and good thing too because he was my last option. Funny, though…" He scratched his greasy head. "He's the best professor here." Landon slammed a fist to his mouth the second the words left his mouth. "I don't mean that you're not an excellent teacher, um… drat! You're an excellent professor, Ms. Day."

I chuckled, and fortunately, he took it as a sign to stop talking. "No harm done, Landon. Where's Mose?"

I scanned the large room. Two walls of windows overlooked the commons where students were sitting on the freshly cut lawn. Some laid on blankets, the surrounding ground littered with books, note-books, pens, and opened bottles of drinks and chips. Many wore shades and bobbed their heads to unheard tunes. Earbuds, those dreaded things. They made them so small these days, it was almost impossible to keep students from using them in class. I'm sure some used them to cheat on exams, but I'd wised up to their schemes quickly. Most questions were difficult to find online. Served them right for trying to cheat.

The summer session was in full swing. These students were ardent, because they showed the initiative to take condensed courses during the time when others were taking trips to the beach, moun-tains, or far away cities. There was something special about summer students. I loved them, and as a way of showing it, I usually let them use their class notes, which was a gift because all the answers came from them anyway.

I glanced over at Mose's empty chair. He'd left his desk in good working order. Only the closed laptop obscured the otherwise empty desktop.

"Oh, ah, he's—"

"Right here."

My best friend stepped into the room, tossing a folder onto his desk. "I see you two have been introduced." Mose grinned first at Landon and then at me. "What do you think?"

"Oh, um..." The heat rushed up my neck, not wanting to say anything distasteful. The poor man was already a nervous sort. "He's very... dedicated."

Mose exposed his shockingly white teeth. "I meant the bones." He pointed at the box sitting on the black laboratory table.

"Oh, that. Yes, it's curious. Where did you say it came from?"

"I didn't. Not specifically. Last night, I told you it was from the Viking era." He ruffled his curly black hair and peered down at the bones.

"Yes, that's right. Viking, huh? That's a broad area. Do you have more specifics? Have they been tested?"

Mose tugged on white gloves and reached into the box, pulling out a femur, holding it up in front of me for inspection.

I leaned forward, paying special attention to the indentations. This was someone who'd had a physical life, one of either hard labor or fighting. Mose held up the ulna, which was rather enlarged. That, and telltale ridges told me that this person was well developed and used their muscles regularly. Then there was the color. Years being buried beneath the ground and yet it didn't have the off-white appearance most would expect. Even though bones are buried for centuries, it doesn't automatically mean that they'll be stained brown. However, if they are buried with any kind of pigment, like bronze or copper, or with died pigments from clothing, then their bones may absorb some of them. So, it's not uncommon to find blackened, brown, yellowed, or orange-colored bones from around the globe. These bones, though, had a distinct yellowish-orange hue marred by black.

Mose carefully replaced the ulna and picked up another, larger bone. A femur. Although I had a hunch, I was eager to get some DNA results for a more conclusive determination of whether this was a male or female.

"Preliminary tests, yes. You'll be disappointed to know that they're male," said Mose.

I glanced sideways at him but kept focused on the bones. Donning a pair of gloves, I reached into the box and hovered above another bone. "What are you afraid of, Didi?" Mose whispered in my ear. The smell of cinnamon lingered on his breath. "It won't fight back."

I took a steadying breath and carefully touched a bone that closely resembled the humerus. Parts of it were enlarged with notches here and there, signifying a person of significant strength. Could it have been a farmer chopping wood? Sure, but after a few years of intense study, this struck me as belonging to only one type of Scandinavian.

I looked at Mose directly and asked, "Year?"

Mose cracked a grin. "Definitely Viking. Probably between 800 to 900 AD."

My hand trembled. "Where? Where was he found?"

Mose took the bone that threatened to topple out of my weak grasp. The room spun in front of me and my stomach swirled, but I stood still, leaning against the old lab table, and waited for the answer, knowing it would either make my hunch or shatter it.

"Denmark. They speculate he was some type of warrior, but more tests need to be done, and we'll probably never know for certain." Mose stepped forward and laid a hand on mine. "Didi, are you okay?"

"Professor Day, you look green. Do you want to sit?" Landon asked, rolling Mose's lab chair beside me.

I nodded but remained silent, staring at the box of old bones.

"Didi, I thought you'd be excited."

I looked up at Mose and blew out my cheeks, patting my feverish forehead with my clammy palm. "Oh, yes. Of course, I'm excited. This... this is an amazing find, and one for the history books."

"That's a little hasty. To be certain, we must wait for the labs. That's what I want your help with. That is... if you're still interested."

When his words registered, I stared at him.

"Sure, I'll help. What do you need?"

Mose clapped his hands together and jumped into his plans, but his words faded into the background as I refocused on the bones. Those ancient bones. They were from the same time as Hulda ... but they were found in Denmark. She was Norwegian.

"That's just for starters. What do you think?"

I snapped back to the present, clutched my hands together in my lap, and stared at Mose. "Um, that sounds great."

I offered a weak smile, which was returned by both Mose and Landon, yet the sense of unease wouldn't shake free. Somehow these bones were linked to Hulda. I just had to figure out how and hopefully not lose anybody else in the meantime.

CHAPTER 8

*M*ose sent Landon off on some errand and we were alone at last.

Mose tilted his head questioningly. "Are you sure you're okay?" He always could read me like a book.

"I'm fine. Anyway, where'd you find that young man? He said you were his last hope."

Mose snorted and picked up an ulna, holding it close to his face and looking at it through a magnifying glass. "Landon's got quite the reputation. Poor kid was treated poorly by both students and faculty at his last university. One of his professors did recommend him, however. Said he was hardworking and loyal to a fault. Anyway, I'm a sucker for lost causes."

He glanced at me and winked.

"Funny, Mose. Real funny." I wadded up a paper towel and tossed it at him. "But seriously, what do you know about him?"

"Why? Are your Jedi senses prickling?"

I playfully punched him once he'd set the bone back in its wrapping. "I'm probably overreacting. It's been a long week."

"I bet." Mose leaned against the lab table and crossed his arms. "Scotland was less than inviting."

"You could say that." I took off the loves and neatly placed them back on top of the pile. "At first, it seemed like a dream come true. You know? It was my first real excavation. It felt like I'd made it. Like I was a real professional, you know Now..."

"Look, I don't know everything that happened, and I'm sure you'll fill me in, but promise me one thing." He stepped forward and took my hands in his. I looked up at him, feeling the moisture pushing against my eyelashes. "Never forget how wonderful you are."

I sighed and stared down at our hands. His tawny beige skin stood in stark contrast to mine, which was shockingly white.

Mose stuck his fingertip under my chin and gently pushed up, forcing me to look at him. "You are one of the best anthropologists I know, Dr. Day. I don't know why you're questioning it, but don't. Whatever happened can't detract from the professional person I see before me."

My lower lip trembled, and I nodded, feeling a teardrop slide down my face. I grinned through the tears. "Now, how about those bones?"

Mose gave my hands a gentle squeeze then released them. I rubbed my palms vigorously against my pants and reached out to pick up a bone.

"Don't!" Mose barked. The second I touched it, I didn't have time to wonder why. I was paralyzed. Jolts of electricity coursed from the charred remains through my finger. Fixed to the spot, I gaped, unable to speak. Where Mose had once stood was a lean, bearded man with shockingly blue eyes. A horrendous *CLANG* rocked the floor, slamming me sideways into the stool. I yelped, regaining my faculties in time to hop over the stool.

"Wh-who are you?"

Although I held my arm up to keep some distance, judging from his sinewy arms underneath his linen shirt, it was clear that if he wanted to harm me, he would.

"*Hjelpe meg.*" His voice, barely a whisper, sent a chill down my spine and echoed within my head before his image wavered and vanished like a puff of smoke.

I blinked. When I opened them again, Mose stood in his place. He stood with his back to me. He turned to hold up another bone but stopped and stared down at the overturned stool.

"Didi..." he said, staring down at the stool, "explain."

I clasped my hands behind my back and shrugged. Anything I said would sound crazy, and I didn't need another talk about calling a counselor. Not from Mose, Laura, or Dr. Gates.

"I tripped."

He frowned. "When?"

"A few seconds ago."

Mose shook his curly black head. "Nope, not this time, Daisy Day. Out with it." He set the bone carefully onto the table and faced me.

"Uh, there's nothing to explain. I hopped off to get a better look, and it tipped over."

"Really?" He pursed his lips. "You were standing. When did you sit? Better yet, how do you explain the lack of sound?"

"Pardon?"

"Sound, Didi. There would have been a bang." He stomped his shoe on the tile for emphasis. "There was nothing of the sort. Don't forget gloves next time."

"I... it's... you were engrossed in the bones, and..." I huffed. "It's not my problem that you didn't hear the loud bang. Maybe you need some sleep. Or maybe get your ears checked."

I planted my hands on my hips and boldly stared at him all the while holding my breath, hoping he'd just let it drop.

His eyes narrowed for a moment then he dropped his arms to his sides and bent to right the stool. "Come on, *Grace*," he chided me. "Go ahead and laugh, Didi. Grace Kelley you are not. I fear you'll end up in traction at some point."

The buzzing sound in my ears eventually diminished and I was breathing again without an all-encompassing dizziness that put motion sickness to shame.

Mose continued to show me all the bones he'd received from across the Atlantic. Denmark, more specifically. He'd called in a favor, apparently. The image of the bearded man for the second time in two days was all consuming. What's more, he'd spoken for the first time.

"Hello… Earth to Didi. What's gotten into you?"

"What?" I refocused on him, long lost in my thoughts, and noticed the slight wrinkles about his eyes and mouth. He was concerned. Something we had in common. Either I was going crazy, or the spirits from the other side were talking, and I had a sick feeling it brought with it a danger I thought I'd left in Scotland.

"Sorry, Mose. I guess it's the jet lag." I stifled a fake yawn, hoping it helped prove my case. "What were you saying?"

"I called in a favor." He paused. "For you. I thought this would brighten your day, and if he's some famous warrior chief or ruler, then your name will be forever attached to it."

My mouth dropped open.

"Didi?" He patted my forearm. "Maybe I should take you home?"

"I…" I fanned back tears. "That's one of the sweetest things anyone has ever done for me. I'm speechless."

I stared at him in disbelief. Sweet? Sure. It was what Mose did, but it wasn't his kind gesture that made me breathless. It was the warrior chief that left my tummy in knots.

"You deserve it." His voice dropped. "You deserve the world, Didi. I wish you realized that. Valued yourself more. Trusted yourself more."

The heady dizziness intensified as the meaning of his words sank in.

"Why do I feel this is about Christof?"

Mose stepped forward and took my hand, holding it tenderly. "He doesn't treat you well. I care about you and—"

"Yes, but—"

"Hear me, Daisy Day. If you tell me to take a hike, I'll shut up and drop it. Promise."

I shifted restlessly and searched his milky brown eyes. "Fine." I sighed. "Speak your peace."

"Christof came into your life when it was a desolate wasteland of trauma, hurt, fear…"

I laughed bitterly. "Wow, I sound so amazing."

"Yes! You *are* amazing. A wonderful, intelligent, brave, young woman who doesn't need any man—any *person*—telling them what to do, think, or feel. He came into your life when you were a hollowed shell. Someone who walked around with death's shadow, never seeing the light from the dark. When Christof noticed you, it was like an explosion of suns, catapulting you into a stratosphere of self-awareness and self-worth. It was beautiful. Honestly." He offered a boyish grin. "I hated it, you know. How he could bring that out in you but I couldn't. It was okay though, because you were living. Living your best life."

I smiled, remembering those early days. Mose was right. I ran around mostly on autopilot, focused on nothing else but my studies. I'd foolishly believed that if I buried myself in coursework I could forget the excruciating pain that pierced my heart and soul since my parents' death. The work drowned out the incessant worries of my sister, my teachers, who meant well with their constant questions and distressed looks, but eventually, after a few months, it turned into something else. It was like I was supposed to grieve in their time. Like a snap of the finger, they expected me to move on with my life. Enough with moping about. It was time to live. Ugh, I remember those talks with Laura and cringe now, thinking about them.

"Then he changed. You changed. He was at your side every waking moment, and at first you flourished, but if you wanted time with your friends… Well, that was it, wasn't it? No time for anyone but him. Christof had to be the center of your world, and if he wasn't, everyone else was to be cut off. Do you remember, Didi? Do you remember the times he read your texts, screened your phone messages?"

I squeezed my eyelids shut and shook my head. "Don't."

Mose pressed my hands against his chest. "Why not? Because it's true? Because it hurts to peel back the layers of your life you've struggled to keep buried and face reality?"

I jerked my hands free and opened my eyes. Mose flinched, and his fledgling hope faded as I stepped backward toward the door. "Reality?" I snapped. "Mosewan, I've lived in a hellish reality for the past fifteen years, and not you, Laura, Dr. Gates, or anyone else can change that."

"I'm not trying to change—"

"Yes, yes you are. I'm not someone to be fixed, Mose. You mean well, but this is my life. I'm doing the best I can." I reached the door and turned. My shaky breaths gave away any suggestion of strength I'd scrounged up. "Please respect that. I'll deal with my life, and you deal with yours."

"What's that supposed to mean?"

"Mose..." I groaned, fighting the urge to flee. Run away from the jagged pain that always hovered underneath the surface. "You haven't dealt with your own perceived inadequacies, even though I and tons of others have talked ourselves blue in the face trying to convince you otherwise. If you want to fix someone, fix yourself. Not me."

The lump in my throat swelled and I coughed to clear it, swiping at the tears with the back of my hand.

"Daisy..." Mose stepped forward, his face contorted in pain.

"No." I sped out of the room, crashing into Landon, who was standing outside the door.

Eyes wide, I stared at him. He tugged at his untucked white shirt.

"Were you eavesdropping, Landon?"

"No!" He held up his palms. "I just got here. Took a wrong turn and ended up in the cafeteria. Since I hadn't eaten this morning, figured I'd stop and grab a bite. Good day, Dr. Day."

He sidestepped me, walking into Mose's office, leaving me standing all alone in the hallway, my mind fixed on the dirty sleeves Landon had just showed me. From the looks of it, he'd been busy with artifacts and not food. Since he hadn't been gone for too long, he couldn't have been to both the cafeteria and the artifacts room.

Curious.

I walked mindlessly to my office and tried in vain to catch up with correspondence before the afternoon's faculty meeting. No doubt Dr. Bernard would be in bright spirits, ready to gloat about his promotion. When the clock struck 3:30 PM, I was no closer to being caught up with e-mails or voice messages. I'd spent the entire time scouring the internet for Landon Fisher. Funny enough, I'd found absolutely zero information on him. It was like he didn't exist. Why was that? Could he be associated with Anice? Or was it all a coincidence?

I shook my head to clear it of all the bad vibes and strode for the door. Anice crowded every waking minute and most of my dreams. I was seeing boogey men when there weren't any. Besides, I had a faculty party to attend. No sense in arriving late and giving Dr. Bernard fodder for snarky comments. Nope, not today. On the off chance I arrived early, perhaps I could pump Dr. Gates about both Roger's condition and these supposed charred bones Mose had received. Perhaps Landon Fisher too, for sure. Dr. Gates knew everyone around these parts, and if there was a story to tell, he'd be the man to tell it.

CHAPTER 9

"**B**ones never lie." Dr. Gates beamed down his bulbous nose at a bright-eyed teacher's assistant. "Your first lesson in the professional world of anthropology, my dear."

It hadn't been that long ago that he'd spoken those exact words to me. However, it wasn't Dr. Gates who'd coined those words, but Dr. Pinnick. The very one who'd died protecting the supposed Viking shield. I'd taken his place simply because someone felt I was easily manipulated.

Being young is a curse in and of itself. You can't get jobs because of the lack of experience, but you can't get experience without a job.

"Hello, Dr. Gates." I stepped up to the Santa Claus-like man and hugged him. The sweet smell of licorice and scotch lingered about him. He was partially retired and only stayed on to teach up-and-coming anthropologists. Fortunately, he'd picked me a few years ago. Without him, let's say I wouldn't be where I am now. "How's the new grandbaby?"

"Fine. Just fine." He patted his burgeoning belly and gleamed. "Though I believe my daughter needs a nap. Poor thing has been up all night since the day she delivered him. No matter. She's a strong young woman, made from excellent stock. He's a lucky little boy."

He was. We all were lucky to be in the orbit with Dr. Gates. If ever there was an angel on Earth, it was him.

He pointed at the button-nosed woman with straw-colored hair, all of twenty-two, beside him. "This is Charity Chase. She's my newest teaching assistant. Charity, meet Dr. Daisy Day. One of the best anthropologists I've ever had the pleasure of working with."

I flushed with delight as I shook the woman's hand. "He's too generous."

"She's too humble, which is another lesson in this field, dearie, especially as a young woman in our career, I'm afraid." He pouted while eyeing the table of pastries behind me. "But worry not. With a lot of determination and grit, you can make it in this profession. It only takes love, my dear. Isn't that right, Dr. Day?"

"Yes, Dr. Gates."

"Ladies, if you don't mind," he wiggled his pudgy fingers, "I'd like to raid the goody table before it's all gone."

Charity and I stepped aside to allow him passage. After he picked up a paper plate, he piled it high with powdered-covered donuts, a cream cheese Danish, a bear claw, two chocolate chip cookies the size of a salad plate, and a couple of strawberries for good measure. Dr. Gates skimmed the room briefly before strolling off to a faraway corner sans people where he could eat his cache of sugary sweets in peace and without judgement.

Charity's soft sigh caught my attention. Tearing away from Dr. Gates's expressions with each delectable bite, some of which ended up in his groomed white beard, I glanced at Charity. While her flawless taupe-brown skin was envious enough, it was her curious amber-colored eyes and supple lips turned up at the corners that left me wondering. Long black lashes, curled at the tips, fluttered closed as her coiled brown locks with blonde highlights bounced about her face when she glanced over at Dr. Gates and shook her head.

"That man will be in a diabetic coma if he's not careful."

"Ah...he's sucked you in, I see." I smirked, unable to contain the warmth I felt for this young lady, only about five years my junior.

Charity's brows shot up. "What do you mean?"

"Not to worry. He's like that to most people. A black hole of kindness. If I didn't know better, I'd swear he was Santa Claus."

We both giggled.

It was true. There was no denying the man's likeness to the red-suited saint.

I leaned in closer to her and whispered, "Have you found his candy drawer yet?"

Charity snorted. "Not even the first hour of working, and he was unlocking his drawer a foot deep and showing me his treasure of candy bars and sweets. How does he not have cavities?"

It was a wonder, but after the first meeting with his wife, all my concerns vanished. I waved off Charity's worries. "His wife takes him to all his doctor's appointments. She's got him on a tight rope."

"I haven't seen him take more than one piece a day. Still, what about his plate of diabetes over there?" Charity hooked her thumb in his direction.

"It happens once a blue moon. I wouldn't worry about it. Say…" a thought occurred to me, "are you familiar with Landon Fisher?"

"Dr. Mose's assistant? Sure. Everybody is." She grunted but quickly straightened up, her brows knitted together in worry. "I didn't mean it that way. It's just that Landon has a sort of… reputation."

"So soon?"

"Yes, he kind of brings it on himself."

"Meaning?"

"Everywhere he goes, chaos ensues. We haven't figured out if he does it on purpose, or if it's just bad luck."

"We?"

Her amber-colored eyes narrowed conspiratorially and she leaned in closer. "Dr. Gates and I, we've talked about it some. I don't know, though. Landon seems genuine enough. He's not the devious sort."

A series of claps echoed throughout the room, drawing our attention to the man standing in front of the pastry table, who was currently shooing faculty and their assistants away.

"Ladies and gentlemen, thank you for coming on such short notice," stated the beak-nosed dean. "There are a few items on the list we must set straight before proceeding with today's announcements. First, I require all syllabi and any changes to curriculum by 5:00 PM today."

After a few seconds of rumblings, he continued. "Second, the Board of Trustees, along with our esteemed President Newton, will arrive shortly."

Exclamations of surprise erupted, leaving the dean waving his arms about, looking like he'd cracked a hornet's nest open. With reddened cheeks, bulging eyes, and a pinched mouth, he shushed the crowd to a deathly silence.

"Please, ladies and gentlemen, let's keep an order of decorum. No need to worry, I'm sure. Third, after their announcements, I'll be making my own. Before all of that, let's give a warm welcome to our returning professor, Dr. Day. Her extraordinary find in Scotland has brought splendid light to our fine teaching institution. Dr. Day, welcome back."

The dean clapped his hands, beckoning everyone else to follow. Soon, there were enough "congratulations" and "great jobs" to bring a pep to my step. Until Dr. Shane Bernard opened his mouth.

"Yes, if you count being chased by a murderer as positive light on the university, then sure. Welcome back, Daisy Day. Bravo."

His lackluster claps stopped everyone in their tracks, dropping the room back into silence. The clatter of footsteps in the hallway drew everyone's attention to the door. People craned their necks, standing on their tippy toes, in order to glimpse the rare visit from our board of trustees and President Newton.

Their unexpected appearance wasn't something to take lightly. Uncommon, but there was something more to the timing of it all. Call me crazy, but the attempted murder of Dr. Roger Phillips, Dr. Gates' friend from the museum, and the trustees' arrival seemed too coincidental.

Each trustee entered the room, and faculty and staff scrambled backward, allowing them space in a conference room stuffed to begin with. On the heels of the trustees came President Newton, stiff and pale as a sheet.

I immediately sought out Dr. Gates, but he'd moved from his corner. A second later, the gentle tug on my elbow alerted me to his presence behind me.

"Something's afoot, my dear," Dr. Gates whispered into my ear. "I believe you're right about Roger."

Before I could question him, President Newton opened his mouth to speak, his booming voice causing many to balk.

"Trustees and faculty, thank you for gathering today. I will not detain you further other than to say that there will be a few changes. The board of trustees has informed me that, due to certain circum-stances, all faculty must undergo a formal interview process. It's all very nuanced, but needless to say, it is necessary. Although there is not much I can tell you at this moment, we will begin these interviews directly. Upon receipt of your request by e-mail, promptly report to your dean for your interview, after which you are free to return to your regular business. Please save questions for the trustees at your designated time. I am sorry for the short notice, but I am confident that you will all rise to the occasion."

With a sour expression on his face, President Newton adjusted his tie, turned, and marched out of the room with nary a glance at the trustees left behind. They stood shoulder-to-shoulder, casting blank stares about the room. While the rest of my colleagues murmured amongst themselves, waiting for the trustees to speak, I scrutinized their body postures along with that of our dean. He appeared as clue-less and surprised as the rest of us.

A man of short stature dressed in a sleek navy suit stepped forward and raised his hand. When the room quieted, he said,

"Dr. Gates, please come forward."

Dr. Gates' gentle palm at the small of my back, and his whispered "Don't move" kept me frozen in place.

As he moved beside me, he stuffed something in my palm and kept striding forward through the parting crowd ahead of us. At last, he stood, towering over the man all of 5'4", and stared down at him convivially. They stood in a way that we all got a side view of them, and while my mentor's jovial nature never wavered, the trustee's expression tightened.

He puffed up his chest, cocked his head back, and declared, "Dr. Gates, while you have been a professor for us for decades, and you've brought attention to our university, bringing in funding for research and otherwise, it is my job to inform you that you will no longer be employed here at our fine institution. As of today, Dr. Gates, you are dismissed. We thank you for your tenure. Please clear out your office and hand over your keys and badge to the dean."

The room started spinning, but the flash of warning Dr. Gates had thrown my way kept me from so much as a squeak. I held my breath, hands balled into fists, and gritted my teeth, praying that all of this was just some prank. A cruel joke that at any time now, someone would yell "surprise" and it would all be over. Alas, it didn't happen. The short man gestured toward the door, and I watched in sheer horror as Dr. Gates ambled out the door and out of sight.

CHAPTER 10

The murmur rose to the level of a jet airplane within seconds as I stood stricken with indecision. While alarm bells rang within my head, I scanned the crowd and landed on the dean, whose face had drained of color. Waving his arms wildly above his head, the crowd kept up its frantic roar until he placed two fingers in his mouth and blew. A high-pitched whistle quieted the room and drew attention to the dean.

He adjusted his jacket and huffed while glaring at the lot of us. "I understand this is all a surprise to—"

The crowd erupted again, throwing accusatory questions his way, and for yet another minute, chaos reigned. I'd collected my wits and locked onto the form of my arch nemesis. The smug smile and arrogant stance made me nauseous. While he didn't have the power to fire Dr. Gates, he knew powerful people that could.

"Ladies and gentlemen! Ladies and gentlemen, please, calm down," the dean called out. "This is a shock to us all, and I can assure you that I will get to the bottom of it. For the time being, however, the trustees have made an executive decision, and whether we like it is not up for debate. Since I'm sure we've all got more pressing matters to attend to, let's get on with the last announcement."

Shane Bernard, who had been within a few feet of the dean, now stood directly beside him, smirking at the crowd.

"Dr. Bernard here, while only working for the university for the last couple of years, has shown the type of work ethic that I dare say most would envy. Late nights, tireless in his efforts to promote the university's archaeology and anthropology departments, he has shown us all a thing or two about leadership. It is with this that I announce his promotion to Chair of the Archaeology and Anthropology Departments. Dr. Bernard," the dean turned to face Shane and offered him his hand, heartily pumping it, "welcome aboard. We expect great things from you."

An apathetic clap followed. Shane folded his hands together in front of him and addressed the crowd. "Many thanks go to the dean and the board of trustees in their generous offer. As the youngest chair of the department, I promise to work diligently to earn your respect and approval. Now," he clapped his hands together, "we'd better get back to work."

His smile failed to reach his cold, hard eyes as the stunned crowd of faculty and assistants collected their belongings and file out. Except me. I stood still until the last person had left, leaving me and Shane alone for the first time in ages.

At first, he stared, waiting for me to speak or move. When I failed to do so, he strolled up, his hands stuffed into his designer suit pockets. "Daisy, it's time to work, or hadn't you heard?" He cocked his head to the side and snickered. "Though I'm surprised you're still here. I thought you'd be running after that old man."

"Inflammatory comments are nothing new for you, Shane, and I expect nothing less. As for Dr. Gates, he's more of a man than you'll ever be, and I'm quite sure your little stunt will fail to achieve its desired effect."

"What is that, Ms. Day?"

I held his stare and thrust out my chin. "Fear."

Shane blinked, a menacing chuckle slipping out.

I stepped closer until there was barely a foot between us. Though he towered over me, I refused to flinch, wobble, or do anything that would betray my thudding heart and shaking frame. "Someone pulled strings for you, Shane. Late nights? Please, you've never finished a full workday in your life. As for your so-called tireless efforts, I'd say all the harassment charges you've swept under the rug with high-powered attorneys attest to that, but make no mistake, you don't work for the university. Everything you do benefits one person. You. Well, and your father, I presume. Ah, there it is. That flash of fire in your eye whenever Daddy comes up in conversation. No matter. Your time is limited."

"Oh, yeah?" He grunted. "How's that when I can fire you with a snap of the fingers?"

I grinned. "Lose the department's fair-haired woman? Nah, that's not happening. You're callous, but not stupid. For now, stay away from me, and keep your hands to yourself for once. I'm sure Daddy isn't all that pleased about shoveling out a fortune every time a young woman catches your fancy."

I hoofed it toward the door and stepped into the hallway, though not before hearing him say, "I'm not your problem, Daisy. You think Scotland was bad? Just wait."

Every hair on my body stood on edge as I turned the corner and sank against the wall. Shane's words echoed within and my breath came in spurts. My theory that Shane was involved was confirmed. He'd gotten to Dr. Gates and Robert... who was next?

CHAPTER 11

I squeezed my eyelids shut and rested my head against the office wall, head pounding. After a few moments, someone lightly cleared their throat.

"Dr. Day? Are you alright?"

Charity's brow knitted with concern, and her warm brown eyes swam with worry. She was holding a Styrofoam cup smelling of stale coffee and a paper plate with a half-eaten Danish.

"Dr. Gates," I mumbled, struggling to stand. I'd been so consumed with Shane that I'd forgotten to speak with my mentor and dear friend. I scrambled for the scrap of paper he'd stuffed in my hand and read the note: "Meet me in my office."

I took off down the hallway at a sprint. After a few turns, I flew into his office, nearly tripping over a pile of books. I flung out my hands and grabbed onto the overstuffed chair where his students usually sat to right myself. I remember those days when I would come in and sit in that chair, talking with him about anthropology and my life for hours on end. It was a treasure I'd never be able to repay.

"Dr. Gates... I...you...?" Nothing coherent came out.

Dr. Gates's arms were stacked high with old books covered in coffee rings and tattered edges from years of use. The sun faded away from the windows like an omen, and the lamps flipped on.

He shrugged, his congenial expression never wavering. "Why, indeed, my dear? The answer lies within you, no?" He carefully placed the books in a moving box and then pushed his bottle-thick glasses up his nose.

I felt defeated and it must have shown because he gestured to the chair. "Sit."

I shook my head. We didn't have time.

"Yes, my dear. We do. Sit."

Prescient? No, he was just a wise, good man that could sense what his students were thinking even if we didn't ourselves.

He leaned against the boat deck he'd splurged on five years ago. It looked like the backend of one. He'd saved up money for a real boat but noted that on a professor's salary, the notion of ever attaining such a treasure would probably never come to pass. Instead of moping about it, however, he'd bought the next best thing—a portion of one that he could take home when he retired. He kept it stocked full of chips, sodas, and candy for angsty, hungry students, bleary-eyed after late-night cram sessions and relationship woes. He was the grandpa we all craved, or as I liked to call him, Santa Claus.

I sank into the chair and noted the orange tint on the mint green fabric. Cheetos had been a favorite of mine and a snack he'd often offer to students. "Dr. Gates, fight this."

He held up his palm. "I will do no such thing, and you would do well to keep quiet. My career has been long and fulfilling, but yours, my dear, is only beginning."

"I don't care," I sputtered, unable to contain my frustration.

"Didi, don't be foolish. This is above my head, and if they want me removed, then removed I will be." He picked up a book sitting on his desk and tossed it into an open box on the floor in front of my feet. "Shane Bernard, or rather his father, has strong ties with the trustees and university administration. This is not new. Money exchanging hands for a few perks is as old as time." He interlaced his fingers against his beach ball-sized belly.

"Yes, but it's not fair."

I cringed. Even to myself I sounded like a brat.

His jovial laugh had me half-grinning. "Life is not fair, Daisy, and you of all people understand that."

For a moment, I couldn't breathe. The air had been sucked out, and I was left alone again like all those years ago, which seemed like yesterday. The loss of my parents had threatened to rip me apart fiber by fiber, but Dr. Gates sensed it from the moment we met, and he had patiently guided me and comforted me ever since. Clamping a hand over my mouth, I fought the urge to cry. I wasn't losing a mentor, I was losing a father figure. Dr. Gates was family. The thought of losing him was almost too much to bear.

I swallowed a sob.

"Didi?" he said softly. "Daisy Day... I'm not going anywhere. I am but a car drive away, and that won't change."

Although I forced a nod my gut churned as if something heavy was sitting on it. The dreaded boogeyman of loss was back, and it was all I could do to keep it together.

"Besides," continued Dr. Gates, "I get to visit Roger and check in on his wife. She called before the meeting. He's conscious, but unable to talk yet."

I sat up straighter. "That's great news. Do they think he's out of the woods?"

"Uncertain, though it sure looks promising."

With a white-knuckled grip on the armrests, I gulped.

"My dear, you look like you've seen a ghost. Are you alright?"

"It's... it's just that... uh... if they've attacked him once, then..."

Dr. Gates rubbed a meaty finger against his brow. "Yes, I too have reckoned that whoever did this will be back, to finish him. Try not to worry. I've called in a favor to one of my detective friends at the local police department, and he's posted someone outside Roger's hospital door. For now, he's as safe as he can be."

I sank into the comfy chair, momentarily relieved. "Do you think they'll go after his wife?"

He shook his white head and waddled around his boat desk to sit in his captain's chair. The swivel chair creaked in protest as he turned to stare out the window overlooking a courtyard. Last year, they installed a Zeus fountain at the behest of Shane Bernard's parents after their generous donation. A replica of the statue Phidias sculpted for the Temple of Zeus in Olympia, Greece circa 430 BCE, the statue of Zeus lacked the ivory, precious stones, ebony, and gold appearing on the original and included as one of the Seven Wonders of the World. Although it was impressive, gold paint replaced the real precious metal while other paints represented the other colors, and various glass parts replaced the precious stones.

While the Bernards didn't demand a replica, they left little room for doubt that they'd be most displeased if it turned out to be anything else. Shane Bernard's area of expertise was Greece. Oh, not because he had a passion for the history and culture, but because his parents did. They owned various properties there, and he'd bragged about the sites he'd gotten behind-the-scenes tours of thanks to his privilege. Sadly, it didn't reflect in his education. His lackluster study of the subject was to appease his parents, and he'd graduated with honors. No doubt those were bought too. Yet the statue itself was elaborate, to say the least. If I was a betting person, I'd say it cost nearly as much as was donated. The trustees didn't care; it stood as a reminder to everyone that they had a rich benefactor, and they were to be taken seriously in their research and in the world of academia.

The statue reminded me of the tunnels underneath St. Magnus Cathedral in Scotland. Then there was Anice's wild face, alive with greed as she watched me decipher the runes on the ancient Viking sword. It *was* authentic and would have brought her a pretty penny, but it wasn't the sword she was after. No, the sword was the tip of the proverbial iceberg. If there was even a hint of more money on the horizon, and proof of a shield maiden would have skyrocketed the value of the sword, then that's what she was after. This whole thing with Roger smelled of the same rotten stench of greed.

"Dr. Gates?"

He tore his gaze off the eagle perched on Zeus' scepter and stared over at me. Deep lines around his eyes and mouth dug in deeper, and his forlorn expression had him light years away from this stuffy office.

"The St. Magnus sword, Roger's attack, and your firing... they're related."

He raised his brow. "Evidence?"

"I'll get it."

Dr. Gates placed his palms on the now barren desktop. "Daisy," he lowered his usually booming voice, glancing over at the door, "these people have reach. My loss means nothing, and Roger will hopefully make a full recovery. But you, my dear... they were mistaken once before about you. They won't be again."

CHAPTER 12

*A*fter I insisted on lugging the multiple boxes filled to the brim with Dr. Gates' books, awards, and mementos of his decades of teaching to his car, I hugged him goodbye and headed off to lock up his office. I stopped on the threshold of his now empty office, except for his desk that would be delivered to his home within the next few days, and scanned the room. Walls barren, all that was left were the dust bunnies and the furniture. An ache constricted my throat and my lips trembled. It was like life itself had been sucked out of the room. Dr. Gates had always been my bastion of strength, especially at work, and he lit up the department with his infectious belly laughs, broad smiles, and sympathetic ear. Dr. Gates made work a haven, and he made magic seem possible. Without him, I was lost. Adrift again in the chaos of life.

I quietly shut the door and locked it, turning to walk the long way back to my teeny office. On the way, I strolled past Mose's office and paused. Hand hovering above the door handle, I imagined his welcoming arms, those soft brown eyes that would understand my grief without one expressed word. How I wanted to fall into him, let him soothe the darkness out of my life. When I gripped the handle, raised voices stopped me cold. I stuck my ear against the door and listened.

"No. I didn't authorize it." Mose's voice was muffled like he was trying to keep his calm, yet he was clearly agitated.

"Dr. Bernard said—"

"Ah, there's your problem. You don't ask Dr. Bernard for permission. You go through me. Got it? What were you thinking?"

When I heard footsteps approaching, I jumped back and ran down the hall and skirted past a column, peeking around it. A second later Landon Fisher stormed out of Mose's office, slamming the door with a loud bang that rattled the frosted glass. Landon's stormy expression belied a different version of the meek and mild young man I'd met earlier, and my suspicions shot through the ceiling about who he really was. I didn't have time to contemplate as he was rapidly approaching. I flattened my backside against the wall and held my breath, praying he wouldn't notice me.

His loud footsteps plodded past me, and soon he was around another corner.

I blew out a breath and slumped against the wall for support. What were they arguing about that had Mose on edge? All the time we'd been friends, I'd never seen Mose lose his temper. Not even with Christof, and that was saying something.

I stepped away from the wall and meandered back to my office. The afternoon flew by. Curriculum sent to the dean, I set about tidying up and drove home, lost in thought. Once there, and after whipping up a Caesar salad and a glass of sparkling grape juice left from dear ole sis, I sank onto my ratty, comfy couch and flipped on the television. Though I stared at the actors on the screen, nothing registered. I couldn't help but think about Roger, Dr. Gates, and Mose.

A couple of hours passed, and it was completely dark in the apartment except for the glow of the television. *National Treasure* was on (one of my favorites to watch with Dr. Gates). My cell flashed twice. I lazily swiped a finger over the lit screen just as Nicolas Cage jumped into the Hudson to avoid the FBI.

Sorry for earlier. Meet me tomorrow morning. We've got some bones to study. Don't worry about breakfast. I've got you covered. Night, Didi.

Leave it to Mose.

And all was right again with the world.

* * *

THE ALARM BLARED four times before I slammed a fist on it to shut it off. I rubbed my tired eyes and threw off the sheets, stuffing my feet into my fluffy pink slippers. On automatic pilot, I wandered into the kitchen and poured the steaming pot of coffee into a mug and thanked my stars for technology. I don't know what I'd do without an automatic coffeemaker. While most people disliked black coffee, I relished it. No matter how many times I explained to people that they only needed good quality coffee, they'd scoff and drown theirs in cream, sugar, and everything else. Unhealthy. Only Mose understood, and that's what I loved most about him. He never questioned my life's choices, sans my boyfriend, and he let me be me. No better friend than that.

I'd drank about half the scalding liquid when my cell rang in the bedroom. Ignoring it, I kept sipping until I drained the mug. Neurons freshly firing, I washed the mug and set it out to dry on the mat. I heard my phone again. Eyeing the stove clock, I noticed it was 5:30 AM. Who would call at such an hour?

Sleep fog conquered, my pulse quickened as the reality of someone calling at this hour registered. In my haste, I tripped over the laundry basket I'd left beside the kitchen garbage can last night and crashed onto my knees. Stars floated within my vision while I grunted to a stand and hobbled to the phone.

"Hello?"

"Didi! Didi, we've been robbed. I... I don't..."

Mose's strained voice dropped until it trailed off into a gurgle, as if he'd passed out.

"Robbed? What do you mean? Where are you?" My palms glistened with sweat.

Mose groaned in response.

"Mose? What's wrong? What's going on?" I raced about, grabbing my keys and wallet, striding for the front door with renewed determination. "Answer me, Mose, or I'm calling the police. Tell me where you are. Are you hurt?"

"*Landon... no...*"

"Landon? You're at work?"

I skipped down the steps and made a beeline for my car. In a matter of seconds, I was tearing down the road, tires screeching against the jerks of the wheel as I maneuvered through the congested city streets. The city had awoken from a light slumber and was in full swing, even at this ungodly hour.

The line went dead, and an icy fear seized my heart. I slammed my foot on the pedal and was soon squealing to a halt in front of the anthropology building. Without missing a beat, I unbuckled my seatbelt, swung the car door wide, and sprinted toward the steps, locking my car with a click of the fob.

While the orange rays of the sun had broken through the darkness of night, it was still too early for staff or faculty to have arrived. I squashed a simper and flung the door wide, hearing the crunch of shattered glass under foot. A piece of metal lay to the left of the door.

Blinded by fear, I raced down the hallway. If anything ever happened to him...

I blinked back tears, rounding the corner to Mose's office.

I slowed to a walk and strained to hear any movement. Since I'd blazed in, I hadn't thought about the possibility of an attacker still on the premises. My only thought was getting to Mose.

When soft whimpers emerged from behind the half-open door, I cautiously stuck out my shaking hand and gently pushed against it. I groaned, hands flying up to cover my mouth. Eyes wide, I followed the trail of blood into Mose's office. I whipped out my cell and called 911. When I got farther inside, I saw him.

His jet-black head was bent over the bloodied and battered body, arms cradling the man's head against his chest like a baby. He rocked back and forth, weeping.

"Mose?" My voice squeaked. The soles of my shoes were suctioned to the floor from the coagulating blood. I gagged when the sickly-sweet metallic smell hit me. I drew in a breath. "What happened? Mose... who are you holding?"

He moaned, throwing his head back and exposing the mask of grief that enveloped him.

I stepped carefully through the blood-soaked papers, shredded like in a fit of rage, and the smattering of charred bones that lay among the puddles of crimson. When I reached him, I reached out an unsteady hand to touch his hand. His eyes popped open, snapping to attention and latching onto mine. His feverish expression and pale flesh spoke of the horror he'd witnessed. Or perhaps experienced?

"Mose... talk to me."

"What?" He blinked down at the man he cradled against his torso and caught his breath. "Um... he's... he's my TA. It's Landon."

Landon? I squinted through the dimness of the room. Through the swollen, battered, and bruised face, I barely recognized him. Only his broken glasses registered from the young man I'd seen just yesterday. Who would want to murder him? Why?

"Mose?"

He'd gone back to rocking Landon, shoulders bobbing up and down with grief. While I understood the shock of it, his behavior was off. Mose usually jumped in with a cool head in stressful situations. I thought about Landon and his conversation yesterday. The tension between the two was evident.

"Mose, have you called the police?"

"The police?" He looked up with a glassy expression, like anything I said was barely registering.

"Have you?"

When he didn't answer, I held up my phone to call.

"Stop."

My finger hovered over the phone as I stared at Mose.

"The bones."

I scanned the mess of his office. Bones, including the charred ones from Denmark, were strewn among the shredded papers. Shards of

Egyptian gods and goddess statues scattered across the office along with some spilled purple flowers from a vase, and ancient Egyptian coins.

"What about the bones?"

"It was the bones."

I tilted my head. "Mose, honey, you're not making any sense."

"They came for the bones!"

A prickly tingle set my hairs on end. I squeaked, "The ones from Denmark?"

My tongue stuck to the roof of my mouth, dry as cotton. "The bones are here." I pointed to the ones surrounding Mose and Landon.

Mose shook his head. "Gone. Except for a couple of them."

I stuck the cell into my pant pocket, knots bundling at the base of my neck. "Okay, tell me what happened."

"I don't know. First thing this morning, I walked in to get everything ready for you, and when I came in…"

"Right. What was Landon doing in here this early in the morning, anyway?"

Mose squeezed his eyes shut. "Because I gave him permission to inspect the bones last night."

I gaped at him. "Why? TAs aren't allowed to examine any type of bones, pottery, or anything else starting off without their advisor present."

"I know, I know, I know, but he was eager, and he promised to examine them in the other room, not here, and put them back."

I searched the room again and noticed the box's contents on the ground by the stool I'd sat upon the day before amongst torn papers smeared with blood. On the ones that weren't, I could make out ancient Egyptian hieroglyphs, hand drawings of the pyramids of Giza, and appeared to be snakes.

"Mose, if someone came for those bones, then this is most definitely linked to Scotland. First things first, let's put the box back with the others. No one needs to know about them. Not yet."

"He's dead, Didi. It's all my fault." He groaned and resumed his rocking.

Mose was in shock, and while I understood, we needed to move fast. I carefully stepped to the box loaned to us from Denmark, picked it up, and made my way to the specimen room, kicking off my shoes the second I was out of his office to avoid a trail. Thankfully, they hadn't tracked any blood. When the box was safely on the shelf, I returned to Mose and dialed the police.

"Alright, Mose, when the police arrive, let me do all the talking. Got it? You're in enough of a state that they shouldn't question you. Not yet."

"What about Landon?"

"That's up to the police."

"No," he snapped. "He wasn't supposed to be here. What will you say?"

I stared down at the unrecognizable student and racked my brain for an answer. "Don't worry about it. I'll come up with something. Pull yourself together. They'll be here any minute."

CHAPTER 13

The forensic team methodically combed through the scene collecting blood, hair, and goodness knows what else while I stood in the hallway watching the scene unfold. Mose had sat on the cold tile floor, knees up, head in hands. An occasional whimper floated up, but my attention was laser focused on the man at the center of it all.

"Detective Soo?" called a beat cop. "Over here."

The lean detective stepped toward the table where the empty box of bones shipped from Denmark had been only thirty minutes ago. Fortunately, Landon had taken multiple boxes, and I'd only returned the one to storage. I wrung my hands, stealing glances at Mose, while the stone-faced detective bent his head over something on the table. Though he remained stoic, a flash of surprise flickered for a moment. He immediately caught my stare and walked over, his steps much like a cat. Agile and flexible, he maneuvered through the white-garbed forensics team and the other cops collecting evidence and was soon standing in front of me.

He had soft brown eyes, smooth golden-brown skin, and straight, jet black hair. If I'd met him anyplace else, I'd say that he was attractive, but as it stood, Mose and I were the prime suspects in a murder investigation, and the hard stare he cast at us left little doubt that he meant business.

He tilted his head at Mose. "He alright to talk?"

I shook my head but stepped aside, intent on the guarded man who caused his fellow cops a sense of dread.

"May I have your name, sir?" asked Detective Soo.

Mose stared down at his hands covered in blood, dried and caking now.

"Sir? Your name."

The detective pulled out a pen and pad of paper from his navy jacket pocket and tapped the pen tip against it. With a hawkish sideways glance at me, he squawked, "Name?"

"I'm Daisy Day, an assistant anthropology professor, and this is Dr. Mosewan Aten who's an associate professor. He found Landon."

Detective Soo's forehead scrunched as he jotted down what I'd said. "How did you know the deceased?"

"I only met him yesterday. He's Mose's teaching assistant."

I wrapped my arms about my torso and shuddered. "Mose—"

"Who?" Detective Soo stopped writing.

"Um, Dr. Aten... Mose to his friends. Anyway, he's known Landon for a couple of weeks, I think. They both examined the newest set of bones shipped to us last night, but that's the last time Mose saw him. Until this morning, that is."

"Thank you, Ms. Day, but I'd like a word with Dr. Aten. Please wait over by Officer Chung."

I wandered over to the officer standing in silence a few feet away. She asked me a few more questions, but I focused my attention on Mose and what he was—or wasn't—saying to the detective.

Officer Chung jotted my number down and made it perfectly clear I was not to leave town. As I wandered away, I looked back to see Mose was still in his seated position, but some of the color had returned to his face.

I ducked under the yellow police tape and pulled out my cell to call Dr. Gates.

"That is distressing, my dear. Have you been to the bone lab? Check to see if anything else is out of order."

Fortunately, the bone lab wasn't near to the crime scene and I could skirt behind a growing crowd of news reporters and their crews. Once out of sight, I snuck to the lab and entered quietly, locking the door behind me. The shelves around the room were neatly ordered, and I quickly found the box of bones I'd stashed earlier. A couple were from the Danish transfer, but an odd chalky white substance covered part of the blackened part of the bones, which fortunately had avoided the contamination of blood splatter.

I whipped out my cell, took several photos, and sent copies to Dr. Gates for safekeeping. I stuffed the phone back into my pocket then noticed a few haphazardly placed boxes.

Huh. I could have sworn I'd squared them all when I rushed in to replace the bones so as not to draw attention to them, but they were all askew, and some were shoved far back against the wall.

I pulled the inventory log and scanned the contents. Nothing appeared out of order, and no one had signed out anything, which was strange considering Landon had taken the bones with Mose's permission. There was nothing, no signature from Landon or anyone else.

I walked over to the boxes and carried them to the black lab table in the center of the room we used to study artifacts and opened the boxes. One by one, I inspected the contents and matched them to the inventory logs we were required to keep. Everything was there except…

I pulled out my phone and dialed, my fingers trembling as I pressed each number. I inhaled a shaky breath and placed the phone to my ear. Each ring was louder than the last until a deep voice answered.

"Lassie, I figure this isn't a casual call."

CHAPTER 14

"Callum, I—" I dared not breathe. A key had been inserted into the keyhole, the handle slowly turned, followed by a soft click.

"Didi? What's wrong?"

The door opened inch by inch until a foot stepped inside the room and the air left my lungs. I ducked, stuffing the phone inside my shirt and praying Callum stayed quiet. I had mere seconds before the person would see me. The blacktop lab tables were tall with long, lean wooden legs. I was a sitting duck.

"Didi?" someone whispered.

I placed my fingers on the tabletop and peeked. Eyes bulging, I shot up. "Mose? What are you doing here?"

He shut the door behind him, locked it, and strode toward me. His weary eyes locked onto the boxes on the table, and he ogled me with raised brows. "Tell me you found something?"

"I might have."

Muffled sounds came from my shirt, and Mose pointed to my chest. "Unless you've got a new type of bra, which I'd have to say I'm a huge fan of, then your phone is on."

I patted my chest and swore. Tugging it out, trying to avoid exposing too much skin, I held it out and placed Callum on speaker. "Sorry, Callum. False alarm. It's Mose."

An audible sigh of relief crossed the phone line, causing me to smile. How that man affected me, I still didn't understand.

"Didi," came his thick Scottish brogue, "where are you? Start talking, lassie."

We filled him in on the events of the last twenty-four hours, and when we finished, Callum remained silent for a moment while Mose and I stared across the table at each other.

"I admit there's a probable connection," Callum said after a long pause, "but Anice is safely locked away. If there's someone after those bones, and it relates to the bones here, then it's not Anice. Has your mystery man contacted you?"

Mose laid his dirty palms on the tabletop and stared at me. "What mystery man?"

I ignored his question. "J did message me, but he didn't say much." I fixated on the box of artifacts to my left, feeling the heat of Mose's stare. "He said she was secure and that a game was afoot, or something of that nature. He also mentioned he injured his hand. Nothing else other than to be careful and keep to my friends and family."

"Aye, a wise statement, especially for you."

I rolled my eyes but kept quiet. He wasn't wrong. I'd always been rather rash when I'd set my mind to something, and this wasn't any different.

I looked at Mose, who'd been burning a hole in the side of my face. "Wait. Why are you here? What did Detective Soo ask?"

"Nothing unusual. Just where was I last night, did I allow Landon to stay afterward and inspect the bones, did I say he could look at the bones in my office... You know, detective stuff. Yes, I think I'm at the top of the suspect list, and so are you."

I jerked my head back. "Me? Why?"

Mose shrugged.

Callum's deep voice boomed in the room, "Because you were at the crime scene, and Didi, your face gets red when you're lying. That detective isn't stupid."

I grunted. "Okay, fine. What do we do now?"

"I can answer that one," said Mose. "Detective Soo would like to question you further, Didi. You'd better get a move on before he sends one of his cops after you."

I replaced the contents of the boxes and re-shelved them, then retrieved my phone. "Mose, please tell me you didn't say anything incriminating."

Mose grimaced. "Maybe? I don't know. He was quick, and I was... I was..."

"In shock," I finished. "It's okay. We'll figure this out. Callum? Any words of advice?"

"Aye... don't get arrested."

Great advice, except I feared it was out of my hands. Time to face the piper.

* * *

RAISED voices had Mose and I frozen in our tracks. The cameras, fuzzy microphones, and dolled up news reporters huddled around Freddie, the janitor, Brian Smith, the benefactor, and Christof, my boyfriend of sorts. A couple of beat cops stood in front of the police tape and held out their arms, not allowing Christof to pass.

"Do you know who I am?" Christof yelled, spittle flying from his mouth. He straightened his tie while Brian Smith placed a palm on Christof's chest, stepping between him and the police, their hands resting on their stun guns. Freddie stiffened when Brian glanced at him. He grabbed his mop and roller cart and strolled off down another hallway.

"Sir," said Officer Chung, "this is a crime scene. Not even the president of the United States could pass these lines."

"I'll have your badge, woman," Christof barked.

Officer Chung stepped backward toward the tape, hands on her police belt. "It's Officer Chung, sir, and you can take it up with Detective Soo."

"I will. You can count on it."

I unfroze from my shock at Christof's presence and strode toward him. When he saw me he lunged forward, wrapping me in his arms.

"Dear heavens, I thought it was you." He buried his face in my hair and kissed my cheek, his strong arms squeezing so hard I thought I'd pass out.

I tried to pull away. "I'm okay, Chris. Promise. But I've got to answer some more questions."

His arms went rigid, and he held me at arm's length. "Don't say a word. Not one word. Do you hear me? I'll call my lawyer."

"You *are* a lawyer, and anyway, it's too late. I've already answered a few of his questions. I've got nothing to hide."

When I tried to pass him he grasped my upper arm, wrenching a yelp out of me. I stared down at his grip. "You're hurting me."

He let go and ran his fingers through his hair. He placed his hands on his hips, a look of both surprise and sorrow on his face. "Sorry," he mumbled as the reporters locked onto our commotion.

One had already stuck her microphone in my face, which he waved off, glaring at her so fiercely that she backed away, though she remained ready to pounce if given the chance. "Don't say another word. Let me call my lawyer."

"You're a lawyer, Christof. If it's that important to you, then come with me."

He grabbed my arms again and bent his head close to mine, whispering, "You need a criminal lawyer, Didi. These reporters are saying you and Mose are the prime suspects. Listen to me for once in your stubborn life."

I puffed up my chest, trying to appear taller than I was, and wrenched free from his grasp. "For once in *your* life, listen to *me*. I can handle this."

I pushed past him and toward Officer Chung. The brunette reporter, foundation two shades darker than necessary and caked with a half-ton of powder, bronzer and shading, shoved the mic in my face, almost hitting my nose.

"How did you know the victim?" she pressed. "Were you in the room when he died? Are there missing bones?"

Officer Chung stuck out her arm, blocking the reporter from harassing me further, and with the other hand held up the police tape, while I gratefully stepped under and hurried down the hallway buzzing with commotion.

"You did this, you son of a—" Christof roared, his face contorted in rage when he laid eyes on Mose.

"Sir," Officer Chung bounded between them both despite staving off the jumble of reporters almost stampeding Mose with their questions. "Walk away, or I will walk you away in cuffs. Do I make myself clear? Sir?"

Christof shoved forward amongst the crowd of camera crews, ignoring the officer, wildly swinging his arms, flailing to catch hold of Mose's soiled shirt.

"Sir! Please leave. Now!"

Officer Chung pushed Christof, catching him off guard. Brian glanced at me. An air of fascination flashed in his eyes as he quickly returned his attention to Christof, trying to pull him away.

Brian whispered something in Christof's ear, and whatever he'd said, it sobered him up. Chris tugged at his cuffs—which I noted covered the beginnings of a tattoo of some sort—straightened his tie, and glared at Mose's retreating form under the police tape. At the last moment, Christof locked onto me, his face an inscrutable mask. He blinked, turned, and trudged down the hallway in the opposite direction, shoved the doors wide, and stormed out of the building.

"So… that went well," Mose mumbled for my ears only, taking me by the elbow. "Let's get this over with, shall we? Then we'll regroup at your place."

CHAPTER 15

Ohile it was good to see color back in Mose's cheeks, this face-off with Detective Soo proved tricky. Like Callum had suggested, he was no fool, and my habit of turning beet red when I attempted to lie would not help.

"Ms. Day, as I understand it, you came after Dr. Aten phoned this morning?"

"That's right."

"Would you tell me what happened after that?"

"Oh, uh, I drove over and found him on the floor with Landon."

He jotted down a few notes on his pad and looked up. "What time would you say that happened?"

"The call? Gosh, about 5:30 this morning, I think."

Detective Soo nodded. "The drive over... how long did that take?"

"A bit. Why?"

"Because I'm establishing a timetable, Ms. Day. How long did it take you to drive here?"

"I don't know... maybe ten minutes. Fifteen at the max."

He scribbled on his pad again and flipped it shut. "So according to you, Dr. Aten phoned at 5:30 AM. You drove over directly and found

Dr. Aten and the victim them on the floor in Dr. Aten's office. Is that right?"

"Uh… I guess so." I rubbed my arms against the chill in the air even though the hallway and office were stuffed with people and it was summertime.

"Okay, then could you explain why you didn't call until 6:30 AM?"

I stood, mouth agape, waiting for the words to come. Crap. What now?

"Uh, I don't know. I checked on Mose, and he was inconsolable, so I made sure he was okay first."

Even to my ears, it sounded hollow. The detective's eyes were unyielding holes boring into mine, and his brows knitted together in frank disbelief.

"Ms. Day, please explain the delay. If you received the call at 5:30, and it took fifteen minutes to arrive, that's only 5:45. That leaves forty-five unaccounted for minutes. So tell me, Ms. Day, what were you doing all that time? Consoling Dr. Aten could have been done simultaneously while calling the police."

I wracked my brain for an answer. "Right, I, um, noted the time of the call at 5:30 because it's an unusual hour to receive a call. At first I thought it was my sister Laura, and that something might be wrong with her or my niece or nephew." I paused and scanned the room, waiting for the detective to cuff me.

Detective Soo ran a hand through his cropped black hair and stared. If it weren't for the other fifteen cops and forensic lab techs in the room with us right now, I'd swear he was going to cuff me and throw me in a cell downtown. Some officers cast curious stares in our direction, though most kept focused on their jobs.

Detective Soo pinched his lips, a sign I'd better hurry or else end up in the back of a police car.

"Anyway, I had to dress, and that was ten to fifteen minutes."

"Why not call the police then?" Detective Soo pressed.

"Because I didn't know what had happened. I wanted to get to Mose as quickly as possible. Plus, he didn't exactly tell me where he was. I only guessed he was at work."

Detective Soo shifted his weight. "Why is that?"

"Because he texted me last night saying he'd have breakfast for me here."

"Why come so early? What were you doing?"

"Excuse me?" I said and folded my arms over my chest. My face flushed, and a wave of heat radiated off my skin and prickled the hairs on the back of my neck. "No, Detective. Mose and I... we're colleagues and nothing more."

He arched a brow. "Then why the rush, Ms. Day?"

"I didn't mean that, I—"

"Then what?" He sighed, clearly tired of the conversation.

"Mose Aten and I are friends. Best friends. I'd do anything for him. So your timetable is all screwed up. He called at 5:30, it took fifteen minutes to dress, I raced over, but due to traffic, it was another fifteen minutes, and by the time I made it to his office, which was another ten minutes from parking and the walk, that only left about fifteen minutes. Is that all, Detective?"

Detective Soo squinted against the bright light they'd set up to gather evidence and inspect the crime scene. He took his time, like he was waiting for me to break down and confess. When he spoke, his voice was raspy and hard. "Don't leave town, Ms. Day. We'll be in touch." He handed me a business card. "If you think of anything, anything at all, no matter how trivial, call."

He turned to walk out when I blurted, "He has a reputation for offending people, Detective. Landon Fisher, that is."

Detective Soo pivoted and faced me. A flash of curiosity within his eyes. "Oh? How so?" He pulled out his notepad again and flipped to a clean page.

"Mose and a few of the teaching assistants mentioned that no one liked him at his undergraduate program. The TAs said that every-where Landon goes chaos follows."

He held my stare blink for blink and nodded. "Thank you, Ms. Day. Your statement has been... interesting."

He raced out of the room, leaving me a sweaty mess in the center of the forensics team and the other officers while Mose stood by the door and studied the layout of his room. From the scrunched brown, folded arms, and tight expression, I'd say something was off. I waved a finger at him and stepped through the door and down the back hallway.

When we were out of sight of everyone, I whispered, "What did you notice?"

He walked out the door leading to the back parking lot and scoured the area. When he was convinced no one was within earshot, he said,

"Something's missing."

"What?"

"My phone."

We stood in silence for a moment. Why would anyone take Mose's phone? Why was Landon in his office at such a late hour? Was he responsible for the torn papers, slashed furniture, and missing phone? If so, who was he working for, and why?

"Curious," I said. "Also, I forgot to mention earlier that something else is missing."

Mose tilted his head. "What?"

"Nordic jewelry. In the boxes sent from Denmark, the inventory logs show a list of jewelry found in the grave with the bones. A couple of them are gone."

"Which ones?"

"A set of keys and a broach."

Mose grinned. "Let's hope Denmark is as anal retentive as we are. We'll check with them, but first, we've got to get out of here. I need a shower, though escaping the vultures wanting their next story might prove difficult."

He gestured for me to walk ahead of him, and after dodging multiple reporters, we made our way to the parking lot. For once, I knew exactly which car was his. A good thing too, because more news vans pulled up with a screeching halt, hopped out, and raced for the doors. We had about five minutes before they'd be directed out here toward us.

Mose's shiny red Porsche was like a beacon in a storm. It was a birthday gift last year from his parents. I remembered how he was hesitant to drive it and remarked it would be offensive not to. His parents loved him and could afford the finer things in life. Why not enjoy them? It wasn't like he'd ever earn enough from his associate professor's salary. We were only young once.

We stepped off the curb and into the lot, and when we were nearing his red Porsche, someone called my name. I stiffened, my stomach in knots.

"Crap. It's Christof. Mose, get in the car."

"But—"

"Mose, don't argue. I'll be there in a minute."

He jogged the remaining feet to his car and slid into the driver's seat. I waved at Christof and prepared for the deluge of questions. Shaking his head, jaw clenched, he glared at Mose and motioned for me to walk closer.

"Why don't you let me drive you home? You'll only get in more trouble with that one."

"Chris, stop. I'm tired. Mose needs to clean up, and we need a breather, alright? I don't need to hash out what happened earlier. If you want to contact your lawyer friend, then fine. Message me his contact information, and I'll be happy to talk with him if that'll make you feel better."

"Feel better?" His voice tightened in a fit of anger that made me want to curl up in a fetal position and shove the covers over my head. "Didi, I hardly think you're in any state of mind to think rationally. You are being investigated for murder. *Murder*, Didi. For once, let me help you."

"No." I scurried off to the passenger side of Mose's Porsche, only a few feet away. "Go home, Christof. Cool off. I'll call later."

I opened the car door, got in, and slammed the door shut. "Start the car, Mose. Get me out of here."

Mose cast a speculative glance at me. "Do you want to talk about it?"

I didn't respond. Christof stuffed his hands in his pockets as we pulled out of the parking lot and tore off down the street.

CHAPTER 16

"Y ou okay?" Mose asked, occasionally glancing at me as he maneuvered through the throng of cars on the road.

"I'm fine." I rested the side of my head on the sun-drenched passenger's window.

Shop owners were opening their doors, eagerly ushering in customers clad in slouchy sweatshirts and leggings or jeans fit for the cool, unpredictable summer mornings, each clutching a coffee cup for warmth.

"We had another argument, and he stormed out. He gave me an ultimatum that I either agree to go to some office party or he'd find someone else."

Mose remained quiet, stealing glances as we stopped and started through traffic. Honking horns, flashing lights, and smells of coffee, tar, and restaurant smoke all faded into the background.

"I didn't call."

"Oh," Mose replied.

Nothing else needed to be said. It was over. Unfortunate? Yes, but I was done with the relationship. It was years in the making, only I hadn't wanted to see it until now. However, forgetting to call him about the party wasn't by choice. I'd forgotten in all the mayhem. Add the jet lag from my trip to Scotland, the attack on Dr. Gates' friend Roger, and perhaps the mystery man following me wherever I went, and the party fell to the wayside. Out of mind. It was probably for the best. Until he'd shown up today.

"Wait a minute." I sat up, the leather seats squeaking under the sudden shift, and looked over at Mose. "Why *was* Christof at the university? How did he find out?"

He shrugged. "The news?"

I sank into the seat a smidge. Could he have heard it from the news and made it to the university that quickly? His office was a good hour away from mine, and he was always at work by 6:00 AM. Early bird and the worm sort of thing.

"Maybe."

I kept quiet the rest of the ride to his home. Something didn't sit right, yet I couldn't put a finger on it.

We pulled into the circular drive by the building and a valet trotted over. With a warm smile he greeted us enthusiastically. "Hello!"

We made our way up to the penthouse floor. The foyer floor was gorgeous, a black-and-white marble checkerboard pattern. We walked through the sliding glass door into the penthouse apartment. The quaint kitchen that could fit six people was stocked with my favorite juices and oodles of liquor in the mini fridge. It was a perfect place for entertaining, even though Mose rarely used it for that purpose. The curtains were drawn, showing the wonders of downtown Boston. To the right of the balcony stood a floor to ceiling bar stocked with thousand-dollar bottles of wine and liquor, but best of all were two six packs of my favorite apple cider ale. This was my place to escape from it all, including the constant fights with Christof and Shane Bernard's latest off comment. It was my home away from home. Gosh, how Chris would throw a raging fit if he found out I'd been to Mose's. Although such insecurity was a total turnoff, I gave him leeway because he'd been so good to me for so long. At least that's what I'd told myself.

Mose tossed his keys in a wicker basket sitting on a modern glass table in the foyer. He started unbuttoning his soiled shirt and bobbed his head toward the fully stocked bar.

"Grab some sparkling grape juice. I'll be a minute."

He tugged off the shirt and tossed it in the garbage, then walked down the hallway leading to his bedroom. The heat rose in my cheeks when he unbuttoned his pants and tugged them down, exposing his lean, tawny legs and skintight gray briefs. I eyed all the juice in the bar. Orange, grape, cranberry… I kept looking until finding the exact one I wanted. I uncapped the bottle with a quick jab on the countertop and took a long drink. The cold apple cider burned as it slid down my throat. I closed my eyes and sighed.

What have I gotten myself into?

I wandered over to his kitchen, and after rummaging through his refrigerator, whipped us up a charcuterie of meats, an assortment of cheese, crackers, and black olives.

When Mose came into the living room, he grinned. "You read my mind."

Rubbing a white towel against his jet-black hair, he picked up an olive and plopped it in his mouth. He slid out a bar stool and sat facing me, choosing a few items from the plate and putting them on a napkin.

"What's on your mind?" he asked.

I snorted. "Other than Landon's murder? Not much."

"Sit. Eat."

I made myself nibble on an olive or two before pushing my napkin away. I flipped through the photos I'd taken on my phone directly before Mose had entered the bone lab and nearly scared me to death. What was I missing? Surely something would stick out. Scream at me the answer to my tired mind. The connection.

"What are you looking at?"

I barely glanced up at Mose when it hit me. Scrolling back to the box of jewelry, I zoomed in.

"Mose, eat up. We're going back to the lab."

"What? Why?" he mumbled over a mouthful of food.

I shoved the phone in his face, and the shock made his features twist. His jaw clenched, and then his cheeks turned ashen.

"Right. If that's true, though, we'll need backup."

CHAPTER 17

"*I'm starting to think you like me, lassie.*" Callum's laugh made me grin.

"On the contrary, Detective, we require your services."

"*That will cost you, bonnie. I'm up for a seafood platter and some whiskey if you care to cross the pond.*"

"Raincheck? We're a little busy."

"*I'm listening.*"

I filled Callum in on everything that had happened, and when I finished, we waited for an eternity before he spoke.

"*Aye, you need help, lassie, but while I cannot physically help, I can give you a lead.*"

Mose and I eyed each other, sitting up taller on our stools. "What lead?"

"*Anice has escaped confinement. She was last seen at St. Magnus Cathedral. Unfortunately, she got away, but I found something you might find interesting. She dropped a piece of jewelry. It's old.*"

"Can you send a picture?"

My phone dinged.

I pulled up the image and my stomach dropped. I drew my elbows into my sides and zoomed in. "Shoot," I mumbled.

"What?" Mose reached over the kitchen island to take the phone from my limp hand.

Sweat broke out on my brow, and I fanned my heated face, trying to make sense of it all. Anice had escaped. She'd dropped some jewelry, which in and of itself was curious, except that the jewelry matched the ones I'd just shown Mose, and they were engraved with all-too-familiar initials.

Mose looked up; brows knitted together. "Do those initials mean anything to you?"

I nodded. "They're Hulda's."

"That means?"

"Anice's escape, Roger's attack, Landon's murder, they're all related."

"I don't follow," Mose replied.

Callum's deep voice boomed across the line. "*Aye, lassie. Although, it wasn't Anice that killed your student. She didn't escape until today. Still don't know how she did it.*"

I rested my elbows on the countertop and held my head in my hands. Anice had her grubby hands all over the police department in Scotland, so it was a lot easier to escape than Callum wanted to admit.

"Uh, guys?" There was distress in Mose's voice. "Someone emailed me from the school. There's another body."

"What?" I whispered, a chill crawling over my skin and settling in the pit of my stomach. "Who?"

His tone was grim. "I don't know. There's another e-mail, but this one comes from an unknown sender." He gulped. "It says to bring the bones to the Zeus fountain at 2:00AM the day after next, or I and Didi will be killed."

My hand flew to my mouth as I processed what he'd said. Another body? Now this? This was getting out of hand!

"*Didi, contact the police,*" Callum said with urgency. "*That detective will keep someone outside your door.*"

"No." Mose shook his head and sighed. "If we go to the police, they'll kill us sooner. They've also hacked our phones and devices."

I gritted my teeth. "We know who took your phone. Any other suggestions?"

"Give me the address," Callum said. *"Let me run it through our system."*

"Won't the mole in your department find out?" I asked. "No, Callum, we play by their rules."

I gestured to the phone and looked at Mose. Fortunately, he understood, nodding his assent.

"Callum, we've got to go. We'll be in touch. By the way," I added, needing to know if her appearance had changed at all in the days since her capture, "can you send me the picture they took of Anice at the psychiatric lockup?"

"I'll see what I can do."

I hung up before he could say another word and stared wide-eyed at Mose. Hopping off the stool, I made a beeline for his pantry, pulling out flour, sugar, and chocolate chips, then I headed to the refrigerator. When I had all the ingredients for cookies and a cake I set the oven to 350 degrees Fahrenheit. I dumped the components together in the blender and switched it on. I turned the sink on full blast, raced to the television and flipped it on, turning the volume as loud as I dared. I beckoned Mose over with a flick of my finger.

I cupped my hand to his ear, but he took my hand and whirled me around, pulling me to his chest. "Turn on slow dance music," he called out, and the television switched from some comedy to music.

He grinned, swayed to the music, and pulled me closer until we were cheek to cheek. He nuzzled my cheek, his warm breath tickling my neck. His lips were beside my ear, and I wondered if he'd lost his mind.

"Do you think they're watching us?" he whispered.

I drew in a shaky breath. Why wouldn't they?

"To anyone watching, we're having a romantic moment. Go with it," he urged.

Mose nuzzled my neck with his cheek, and I giggled, but it sounded more like a strangled duck. I squeezed my eyes shut and hesitated for a second before throwing all caution to the wind and kissing his clean-shaven cheek. Working my way up to his ear, I felt his arms tense, but I was in this one hundred percent. I kissed his lobe before speaking.

"We need burner phones, a new place to stay, and a new form of transportation," I whispered. "Once we get those, I'll contact Nick and see if he can trace the e-mail."

Mose gripped my palm and pushed me out, twirling me once, and then pulling me back in. Breathless, I slammed into his chest and tried to get my bearing before he extended his arm, pushing me away and back again. Dizzy, I laid my head onto the crook of his neck.

He gently tilted my chin up to face him, mouthing, "Go with it."

His lips brushed mine and my breath caught. His hand slid against my upper back, forcing me to arch against him. His lips touched mine. At first it was soft... sweet. Then he pressed harder, parted his lips, and I was putty in his arms. When his mouth slid over to nibble on my neck, I gasped.

He pulled back, gauging my reaction before he tangled his hands in my hair and hungrily kissed my mouth, my throat, my jaw... My body molded to his and we flopped onto the couch, and I didn't know where I ended, and he started.

BEEP! BEEP! BEEP!

We froze, our clothes half off.

"Crap!" I shot up and ran to the oven, jerked it open, and flailed my arms at the heaps of smoke that wafted up, stinging my eyes and nose. I turned it off and, coughing in fits, I grabbed a hot mitt and retrieved a flat sheet out of the oven and dropped it with a clang on the stovetop.

Mose was on the stool next to me on his knees, waving a towel up at the smoke alarm, as

"Why did you leave cookies in the oven?" I said, my lungs spasming against the smoke. Jogging over to the balcony windows, I slid them open and breathed in the clean air.

"I didn't." Mose hopped down after most of the smoke had cleared out. He walked to the cookies and picked up a singed note and groaned.

"What?"

I trotted up and stared at the note. The artistic swirls of a woman's hand were clear.

Hope you have a wonderful day. Can't wait for our dinner tonight.

Love,

Olivia

I gawked up at him, face flushed, and a hand to my white, lacy bra. I bolted for the couch where my shirt had fallen and yanked it on. Crossing my arms against my chest, I waited for him to speak. But he didn't say a word, just watched me. After a few more awkward moments, he tossed the charred note onto the granite countertop. He ran a hand through his thick hair and studied my confused expression. Walking over to me, he gently brushed his thumb across my cheek, eyes locked on.

"We'd better get going," Mose said. "Lots to do."

CHAPTER 18

The car ride to the local strip mall was awkward at best. I kept sneaking glances at Mose, who was solely focused on the road.

I watched the crowded sidewalks, lost in thought and unexpected emotions. An attraction to Mose hadn't ever crossed my mind. Never. Sure, he was handsome, but he'd been more like a brother than anything else. Besides, there had always been Christof.

Mose swerved, an epithet on his tongue. I fought the urge to laugh seeing his white-knuckled grip on the steering wheel. I always found it interesting that he cursed in ancient Egyptian. He was born in Egypt, though had attended school in the United States. Although he'd gone with his parents on their work trips when he could, he was as American as it gets. Football games on the weekends, hot dog lover since forever, and his favorite pie was apple.

He parked in a parking garage, and we got out and walked in silence into the phone store. I gave a precursory scan of the crowd before entering, noting anyone acting suspicious. Well, we were in Boston. Everyone is suspicious of something. It's what I loved about this city. We took people for who they were, and if you didn't like it... tough.

"Here."

Mose tossed a few phones at me along with prepaid cards and then stomped off to the checkout, leaving me jostling the armful of items.

I jogged after him when I kept everything from toppling to the floor in the crook of one arm. Placing my hand on his as he pulled out his wallet, his platinum credit cards in full view, I lowered my voice. "Wait. Won't they have those tracked too?"

Mose blinked twice at his platinum credit cards before stuffing them in his back pocket. "Now what? Do you have a better plan?"

I smiled nervously at the impatient cashier, who glared at us like we were escaped convicts on the run. "Not exactly. Give me a second."

I whipped out my phone and dialed. After a long ring, a voice groggy with sleep answered. *"Hello?"*

While I was sorry for the late call to Scotland, it was necessary. "Can you do us a teensy, weensy favor? I forgot my card at home. Would you buy this stuff for us? I promise to pay you back."

The store clerk sat on his stool and glared at me. I handed my cell to him, and he started exchanging words with Callum, my rescuer of late.

"Yeah… yeah… Have a good one." He turned back to us, cracked his knuckles, handed the cell to me, shoved the bag of items toward Mose, and started ringing up the next customer.

Mose frowned, staring at me with an arched brow. "He's not your boyfriend?"

I shook my head and followed him out the door. A half block down, Mose nudged me with his elbow. "Then what's going on between you two, anyway?"

"Who?" I glanced distractedly at Mose.

When we left the store I caught sight of a man in a red parka. It was the same person who had parked beside us in the parking lot. He'd apparently waited while we were in the phone store. Talk about conspicuous. Not to mention his shaggy haircut, which couldn't cover all the ink on his neck. The most prominent tattoo was a dagger next to a black cat with piercing green eyes. But it was the snake slithering through a green vine that gave me pause. Snakes. I shuddered. Never a fan, and as if fate were playing a trick, snake symbols seemed to pop up wherever I looked recently.

I picked up speed and glanced at Mose, noticing his inquisitive stare. There was no way of telling him without alerting the man who was hot on our heels. From the looks of it, Mose was completely oblivious to our situation. When I looked at the reflection in the next storefront to see if we'd lost the man, Mose spoke again.

"Callum," he stated flatly, though he spoke the name like it left an acrid taste in his mouth.

"Him? Oh, uh, he's a detective." Nope, still on our tail.

"Now tell me something I don't know."

"Like what?"

We came up on the next cross street and waited with the crowd to walk on the next green light. I snuck a peek behind us. Crap. He was now an arm's length away.

"You know... is there something *between* you two?"

The light turned green and off the crowd went. I yanked Mose at the last second and took off running down a different street, peering back whenever I could.

"Hey! What's going on?" Mose snapped, matching my strides.

"We're being followed. Shut up and run."

His long, lean legs soon had him leading the way and we swerved through tourists and natives alike, some flipping us the bird as we flew past. The muscles in my calves burned, and my lungs ached from the effort to breathe while we ran full sprint block after block. We couldn't shake the guy. Left, right, left. We kept running, each breath more painful and ragged than the last, yet I dared not slow down. Mose was getting farther ahead. We needed a distraction and fast, or I'd slow us both down to the point of...

"Right!" I barked, sweat trickling down my face and back, even in the cool air.

Mose's lean frame swerved down an alley. The man was catching up, but his sights were on me, not Mose. When I went around the corner to the alley Mose had entered, I shoved with all my might at the fruit stand and sent the melons, apples, oranges, and watermelons tumbling to the ground and rolling down the sidewalk.

Legs shuddering with exertion, I caught the curse words in the wind of the cart owner, but I didn't waste time looking back. At the first door on the left, I grasped the knob and turned, thanking my lucky stars. I flung it open and slammed it shut behind me. My back against it, gasping for air, I sank down until my knees were up around my ears.

"It's about time." Mose yanked me up.

I glared at Mose. "Go. He's… coming."

A couple of servers threw us curious stares but no one said anything as we wound through the kitchen and out into the main room. Strobe lights lit up a dance floor that had seen its height during the 1970s. Familiar territory at last. I knew the owner of the place, someone I knew from grade school, and she'd shown me around just a couple of months ago. Her intent was to revive the place into a teen and young adult club. What better way to keep them off the streets? I'd been impressed with how she'd cleaned it up, keeping some of its unique 70s features. Better yet, she'd told me to stop by anytime I wanted. While I'd wanted to come a few weeks prior when it opened, I'd been in school and then Scotland.

Now was as good a time as any, and the crowd that I'd hoped for didn't disappoint. Loads of jumping, gyrating teens pumped their arms up high to the rhythm of the music. Packed like sardines, both Mose and I blended in surprisingly well. We both looked young for our age, which in any other situation, career-wise, would have been a con.

When Mose hesitated, I stepped into the pulsing mob. A few guys eyed me with approval and a couple of young men pressed against me, grinding to the music.

"Un uh, guys. Hands off." Mose shoved his hand between us, and both men immediately backed away, holding their hands up in surrender.

"No problem, man. Don't get so bothered." The young guy wore a white undershirt with a pale blue jacket, his sockless feet stuffed into swanky hundred-dollar shoes. He cocked his bright, purple-colored head. "Hey, aren't you Dr. Aten?"

Three to four more people turned their attention to us. I stiffened, searching for our hunter, then one young man tapped Mose on the back.

"It is you. Hey, guys! This is Dr. Aten. This man's got women everywhere. Is this your pocket girlfriend, doc?" The young man winked at us and gave an approving nod. "Nice."

"What?" Mose asked, looking from one smiling face to the next.

"Pocketing," said the young man. "Having more than one woman but not posting about it."

"Ah, I think you have me mixed up with someone else." Mose tried ushering me through the crowd of now ten deep onlookers.

"Then what about Oliva? I thought she was dating you. That's what she's told everyone," the young man said.

Mose stopped, his hand on my lower back, and turned. "I don't know what pocketing is, and I don't care. My relationships are for me alone. Got it?"

"Ah," he said. "No problem, man. Relationships, as in plural. Nice." He winked again at Mose, who rolled his eyes and pushed me on into the middle of the crowd.

Mose's long fingers curled over my waistband, and he pulled me closer to his side. I tried not to squirm against the intense heat. He was staring off into the distance, and I followed his gaze to the right wall. A hazy mirror reflected Mose and I surrounded by psychedelic lights and images of floating spheres and starbursts. Right next to us was a surfer man clad in a white tank top, bleach blond hair, red swim trunks, and flip-flops. On our other side was a pineapple crate, on which an attractive young woman leaned lazily back and forth, studying the crowd through half-closed lids like they'd been almost glued in place. She was beautiful. Innocent and sweet. Then I saw the red jacket and my blood ran cold.

Was this Anice's doing?

The song changed and the bass thrummed in my chest. I turned toward Mose and pressed against him. The tune was a slow one. Mose went rigid at first, then gradually relaxed, following my lead.

I moved near his ear and said, "He's here."

Mose nodded tightly, looking from me to the door. "Any ideas?"

I shook my head, then took his hand and led him further onto the dance floor, yelling into his ear, "Dance! Or he'll see us."

This was the only time I thanked my lucky stars for being born of average height, like Mose, and we blended into the crowd with ease. Most of the others had lost interest in us by this point, and everyone jumped and swayed to the rhythm. The ultra-sweet scent of marijuana made me green, but it was my sticky clothes that I noticed the most. Mose's white shirt was nearly translucent, exposing his muscular biceps and chest. Packed like sardines, we bumped against each other. Not even a slip of paper could get between us.

"Stay calm," he whispered into my ear, jerking me close. "He's walking into the crowd."

"Hey, jackass. What are you, a perv?" the young bohemian woman who had been parked on the pineapple crate snarled. Parka man had shoved her aside in his haste to find us.

"Don't look." Mose gripped my chin and looked me dead in the eyes. "Do you trust me?"

My heart beat wildly and my knees wobbled, threatening to let go. All I could do was nod.

"Good. I won't let anything happen to you."

The music faded into the background as I kept laser focused on his brown eyes searching mine.

"Ready?"

Ready for what? To run? To fight?

Mose wrapped his arms around my waist, his warm breath cooling the perspiration on my face, then pressed his lips onto mine. He moved us expertly to the rhythm, my feet practically floating off the floor.

Sinking into his arms, I melded my body against his and let go. My hands flew up around his neck. I stroked his sweaty hair and face, pulling at his shirt, pulling him closer... closer to me. And then...

"Run!" he hissed into my ear, shoving me toward the door.

I shook my head, not understanding. I touched my bruised lips.

"Didi, run! Run!"

He grabbed my upper arms, thrusting me forward out of the crowd and toward the front door. "I'll go left, you go right when we get out. We'll meet up at the bone lab. Don't worry, Didi. Just run!"

CHAPTER 19

I tripped running up the stairs. My ankle wobbled, and I slammed onto my right knee. I stifled a moan, shot up to my feet with the aid of Mose's muscular arms, and dashed to the door. Shoving it open, I took off running to the right like he'd said. I couldn't resist the urge to look back.

My hair whipped about my face, stinging it where it struck as I whirled my head around, catching Mose's black head zigzagging through the crowd and disappearing among the masses.

I tore around the corner and down another side street. Sweat stung my eyes, yet I ran faster. I passed person after person and felt their curious stares follow me. After about a mile I slowed, my legs crying out for relief, and searched for a marker that would place where I was. I spotted the familiar knotted tree on the university grounds a few blocks away. I pushed through the pain until I reached the university steps of the anthropology building, staring at the perimeter of yellow police tape in front of the entrance. A gaggle of reporters lingered behind trees in the shade, either on their phones or being recorded by their crew.

I stole around to the side entrance, which hadn't been cordoned off, and traversed the halls until I reached more yellow police tape. A swarm of reporters crowded the area. The brunette reporter from earlier, whose caked makeup dripped beige in the sweaty confines of the tight corridors, had stuck her microphone up to a cop's face, firing question after question.

I hid behind a corner and strained to hear.

"Can you tell us the identity of the deceased?"

"No comment."

"What about the gender?"

"The chief will address your questions when she's ready. No further comment."

"Chief! Chief!" the reporter called out. "What can you tell us about the deceased?"

The chief was an average height female in her mid-forties with severely tied back hair, and a permanent grimace. Her crisp blue uniform strained against her biceps and cinched in tightly at her fore-arms. The severe expression she held for the reporter was enough to silence a man twice her size.

"Ladies and gentlemen, I'll answer your questions one at a time. First, let me confirm that there has been another death on the premises within in the last few hours. We don't know yet if the two are connected."

"Chief, can you tell us the gender or identity of the deceased from either death?" another eager reporter asked over the roar.

"The one early this morning is of a male between the ages of twenty and twenty-five. The second is a man somewhere between thirty and thirty-five."

"Chief," said the female reporter, "can you give us cause of death?"

"The one from this morning was from a bullet wound to the chest while the other one was from strangulation. That's all for now."

The chief ducked under the yellow police tape to the clamoring of reporters' questions while I stood flush against the wall.

So Landon was shot. Not surprising with all the blood I'd seen, though from the splattering and state of the room, he'd put up a good fight. But who was this other man that had died?

I tiptoed down the hallway undetected and climbed up to the

second floor then descended to the other side of the building. The bone lab was a few feet down the hall. Fortunately there weren't any lurkers; unfortunately that dreaded yellow tape crisscrossed the entrance.

I grimaced. Now what? Breaking and entering was a crime, yet Mose wanted to meet here and I couldn't do it standing out in the hallway. I'd last two seconds out in the open with all the reporters crawling these halls. I stared at the shiny police tape for a second. You only live once, right? I popped the door open and crouched, stepping under the tape. Once inside, I closed the door with a soft click.

"About time."

I whirled on the balls of my feet. "Mose!" I screeched. His brown eyes were calm below long, sleek lashes. My heart started beating again when I saw his sweat-soaked clothes. "You about gave me a heart attack. When did you get here?"

"A few minutes ago."

"Did you find out who the other murder victim is?"

Mose's grin slipped. "Uh, Didi, why don't you have a seat?"

I waved off the stool he pulled out from underneath the lab table. "Tell me."

"It's Francisco."

I crumpled onto the chair. The room blurred as tears stung my eyes. "Freddie? But why?"

Mose shook his head and patted me on the back. "Hey, have you still got the phones?" he asked.

I pulled out a few that I'd stuffed in my pockets before ditching the bag halfway through the run. He took one and set to charging it while I found the prepaid phone cards.

"We'll have to be careful with these," I sniffled, wiping my face with the cuff of my sleeve. "Not much on here."

Mose motioned to my phone. "Bring up the photos again. Let's have a good look at the initials."

I sighed and stared up at him. "They're Hulda's initials."

"Who's this Hulda?" Mose pulled out an adjacent stool and sat next to me.

I eyed him carefully and pursed my lips. How much should I tell? The answer, of course, was everything. I'd wanted to keep these "sightings" a secret for a tad longer though. "Hear me out before judging, alright?"

He held up his palms.

"Fine." I sighed. "Hulda is a shield maiden from the Viking era. She's appeared to me a couple of times, and she saved my life in the tunnels under St. Magnus Cathedral."

He arched his brows and sat forward, leaning his elbows against the tabletop. To his credit, he kept quiet.

"When I searched for her, I found she's from some small town... um, Kaupang, I think. Anyway, it's in what is now Norway. I suspect these missing jewelry pieces from Denmark are hers. If the initials prove to be hers, that is. from the missing jewelry, the initials, the missing bones, and the deaths of Landon and Frankie, I'd bet my life on it all being related to Scotland and—"

"Anice Foster."

I nodded and pointed to the charging phone. "Is it ready to make a call?"

"Sure. Why?"

I snatched it off the table, keeping the cord intact to continue charging, and dialed.

"Aunt Didi? Ready to go back to Scotland?" Nick's sixteen-year-old voice squeaked on the last word, which made me smirk. He'd nearly lost his life when Anice abducted him in Scotland less than a week ago. Why he'd want to go back so soon was a mystery.

"No, but I need your help."

I heard him clap his hands and rub them together. *"Is this related to the shield and those two deaths at your university?"*

I blinked. "How did you find out about that?"

"Uh, I listen to the news from time to time. It's boring here. With the baby crying all night and day, Mom and Dad yelling at each other for diapers, bottles, and pacifiers, I turn the news on to drown out everything."

Huh. Laura hadn't mentioned anything in our last talk. She'd painted a rosier picture. "Can you look up an e-mail address for me? We need to know who sent it."

Two minutes later, and a few rounds of knuckles popping, Nick's crackling voice returned. *"It's untraceable. Whoever sent this didn't want to be found. Sorry, Aunt Didi."*

I groaned. "No problem, Nick. Be kind to your parents, okay?" I said as an afterthought. Trouble was brewing there, clearly.

"Alright. Maybe I can help you though, like in Scotland?"

"Not this time, Nick. Take care of your parents, and I'll be in touch."

"Bye," Nick grumbled. I hung up.

"What now?" Mose asked.

"We wait."

"For what?"

"A plan."

We had to connect the pieces we uncovered, and we didn't have a lot of time. First, I needed a cold shower. The two encounters with Mose had left me discombobulated, and a clear head was necessary.

"We need a place to stay. Somewhere no one will expect to find us."

Mose's devilish grin gave me pause. "I've got the perfect place. Let's go."

CHAPTER 20

*T*he texts and calls from Christof were into the double digits, and at some point I'd have to address them. I wasn't the only one. Mose had reached out to Olivia, and he'd been receiving call after call too. He'd already canceled their dinner date, promising to make it up to her in a few days. Judging from his hardened jaw and stiff posture, he was placating her. Their whirlwind relationship left me dumbfounded. He'd never kept a dating partner secret from me, and from the sound of it, they'd been together for some time.

Another ding on my phone. I tossed it onto the seat between Mose and me on our Uber ride. We had to ditch them, and what better way than to drive all over Boston? We planned to leave our cells on this first ride, then get multiple other Ubers to make certain we weren't being tailed before ending up at the secret hiding spot Mose had picked.

We paid the driver and exited the car. It was late afternoon now. The air was thick with warmth, though not enough to drive people indoors. Parents with children clustered at ice cream shops or sporting venues while groups of boisterous teens lounged in coffee shops and restaurants, or just milled about downtown. The blocks were packed with cars, and honking filled the air with a rhythmic pulse. People bustled about carrying bags of groceries or the latest fashion trends, and they scowled at each other when someone was in the way or bumped into them. It was busy and chaotic and wonderful.

We stopped at a local hot dog vendor to scarf some food and drinks before taking yet another Uber.

Once inside the next car, I leaned my head back and closed my eyes, enjoying the lack of calls and beeps of texts. The bumps of the road, Mose's soft breathing, and the sweet songs of Selena Gomez and Taylor Swift lulled me into a twilight sleep.

Images of Hulda came to mind, along with the ancient wooden shield speckled in blue and red. Even after centuries-long decay, it spoke of strength, courage, and determination. Did it belong to a shield maiden? To Hulda? That would be extraordinary. Then there were the initials on pieces of jewelry found in Scotland and the same initials on jewelry from Denmark several hundred miles away. It was common knowledge that the Vikings sailed the deep blue sea, so it wasn't out of the realm of possibility that Hulda had traveled to Denmark. If she'd been in both places, to hold actual evidence of it... that would be too coincidental. On top of all that, there were the deaths today. Landon and Frankie. What about Roger clinging to life in a hospital down the road? How were they all connect—

It hit me like a baseball bat to the gut. I sat up straight. "Stop the car."

The driver gripped the steering wheel so hard his knuckles turned white. "We're still several miles away."

"Stop the car. Now."

Mose stared at me like I'd grown horns. "What's wrong, Didi? Have you remembered something?"

We screeched to a stop. I flung the door wide and jumped out. A quaint cafe with outdoor seating stood half a block away. I bolted toward it, sitting at the last table for two pressed up against the restaurant's front window. If we needed a hasty exit, it would do well.

Menus and glasses of water were placed before us, and only when the waiter left did I open my mouth.

"The initials. How could I have been so stupid?"

"What do you mean? The ones in Scotland?"

"No... Yes... I mean both. Look." I brought up the photos on the burner phone. I'd copied them before leaving our actual phones in the first Uber. "See the initials?"

Mose bent his head close to mine, and the smell of cinnamon and ginger wafted up. What was in his cologne, for Pete's sake?

I gave myself a mental shake. "These initials are the same from the Scotland site and the ones from Denmark. That means Hulda traveled. To Denmark."

I waited, giving him plenty of time to piece everything together.

His mouth dropped open. "Those bones... the ones someone's so keen on stealing—"

"Yep." I bobbed my head so fast I thought the world had turned sideways. They were almost exact replicas of each other. Scotland and Denmark. Maybe Hulda was some kind of ambassador. Yet something about that didn't sit well. Even though women could legally divorce, own land, and be chieftains, lots of scholarly articles cast serious doubt on women traveling outside their villages. But if that were the case, then why would her initials, carved with the same flare and curls, much like a fingerprint, be in two places several hundred miles away from each other? The logical reason nearly leapt off the phone at me and whacked me about the ears. "Don't you see? They're undoubtedly linked. They're Hulda's. I can feel it. Whoever wanted these relates to Anice in some way. The only thing I can think of is that black market operation racket, except Anice isn't the top dog." I shook my head, unable to conceal the grin. "She's not Boss Man."

Mose's brow knitted in confusion. "If she's not Boss Man, then who is? We have not only Anice on our tails, but also whoever this nut is."

He was right. From our dealings with Anice in Scotland, the tentacles of Boss Man's power had worked into local law enforcement and goodness knows what else.

I scanned the crowd before speaking. "Mose, we've got to get to our hideout," I whispered. "How far is it from here?"

"Not far. Let's go."

* * *

MOSE PAID with money he'd withdrawn from several ATMs around Boston on our Uber drives in order to throw off the people tailing us. It also left us with a good amount of cash to live on for a few days until we got this all sorted. I wanted a safe place to take a shower, take a nap, and focus my thoughts. It was difficult with all the running around, and I couldn't help but think that was part of their strategy. Whomever "they" were.

"Here we are." Mose waved his arms wide after stepping out of our final Uber.

I stood with my mouth open, momentarily speechless. "Are you crazy?" I said when I found my voice. "The *Ritz*? Why don't you just put a neon sign on our heads?"

I stomped off toward the entrance. A uniformed man opened the door with a pert grin, eyeing Mose groveling at my heels.

"Doesn't my love approve?"

I spun around and glared at him nose to nose. "What did you say?"

Mose wrapped his arms around my waist and tapped my bottom with one hand. "You are a most demanding lover." Mose winked at the doorman. "Isn't she marvelous?"

"Indeed, sir." The doorman smirked. I fumed.

Mose linked my arm through his and pulled me with him through the door, where another smartly dressed man emerged to greet us. Smiling broadly, he addressed Mose.

"Dr. Casper, it's wonderful to see you again. We've prepared your usual room for this evening. Are we to order in or eat out this evening?"

My eyebrows shot up and I looked from Mose to the finely dressed man.

"We'll be dining in." Mose pecked my check and winked at the man, who grinned.

"Of course, sir. Please, follow me."

We rode the elevator to the top floor and were at long last alone.

I yanked my arm from Mose's and marched into the suite, spinning around, hands balled into fists by my sides. "Dr. Casper? The Ritz? Your... usual? What the—"

Mose held up his hand. "It's not what you think."

I hmphed. "Tell me, Mose, what am I thinking?"

"I don't bring many women here, and I rarely visit. When I do, however, I like to live it up a little. It can't hurt. My parents pay for it anyway."

"What?" I groaned and pressed my fists to my forehead. "Your parents?"

"Genius, right? They'll never track us here."

I scowled. "Mose, they'll easily track your parents. You want them to hunt them down? It's not a far stretch to connect you with them."

Mose waved off my hesitations. "I use the name Dr. Casper. No one knows who that is, and the staff here won't divulge that kind of information to anyone."

"You'd better be sure, Mose, because these people have infiltrated the Scotland police force, and who knows what else?"

I whirled around, then stopped. From the center of the living area, walls of windows overlooked Boston Common and Public Garden. The gas fireplace was lit and warming the room, above which was a large LED TV. Plush seating lined the opposite wall from it, and as I walked through an opening beside the fireplace, there was a wood floored dining area with seating for eight.

"Where in blazes are we?"

Mose flopped onto the couch and flicked on the television. "The Ritz."

I shook my head. "No, what is this place? It's gorgeous."

He flipped through several channels before settling on the local nightly news. "It's the Presidential Suite."

I gasped. "The... Presidential Suite? Mose..." I fanned my face and sat down beside him. "This... your parents... it's too much."

"Forget it." He kept laser focused on the TV. "It's a drop in the proverbial bucket for them."

I placed a clammy palm on my wildly thumping chest and scanned the room. He definitely dropped far from the familial tree. He was a hard worker, and he detested using his parents' name to advance his career.

He cast a sideways glance at me. "Weren't you wanting a shower?"

"What? Oh… yeah."

I got up and drifted into the oversized bedroom, complete with a walk-in closet. The bathroom was ten times bigger than my closet of an office.

"Grab something out of the closet to wear. Mom keeps it stocked with various items. She hopes someday I'll grow up and get married to a respectable girl," Mose called. "There are clean towels set out on the vanity. I'll order us some food. Take your time."

I ran my fingers over the sparkly and sheer gowns. They were for a young woman, and the sheer beauty of the bright red, yellow, and purple fabrics flowed over my skin. Soft as silk. I dare say a few of them were. Even though I itched to try some on, I found a soft cotton t-shirt, some fitted jeans, and underthings and headed off to the shower.

When all the knots in my back had been massaged out from the vibrating streams of water, I dried off and dressed. I even applied a bit of makeup since Mose's mother had seen to a stock of foundations of varying skin tones and lipsticks, blush, and powder to boot.

I looked at the woman in the mirror and touched my full red lips. I tucked a few stray hairs behind my ear and gaped at the cat eye I'd perfected for once in my life. It was a rare transformation, and one I rather felt awkward doing. My job meant dirty nails, sticky clothes, and grit in my hair. My only vanity product was the tinted sunscreen I usually wore.

I walked into the TV room while Mose was lounging on the couch, intent on the weather report for the night. He scrambled to his feet and took in every inch, starting from my head to my feet.

"Wow."

I tugged at the hem of my white cotton V-necked shirt under his intense gaze.

"You look… amazing." I fidgeted under his approval. "Would you care for some wine?"

"Sure," I said with a small smile.

He jogged into the dining room and came back with two glasses, offering me one. "Be careful. We don't want you hungover. No repeats of junior year."

I smirked and took a sip. "Oh."

Mose chuckled. "Non-alcoholic. I made a judgment call."

"Ah, good choice." I held it up. "Skalle!"

"Yes." He held his glass high in the air. "It's only appropriate. To Hulda. Skalle!"

I downed half my glass while Mose stared on, not having touched his drink yet.

"Is there something on my face?" I instinctively patted my cheeks.

"No." His voice went deep. "It's... It's just I haven't seen you dressed up like this in a while."

I looked down at my top and jeans. "I hardly call this dressed up."

He arched a brow. "We can fix that." He stepped closer and the air evaporated from my lungs, leaving me dizzy. He strode confidently across the room and reached a hand to touch my cheek when a loud BRRING interrupted us.

Mose grunted. "One moment."

He went over to the suite phone and returned a few seconds later. "Our dinner is ready. They're bringing it up now."

He met the staff at the door while I blew out my cheeks, thankful for the disruption. I needed to get my head on straight.

"Good evening, Dr. Casper. We'll set this up and leave you to your own devices as requested. If there is anything else you require, please call."

They set up the food in the dining room and took their leave, leaving me staring across the table at Mose.

Things were only getting weirder. Christof, Callum, now Mose... Geez, I *was* a walking disaster.

CHAPTER 21

*D*inner went smoother than I expected, and then we caught the news, checking to see if there were any updates. It was only the same stuff played in a never-ending loop. However, it gave me an idea.

"Hey, listen. Frankie surely wasn't a target. Think about it? Why kill the janitor?"

Mose bunched his forehead. "Maybe he saw something? The killer, perhaps?"

"Exactly. Frankie was in the wrong place at the wrong time. What about Landon? His killing wasn't an accident. He removed the bones without your approval from the bone lab and took them to your office sometime either last night or early this morning. Was he in different clothes?"

Mose knitted his brows together. "Wow, Didi. You amaze me. Why would I pick up on that?"

I huffed. "Think, Mose. Was he wearing the same clothes last night and this morning?"

Mose slowly nodded. "Yes, yes, I think he was. So that means he didn't go home."

"Right. So the murder probably happened before you got there this morning." I shivered thinking about how close Mose was to getting killed himself. With the threatening e-mail, he was probably next on the list. "You mentioned placing the Denmark bones back before leaving. Where did he get the keys to your office?"

Mose licked his lips and winced. "They're mine. I gave them to him. They're on a key chain, and instead of taking the bone lab key off, I gave him the lot."

"Okay, so he took the bones to your office. Why?"

"I don't know."

"Mose, there were papers everywhere, like someone had torn up the place looking for something. What could they be looking for?"

He shook his head, yet the telltale nibble on his lower lip spoke louder than a twenty-one-gun salute at a funeral. "No idea. Although..." Mose got up and strode across the room to the other phone laying in the middle of the dining room table. "There was some correspondence from Denmark. They sent a letter about their findings. Here."

He handed over the phone. A picture of a letter was showing.

"They noted the remains were probably of a man approximately twenty-five to thirty years old. It's also mentioned that the jewelry and keys were initialed with an H and some other letter or rune. The artifacts found with him had a rune in the shape of an R and..." I squinted but couldn't make out what other letter it could be.

"They don't know either. I called them yesterday about it when I took a picture. Things go missing in our office, especially as of late, and I didn't want to lose this correspondence."

I flipped between the pictures of the letter, the bones, and jewelry from Denmark until my eyes turned gritty and tired.

"We need a good night's rest, Didi. We can hit this again in the morning."

"Mose, these people aren't fooling around. We need to figure this out now. Tomorrow may be too late." I scrolled back to the bones. I zoomed in and stared at the chalky substance. "What do you think this white substance is on the bones? Were they like this when you got them?"

Mose bent over me. He twisted his head this way and that until he stared at me wide eyed. "Huh, that's weird. Nope. I wonder what it is?"

"I don't know, but I think I've figured out a way to protect you, the bones, and everyone else."

"What? How?"

Although it was a long shot, it was worth taking. No need to lose another soul tonight or any other night.

"First, we'll need some black outfits."

"No problem." Mose drained his glass of wine and refilled it.

"Next, we'll need back in the bone lab."

Mose groaned and pinched the bridge of his nose. "It has to be the lab? Do you love tempting fate?"

"No, but it's necessary."

He stared at me for a few minutes and then sighed. "Fine. What next?"

* * *

AMID THE DETAILS, my new phone rang. I'd given Laura the number without so much as an explanation, and she'd wisely not asked.

"Hi, Laura. Is everything okay?" I glanced at my watch. It was after midnight.

"Yes, everything's fine. I wanted to check in and make sure that you can make Nick's birthday party this weekend."

Crap! I'd forgotten my nephew's birthday. What kind of aunt was I? "Uh, sure, but why call so late? Is the baby alright?"

Laura's forced sigh followed a high-pitched wail. *"Her vocal cords aren't broken, if that's what you mean. No, she's great."*

Laura's clipped words didn't fool anyone, and a little red flag popped to mind of who wasn't heard across the phone line. "Laura? When's the last time you slept and let your husband help?"

Laura cooed to the baby then said to me, *"I'm fine."*

"That's not what I asked."

"Didi, drop it."

It was happening all over again. My accomplished sister, thinking she could handle it all, probably had banished her husband from any of the child-rearing. She had this fear that only she could take care of Nick when he was little, and it nearly drove her husband to the brink. This time she would co-raise a child with her husband. That was the plan, and Timothy was an upstanding man. Sweet, funny, empathetic... he was the perfect husband. He even put the seat down on the toilet from get go.

"Laura, honey, let Timothy help. Take a nap. Don't forget a shower. Goodness knows how awful you smell."

"Yeah, when you've had a baby, then we'll talk," she snapped.

I paused and waited for her sanity to return, but when she failed to respond like usual after scolding me, I jumped in. "Sister mine, enough. It's past midnight. Your husband wants to help raise this child, and you need some food, sleep, and a shower. Tap him in and get on with it, alright? Don't be a martyr. That baby needs both of you, and right now, she's got half of a mom because you're too stubborn for your own good."

I held my breath and waited for the torrent to follow, but instead, I heard the quiet sobs that usually followed an argument with Timothy about parenting.

"He's right. I'm an awful mess." She sniffled. *"I'm screwing it up again, aren't I? She'll end up hating me like Nick, and Timothy will leave me for... for... for Esmerelda."*

The soft sobs crushed my heart. She'd been this stalwart of strength since we'd lost our parents, and I'd never seen her openly weep about our parents, or anything upsetting for that matter. Bottled up for decades, she'd single-handedly finished med school, residency, and fellowship, all while raising Nick and with rarely a wink of sleep. As for her marriage, the tension between them was palpable, and what Nick had confessed during our brief trip to Scotland, it was anything other than strained, but this new baby was a gift for them both. However, if she didn't let him help, I could only imagine the old wounds splitting open, afresh with memories best left alone.

"Esmerelda? Who's Esmerelda?"

"*His... his colleague,*" she hiccupped. I imagined her tidying up her signature ponytail she'd sported since med school.

Timothy was a financial planner, and a darn good one. Though not stunningly gorgeous, he was attractive, funny, and loyal. The idea of him with another woman was laughable, but Laura wasn't in her right mind, and saying so would only bring another round of arguing, which was the last thing she or I needed.

"Okay, so tell me about it. Why do you think Timothy and Esmerelda are having an affair?"

"*He's always talking about how great she is with this and that. It was Esmerelda who scored the big account. Esmerelda makes the best jokes. Esmerelda makes the best coffee.*"

I snorted. "Timothy doesn't even drink coffee."

"*I know!*" she wailed.

"Hey, Laura? He's *not* having an affair."

"*How do you know? She's all he talks about.*"

Somehow, I doubted it. I had to steer the conversation elsewhere.

"What about Nick? How can you say he's screwed up, huh? He loves you."

She sniffed. "*He does?*"

"Laura, of course he does. He wants to live up to your expectations, which, by the way, are exceptionally high. Plus, he's quite the computer whiz. I'd say you've raised an excellent young man. As for Timothy, have you talked with him about this?"

"*Are you kidding? He'd think I'm crazy.*"

I rubbed the back of my neck and leaned my head against the fluffy pillows. Mose had taken several pillows and an extra blanket to sleep on the couch in front of the bedroom window, and as Laura scoffed, I stared at the rise and fall of his chest. Always the calm in the storm, he was the absolute best thing that had ever happened to me, and the thought of losing him to some psychopath left me cold.

"No, no, he won't," I whispered. "I'm sure he's got some insecurities about you as well. All those late nights with those hunky docs? Please, Laura, that man is a freaking saint. He's only got eyes for you. Ask him. He'll tell you."

"You're right." She stifled a yawn. *"What am I thinking? Ugh, these late nights, work... I tell you, it's enough to drive anyone—"*

"Crazy?"

We both chuckled, which stirred Mose. He popped his head off the pillow and squinted into the darkness, murmuring, "Are you okay?"

"Time to go, sis. Seriously, get some rest, food, and a shower. You'll feel a million times better. Start with waking up your husband. He'll be more than happy to help. Trust me."

"What about you? Since when do you sleep over with Mose? On a school night?"

The heat rose high on my neck and cheeks. "How did..."

Laura snorted. *"Is that not his voice I overheard? Please, Didi, I have a teenage son. He sneaks people in and out of his room on the regular."*

Nick was having girls over? That little bugger. We'd have to have a proper talk the next time I saw him.

"It's not what you think. Mose and I—"

"It's none of my business other than to say have fun, Didi."

My eyebrows arched in surprise. Was this the same sister who told me I couldn't date until I was thirty?

"Didi, all I'm saying is play the field. While there are a lot of losers out there, Mose isn't one of them. If you like that Scottish guy, then why not? The more the merrier."

"Laura!" I gasped.

"There's no denying it," she continued. *"You absolutely beam when you mention the Scotsman. Give it a thought, alright? That's all I ask."*

Laura thanked me for the proverbial cold shower, and we hung up.

"Everything okay?" Mose asked, sitting up and stretching his hands high above his head. I averted my gaze, putting my phone on the nightstand, as he'd taken off his shirt sometime earlier.

"Fine. Let's get some sleep. We've got some bones to duplicate."

CHAPTER 22

The phone rang, jolting me from a deep slumber. I fumbled in the inky darkness of early morning, finding it on the fourth ring.

"Hello?" I croaked, rubbing my eyes.

"They're leaving. Now's the time."

I stretched out a leg, tossing the blankets off, stifled a yawn, and stood. In the fogginess of o'dark thirty, I stepped forward without fully extricating myself from the blankets and tripped. Falling sideways, I slammed into the nightstand, sending a notepad, keys, and my cell phone tumbling to the floor. I swore under my breath, massaged what was sure to be an ugly bruise on my thigh, and yanked free of the sheets. Stuffing my feet in the pink slippers Mose had set out for me during the night, I trudged toward the bathroom and picked up the cell. Fortunately, the call hadn't dropped.

Nick sounded way too chipper this early in the morning. Then again, he was sixteen. Almost seventeen. Ah... seventeen. I remember the angst-filled days of college prep, exams, and college applications.

Nick was a typical teenager. Able to stay up for long stretches of time with little sleep, irritated at both his parents, and exhibiting a brooding sense of self-righteousness and rebelliousness. However, he was also a hacking mastermind, and it was due to those skills that I'd broken my oath to keep him out of this mess. While Mose and I got a couple hours of sleep, he'd stayed up tracking police systems for updates on the university murder cases along with police where-abouts. It wouldn't do having them spot Mose and me entering the bone lab. Nick agreed, but there was always a quid pro quo with him, and this time was no different. So, it appeared he was coming with me to Scotland again. Though I had misgivings, he was a great help last time, minus the kidnapping, and he proved quite useful in the hacking department. Thankfully, he could hack safely from the privacy of his own home.

"Thanks, Nick, but we're still talking about those girls you're having over in the middle of the night."

"What girls?" He feigned innocence.

"The cat's out of the bag, buddy. Your mom knows."

After a few expletives, he grumbled, *"Fine, but it's not like I'm snorting drugs or anything."*

I fought the grin pulling at the corners of my mouth. "I should hope not. Laura would kill you. Then your father—"

"Then you. Yeah, I got it."

After we hung up, I giggled. My, how much he'd grown over the last few weeks. Even though he was sixteen, I still imagined him as a cute little five-year-old who loved his aunt's treats, trips to the zoo, and secret candy stashes that his mother would abhor. These days he'd rather take trips to Scotland filled with murders and secrets and have girls over in the middle of the night. Where did the time go?

"Get dressed," Mose mumbled. "I'll take another shower. Breakfast is in the frig."

He lumbered past me in his striped pajama bottoms into the bath-room and closed the door. I scrounged around in the closet, finding an all-black ensemble, and then traipsed out of the bedroom toward the kitchen.

Sure enough, there was a platter in the refrigerator with an assortment of cheeses, crackers, toasted bread, jams, and olives. I pulled it out and set it on the dining room table then headed back to the kitchen for napkins and utensils.

Mose appeared in his all-black outfit, looking like an Egyptian god. I stopped in mid-step and stared.

Mose looked about him, forehead furrowed. "What? Did I put something on backwards?"

I shook my head. "Nope. You look... fine." I walked into the dining room for a piece of toast, which snapped in half when I tried rubbing jam on it. I wiped the crumbs off my pants and grabbed another piece, repeating the process.

A whiff of cinnamon hit me full on when Mose sat by me. I swiveled in my seat, blurting, "Why do you always smell of cinnamon?"

Mose stopped eating olives and looked at me. The dried toast stuck in my esophagus when I tried to swallow it. Tears prickled my eyes when the piece of toast lodged. Soon my face was hot, and I flailed my arms about, motioning toward the carafe of orange juice.

Mose filled a glass and raised it to my lips, gently patting me on the back while I sucked it down.

I sputtered and hacked when the toast dislodged and sank into my stomach.

Mose stepped aside, popped an olive in his mouth, and leaned against the table. I set the toast aside and picked up a piece of cheese to nibble on.

"I didn't realize I smelled like cinnamon." A faint smirk flashed across his face.

"You do. So..." I folded a corner of the napkin repeatedly without looking at him.

Mose slid closer so that only half a foot remained between us.

"What else do I smell like?" His voice was low. Intense.

I couldn't gather the courage to peer up from the napkin, which I'd now torn into pieces. When I reached for an olive he laid his hand over mine, stopping me.

"Didi? Look at me."

I licked my dry lips and shook my head.

"Didi... please look at me."

I tore my gaze from our hands, and the way his bronzed skin contrasted the pale white of my own.

"What?" I focused on his eyebrows. Anywhere but those intense brown eyes.

"There's something I've been meaning to ask for a while now, but it's never been the right time."

The butterflies in my stomach swarmed to a feverish pitch. This was Mose. Same old Mose. The one from freshman year when he was a teacher's assistant, and I was his student. The same one who'd gotten me through the through the painful early college years, fights with Christof, and the nights I cried myself to sleep on his couch over the death of my parents. He was the only person who knew all my secrets. We cried together, laughed together, joked together, and reminisced about life. We were the best of friends, always remaining close over the years, and never once had I noticed his full lips, his long, curly, black lashes, or his lean muscles. He'd always been just Mose. The friend, the protector, the confidant—my best friend.

He squeezed my hand, and I gulped for air that felt thin and dry. Inside, I was dying... dying to kiss him, dying for him to hold me, dying for him to stay close to me for a lifetime.

"Have you ever..." His lashes fluttered downward like he was carefully planning each word. "...thought of me... differently?"

"Mose, I can't answer that."

"Why?"

I shook my head, tears building, and peered at our joined hands, then stroked my thumb across the lines of his palm. "You're my best friend. I can't lose you." I looked up into his beautiful brown eyes.

"You won't."

A relationship between us would threaten everything—Mose with his girlfriend, and me with my safely constructed world of work and friendship. I needed to keep it the way it was, or it could all go to Hell in a handbasket. We were friends and that was it—no matter how sweet he smelled or how many times I longed to kiss him. I looked into his brown eyes and my stomach flip-flopped.

"You can't promise that, Mose. I can't lose someone else that I love. We're friends. That's it. Besides, you've got a girlfriend, remember?" I withdrew my hand. "We have a murder to solve. Let's get started."

CHAPTER 23

The darkness of night and busy city streets helped cover our tracks. The hotel staff's use of their private limo also helped. We sat across from each other on the ride over in silence, and all I could do was stare out the tinted windows and watch the blur of streetlights and shuttered stores pass by.

We'd asked the driver to drop us off about a block from the university in case we were followed. The ever-present feeling of being watched left me constantly scouring the area before we made it to the side door of the university building. Thanks to Nick's tutoring, I picked the lock on the lab door, and we were gathering the supplies to make casts of the original bones.

Mose kept stealing glances at me, but I remained focused on the task at hand and stuffed the sadness down into the abyss of my heart.

"So," he said after twenty minutes of silence, "do you miss the craziness of Scotland now?"

My smile fell flat at his masked expression. He pulled a femur from the firm mixture, forming the cast, and brushed it clean of any further debris, then placed the original back in the storage box. I noticed a few other specks of white debris that landed on the black tabletop.

"Come on, Mose. Don't make this difficult."

"I'm not." He turned his back on me and started mixing the contents of another bucket to form another cast.

"Yes. Yes, you are. We're friends, Mose." I hopped up onto the black-topped work bench where my bone was setting in the gelatin-like mixture and swung my legs back and forth. "Tell me about this woman friend of yours."

"No."

"Come on. What's she look like?"

Mose huffed and turned. "Can we not do this?" He flung the casting goo off his fingers and wiped them with a paper towel.

"Olivia, right? It's a beautiful name. What's she like?"

Mose inhaled measuredly. "She's like any girl."

I snorted. "Right. Not buying it. Olivia is...?" I stopped, hoping he'd fill it in.

"Smart, witty, sexy..."

"Go on."

Mose tossed the paper towel in the metal trash can and walked toward me. He placed his palms on either side of my hips and pushed my knees apart, his nose inches from mine.

I swallowed hard.

"Olivia's a thunderstorm on a clear day. She's energetic, a butterfly on the wind of a hurricane. She's the exact opposite of you."

I gulped, unable to breathe.

Mose stepped back to test the firmness of the cast.

I stuck my trembling hand in my bucket and fished out the remnants of a man's pelvis. Pouring in another mixture to fill the mold and complete the cast, I set down the canister and kept quiet.

Mose spun around, his face a mix of resignation and sadness. "We'll be friends if that's what you want, Didi. I'm good. I can wait, but I doubt you can."

"What's that supposed to mean?" I hopped off the table and landed with a thud.

"Don't pretend that you don't react to me."

"Mose, I—"

"Let's finish these casts before someone finds us."

He was right. He always was, and the point hurt, but there was one thing I couldn't do, and that was lose him.

"Fine."

A few more minutes passed in silence.

"I would have told you about Olivia. I didn't want you to find out through Shane Bernard."

I pulled apart the forming material and found the hardened cast of the pelvic bone. "I appreciate that. By the way, what do you know about his promotion?"

"Not much. He's gotten an assignment overseas from the rumor mill. Somewhere in Spain."

I stopped and turned my attention to Mose. "Wait. Spain?"

"Yeah, why?"

"Anice taunted me about getting her claws in Shane before she almost killed me in Scotland. Apparently, she contacted him about taking over when I was gone."

"Curious." Mose checked his watch. "Why don't we search his office? We've got about an hour before anyone arrives. That's if we have work today."

We raced to tidy up the lab, making sure it appeared as untouched as it had before we entered, then we snuck out and headed to Shane's new office.

Mose pulled out a tiny flashlight and held it between his teeth while he extracted a couple of pairs of black leather gloves from his skinny jean pocket.

"Where did you get these?" I whispered and tugged them on after he'd offered them to me.

He winked. "Always come prepared, Didi. To a dig, and to a break-in."

Mose rifled through Shane's desk drawers while I noted his passwords on colorful, sticky notes stuck to his computer. I logged in to his accounts, scrolling through e-mails. Though nothing caught my attention, I printed off the ones from the last several weeks and stuffed them in my pants, keeping them for a more thorough review later. Then I set about helping Mose tidy up.

"He needs a woman," Mose mumbled.

I arched a brow. "Who says he doesn't have one?"

"Right, and I'm the next pope."

I snickered. "That would mean learning Italian. Somehow, I don't think so."

Mose mocked offense. "If required, I can learn or *do* anything."

I smacked my gloved palm on my forehead and grinned. "Remember that language you and I made during freshman year at undergrad? Gosh, that was crazy fun. Belinda never figured out what we were actually saying." I chortled.

"It wasn't like we were calling her anything crude. I like that anthropological system of words we created, and if we can create a language, why can't the ancient people of Greece, Ur, or the Mayans?"

"True." I jerked in the direction of the door when I heard the squeak of a rubber sole. "Hurry!" I hissed. "Someone's here."

We quickly finished tidying up and snuck out in time to see the junior janitor arriving for work, his earbuds in and dancing along to music.

"Phew, that was close." I high-fived Mose once we were safely outside and more than a block away. The sun was rising, and we had to get off the streets and away from prying eyes.

"Limo's coming," Mose said and stuffed his cell into his pant pocket. "What do you say to a second breakfast, and then I'll drive you to work? We can't call in sick. They'll be onto us."

"Right. Easy on the second breakfast though. We're not hobbits."

CHAPTER 24

"Ugh." I groaned and held a hand over my tummy. "You'll have to wheel me in. Why did I agree to pancakes?"

"Why not?" Mose asked.

"I asked for Swedish pancakes. Not overstuffed."

Mose patted his hardened abs. "We both need to pack on a few pounds."

"Speak for yourself. I'm perfectly fine with my boyish figure. It's all the running, climbing, kneeling, and everything else we do."

"Daisy Day," Mose clucked, "you are anything but boyish." His eyes lingered on my chest.

"Uh... okay. Keep your head down, teach, and we'll meet up after work. Agreed?"

Mose saluted and turned, walking off toward his lofty office while I went to mine. Classes were nothing out of the ordinary, except for the constant interruptions of students whispering about the murders. While it was curious classes hadn't been canceled, Shane's new tenure was probably to blame, and since I was walking around on eggshells with him anyway, I wasn't about to give him an opportunity to fire me too.

The last class of the day over, I trudged to my office, arms piled high with books and my laptop, when I nearly ran into a dark-haired woman of about thirty. My surprise turned to sadness in an instant.

"Lola... how are you?"

Her big brown eyes filled with tears. She swiped them away and hugged me. "Ms. Day, you were so kind to my Francisco." Her lips wavered. "*Gracias.*"

"Of course. But what are you doing here? Where are your children?"

"Mr. Bernard says I must clear out Francisco's locker. They've hired someone new."

My jaw dropped open. "What? Already? Oh, Lola. You don't need to be here right now."

"It's okay, *professora*. My *abuela* has my children. It's better this way."

She stepped to the side when I reached a hand out to stop her. "Let me help you. Please?"

Lola paused, then nodded.

* * *

THE DAMP LOCKER room of Francisco Ramirez Garcia, his manager, and his assistant were in the basement. There was only a swinging yellow light to illuminate the area. A room like my office, it smelled of rotten eggs and grease.

I wrinkled my nose and set down the cardboard boxes I'd gathered from Dr. Gates' office that had been left over from his unexpected firing.

Lola stood facing Frankie's military green locker. Pictures of Lola and their two kids beamed back. The son, around five years old, sported two missing front teeth and slicked back hair with a beast of a cowlick popping up like the character Alfalfa in *The Little Rascals*. The daughter, only two years older, stood beside her mother with her hands behind her back, hair braided and laying across one shoulder.

My heart ached. He'd never see them grow, marry, or have children of their own. It wasn't fair.

Lola brushed her fingertips across the smiling faces of her children before peeling back the tape around the corners of the photograph and putting it in the cardboard box. As for the pictures of herself, she ripped them off and tossed them on top of the others, then opened the locker.

A whiff of Freddie's aftershave lingered in the air as she picked the bottle up and ran her thumbs over the label. She sniffled and rubbed her nose on the sleeve of her shirt, gently placing the glass bottle in the corner of a box. She picked out all his tools and neatly placed them in a box, leaving the hardest part for last.

Lola tenderly placed her palm on top of Frankie's red and black plaid button-down shirt, her lips quivering.

I stepped beside her. "Let me help you with that."

She shook her wavy, black hair. "No. I'm fine."

Lola picked up the shirt, a pair of jeans, and his black work boots. He'd kept them polished to a shiny sheen, almost like they were brand new, but I knew better. Though they'd barely had enough money for Lola's latest intravenous treatment for her lupus, Frankie had declined any help. I'd eventually set up a Go Fund Me page with my colleagues, mainly Dr. Gates, Mose, and a few others, and collected a few thousand dollars, which almost brought Frankie to his knees. Still, the improvement in Lola, while modest, had brought the glow back to his wife's face and a bounce to Frankie's step.

Lola and I finished cleaning out his locker, and I helped her take the boxes to her beaten up pickup truck.

"Is there anything else I can do?" I asked after the last of the boxes was placed in the bed of her truck.

"Thanks, but no. This is my road, not yours."

I hugged her and she got in the truck. She rolled down the window, beckoning with a flick of her delicate finger, looking around like a cat burglar.

I rested my palm on the windowsill and bent low to hear her.

"Didi, I think someone threatened Frankie. He didn't want me to tell anyone—especially not the police." The worry on her puffy, reddened face was now accompanied by a hint of anger. "He said I should trust you, that you would know what to do." She let out a jagged sigh. "Oh my God, he really is dead." She pressed her hand to her mouth and dropped her head, shaking it back and forth.

"Someone here threatened him?"

Lola shrugged. "Here or the law offices... he didn't say who. He only said that you would understand."

I reached through the window and grabbed her frail hand, giving it a gentle squeeze. "Don't worry, Lola. You take care of those babies. Let me handle the rest."

"*Professora*, please, be careful." Her tight expression lingered as she returned the squeeze.

After encouraging her to call for anything, she drove off, the truck puffing black and white smoke and chugging its way out of the parking lot onto the busy street. I stood there for a long time mulling over what she'd divulged. Frankie assumed I'd figure out who killed him. He trusted me, not only to find his killer, but to protect his family. The problem was that I hadn't the foggiest idea of who it could be other than Anice. It was definitely linked to Landon's death. I thought of anyone who might want to see him dead and came up empty. It wasn't until my skin sizzled from the strong sun overhead that I made my way to my office, packed up for the night, and hailed a taxi.

As the driver hastened through the busy Boston streets, I wondered how Lola and the kids would survive. She'd assured me they were fine, moving in with her parents and grandparents in a cramped three-bedroom apartment. Though faced with the hardship of raising two young children on her own, she seemed determined and even a bit stronger. With the help of her parents and grandparents, who I'd only heard about in passing from Frankie, she was in excellent hands. They were the village she needed now.

The taxi veered off the main road and drove up to the outside of my apartment complex. After paying, I bounded up to the second-floor landing, only planning to take enough time to grab a shower, pack a small bag of clothes, and then follow the same procedure Mose and I had taken the day before to evade any watchful eyes. When I opened the front door, a note fluttered down to the doormat.

Half expecting another note from mystery man J, I picked it up. My excitement quickly turned to concern. The unfamiliar pigeon scratch leapt off the cream-colored envelope.

I kicked the door shut behind me, opened the envelope, and read the note:

You'll pay for that stunt in Scotland, Didi. Solitude doesn't agree with me, but maybe it will for you. Time to pick. Christof or Mosewan. Better hurry. They're both up for a nasty surprise. Fireworks will fly tonight at 8:00 PM. Don't worry that pretty little brain of yours though. I've informed Mosewan the timeframe has moved up.

So who will it be, Christof or Mosewan? Either way, it'll be a blast. Don't bother telling them or the police. One peep, and I'll kill them both.

Happy choosing, Didi.

Anice

CHAPTER 25

*H*er words painted a bleak future for both of the most important men in my life. The meaning was clear. One was to die.

I crumpled the note into a ball, threw it down on the counter, and kicked the trashcan. It bounced off the refrigerator, spilling yesterday's coffee grounds onto the floor along with empty boxes of oat milk and a half-eaten donut.

I grabbed tufts of my hair and screamed at the top of my lungs, slamming my fists down on the countertop. The pain barely registered.

Get a grip, Didi. There's still time.

I snatched a glass from the cabinet and filled it with water. The clock above the oven indicated 5:00 PM.

How was I to save two men in less than—

"Crap!"

I drained the glass and set off for the closet. A formal gown, shoved between two other dresses half a decade old, hung on a black velvet hanger in the back. They were the only ones I'd kept. The day job didn't require too many social appearances, and I liked it that way.

I tugged the baby blue silk gown off the hanger and held it against my body. The plunging neckline, the tight fit, wasn't my normal choice. It exposed too much skin and left little to the imagination, but Christof had gifted it to me last year and had begged me frequently to wear it. I had many excuses for not doing so, although the real reason was that it wasn't my style. Jeans and a t-shirt were practical and comfortable. Right now I required something far dressier, and I either chose between two sequin-covered pieces with gobs of ruffles, or the baby blue pinup model dress.

I quickly showered, dressed, and ran down to the Uber that awaited me at the foot of my apartment stairs. Once inside, I pulled out my cell and typed a message I hoped Mose would understand. It was the only idea I had while dressing, and I hoped it worked.

"Can't meet tonight like planned. It's time to confront Christof. Know you'll understand. Wish me luck! Remember, llaack non tag. Koshtighet. Fyrverpompa droplet. Love, Didi."

Would he remember our invented language from years ago? Regardless, there wasn't time to rethink it. The drive was short, almost too short, and I'd formed the thinnest of plans, setting off as fast as my pale blue silk heels allowed. Not used to wearing them or the form-fitting shift dress, I shuffled across the marbled lobby floor to the elevator doors of Christof's office building. His practice owned the upper floors of the skyscraper and employed their own doorman. A young man of about twenty, no doubt looking to rub elbows with a network of men who could propel his job outlook in the next few years to extraordinary heights, stood at attention by the elevator doors.

"Ms. Day," he half bowed in his black tuxedo. "Let me escort you up."

He extended his arm and I held onto the crook of his elbow, wobbling on my high heels and cursing my sore ankles. I was sure I'd twisted them twice between the car and the door, which were only ten feet apart.

"Lovely weather we're having," he said, looking forward and walking like a broomstick was shoved up where the sun doesn't shine.

"Uh, yeah." I swatted at an errant hair that had fallen from my loose ponytail. It was a more formal one than the usual, and it was all I could do on such short notice. Whether Chris would approve fell between "who cares" and "meh" on my scale of give a hoots.

The young man pressed the elevator button, and we waited. I tugged at my spaghetti straps while he stood stiff as a board and tweaking his bow tie. We made quite the fidgety pair.

The ding of the elevator doors reverberated in the marbled-floored and crystal chandeliered lobby. I wobbled into it with his help and waited for the young man to press the penthouse button, entering his secret code. At the last second a hand jutted between the nearly closed sliding doors and in stepped Brian Smith.

"Good evening, Harold," Brian said and patted him on the back. "Top floor, please." He stuffed a roll of money in the young man's jacket pocket and grinned. "Tell your father everything's working according to plan."

Brian stepped beside me and cocked his head. "Dr. Day, what a surprise." He took my hand and, keeping his eyes locked on mine, kissed the top of it. "Who has the pleasure of your company this evening?"

My clammy palm remained in his firm grip while I shifted on my heels. "Oh, uh, Chris. He's the newest junior partner of the firm."

"Christof?" He grinned. "I feel sorry for the elusive girlfriend he's mentioned before. She's not real. The office has a bet going ten to one that she's a figment of his imagination."

"Oh?" The chuckle that came out sounded more like a cacophonous squawk.

"Yes, it's frowned upon not to be engaged within a year of junior partner, and to be a senior partner, you'd best be married or… let's say it would be rather difficult. So, you mentioned Christof and you are friends? I must say he has exquisite taste."

The initial press of gravity lessened and we were shooting upward in a glass elevator. The dizzying heights made me grab my empty belly and thank my lucky stars I had not eaten nothing recently.

Was Christof only in a relationship for the office perks? This bet… I slid my hand from Brian's and forced a smile.

"Have you given my proposal any thought, Ms. Day? It's been more than a day."

I bet this man had people swooning to get in his good graces, or his bed, but my mind was still mulling over Christof's motivations. Was he in a relationship with me for promotion opportunities, or were his intentions real? He wasn't the type to stick around for long if he lost interest. I witnessed that firsthand years ago in college. He'd stayed with me through thick and thin, but was that because he loved me or was it to show his partners and firm that he was a stable gentleman worthy of promotion? His job ruled his waking and sleeping hours, and I had always supported his ambitions...

"There are other things on my mind at the moment." I tugged at the spaghetti strap that had fallen onto my arm.

"Forgive me. I'd almost forgotten about the young man who died yesterday at your work."

The young elevator attendant turned around and pointedly stared at me. "Do you teach there?"

"Yes."

"Was it as gruesome as they say?"

"Harry!" Brian snapped.

"No, it's okay," I said. "It's human nature I guess."

Harold looked from Brian's taut face to mine. "They say it was murder. I can't believe anyone would want to kill Landon Fisher. I mean, he's annoying, but to kill him?" He shook his head.

"You knew Landon? How?"

"We went to undergrad together. He's nosy, and some people hated how he sucked up to the professors. He was harmless enough though."

"Have you kept in contact?"

"Oh, he wasn't a close friend. We'd text from time to time. My dad got him the job at the university. He called and begged me for help, and when I mentioned it to my father, Landon had the job in a few weeks. That's the last I ever heard of it."

"Who's your father?"

Brian buttoned his gold cufflinks. "Dr. Day, you must start

watching television every now and again or take up social media. Harry's father is the biggest philanthropist in Boston."

"Yes," Harry piped in, "he's worked hard for funding to clothe, house, and educate the homeless, funds for museums, and other worthy charities."

Harry looked the spitting image of Prince Harry of the United Kingdom, and his mannerisms were similar too. All that was lacking was the accent.

"Anyway," Brian continued, "how about the charity event? Are you up for it? You can talk about your latest adventure in Scotland. From what Christof said, it was quite the trip."

"If kidnapping, murder, and mayhem are your definition of adventurous, then yes."

Brian laughed heartily. "Charming too, I see. How has Christof not introduced us before now? I'd say he needs to dump that dolt of a woman he's dating and ask you out."

My cheeks flushed hot. "Dolt?"

"Anyone who regularly misses out on a significant other's accomplishments is a dolt, Ms. Day. She's crazy to keep him on a long leash. Poor guy."

Poor guy, indeed. I had a few choice words for both Christof and Brian. For now I'd settle for finding Christof and vacating the premises as quickly as possible.

The elevator dinged.

"Here we are, madame." Harold smiled and extended his hand to me. "Please, watch your step and have a wonderful evening."

The blast of music when the doors slid open nearly toppled me backward. Harold's glistening white teeth and bright brown eyes beckoned me out of the elevator and into the murmurs of a packed ballroom equipped with black-clad waitstaff in white gloves, a grand piano in the far back corner, and a wooden dance floor made for a championship ballroom competition. A flowing fountain of crystal-stemmed glasses with champagne flowing from the top to the bottom of the pyramid was showcased in the right corner of the pricey selection of food. Shrimp, lobster, caviar... nothing but the finest for the elite law practice and friends.

I clutched at my bare neckline, scanning the room for Christof.

Brian leaned forward his mouth close to my ear. "Christof will surely dump his girl now. If he doesn't, Ms. Day, please call me." He winked and plucked a champagne flute off a passing waiter's tray and wandered into the crowd.

I mentally shook off the deluge of information I'd been given in the last few minutes. First things first, I had to find Christof. I craned my neck, searching the crowd for him. A few feet away, among a crowd on the jammed dance floor, stood my boyfriend, who was gliding across it with a petite brunette in a navy dress with barely enough room for her to breathe. I gaped at her ample bosom bouncing in step with Christof as he expertly maneuvered them through the crowd of approving onlookers keeping in step with the upbeat tempo.

Ordinarily, I'd have marveled at his confidence, his handsome frame whipping about with ease. Not tonight. Tonight, there was only one goal. To keep Christof, me, and everyone else alive.

I took off a little too fast and my ankle buckled, then I was falling sideways into the poor waiter waitstaff holding a tray full of hors d'oeuvres. The silver tray flew out of his outstretched palm, splatter unsuspecting rich patrons in the near vicinity with shrimp and lobster rolls. To top matters off, it occurred during a lull in the music, and the tinny clang of the tray on the wooden floor drew every eye in the room.

"I'm so sorry." I picked an errant shrimp off the waiter's black jacket and stuffed the crustacean in my mouth. "Mmmm... so good," I garbled. I gave him a thumbs up and cursed the high heeled shoes, wishing for my usual dig boots.

Christof's bewildered voice broke through the silence. "Didi?"

I TURNED SLOWLY and plastered on a smile. The crowd hadn't moved even though the DJ was doing his best to get the crowd dancing again.

I was the caterpillar amongst butterflies. A pig in a dress was still a pig, and I wasn't one of these uptown people flush with money, nor did I care to be. It was only because of Christof that I even tried occasionally, and every time I did, I regretted it. Something *always* happened. Mostly at my expense.

"Chris, may we talk..." I eyed the unmoving crowd and noted Christof's stiffened posture, "...privately? Now," I added through clenched teeth.

He cleared a path to the back, behind the champagne fountain and food tables. Farther down the hallway there were three larger offices, closed off from prying eyes. These offices were unlike the others, which had glass walls and lacked privacy. As a junior partner, Christof had an office with closed doors.

"Quite the entrance, Didi," he remarked. Christof leaned against his desk, arms crossed. His tailored tux fit him like a glove. He scanned me from head to toe and whistled. "You. Look. Lovely."

He stepped toward me, but I held up my palm. "Not now. We've got a problem."

His forehead creased into a frown. "She's my new assistant. I'm supposed to show her around. Don't worry about my partners. I'll explain that you were a little woozy from champagne."

"What? No, not that. We've got to leave."

Chris chuckled. "Why? The night is young, and you look ravishing." He strode up, bent his head, and kissed my neck.

I pushed against him, my palms on his chest. "Chris, I mean it. We must leave now."

The humor drained from his eyes and he stepped back, shaking his head. "Didi, not this again. Let's get through the night, and then we can talk about—"

"No. I can't explain it now, but we're in danger. We've got to leave and get these guests out of here before someone gets hurt. Something happened at work, and I don't have time to explain."

Chris glared down at me. "Daisy, I love you. But your hobbies are just that—hobbies. I've put up with your harebrained schemes, but this stops tonight. I thought Scotland would have been your wake-up call. Clearly it wasn't. Either you give up that dangerous *hobby* or... or we're through."

Chris stuck out his chin. While his stubbornness had been charming once, today it could get us and countless others killed.

"Fine." I spun and reached for the door. "I'll do it myself." I flung the door wide and stormed off. Slipping off my torturous heels, I marched down the hall. Better to not break an ankle.

Ignoring the calls from Christoff I rejoined the crowd, which was slow dancing. Brian, who'd positioned himself between one of the smaller offices and the food table, eyed me curiously. He dipped his head when I sped past him and wandered toward the office area I'd just come from.

My eardrums buzzed with the assault of the booming bass shaking the walls, while the liquor flowed and the champagne corks popped. I searched for a fire alarm or anything that would get a large group of people out fast in an emergency. All I saw was a group of partygoers. Everyone was busy dancing, bobbing up and down. Then I spotted a red fire alarm against the wall surrounded by... the elevator doors! After bumping into the umpteenth millionth couple pressing forward in the mob, I reached it. When my arm was halfway raised to the alarm my smartwatch binged with a message and bile rose in my mouth when I read it:

"Hurry. It goes off with a bang at the top of the hour."

I noted the time: I had five minutes.

"I advise you not to pull that alarm. Nothing you do goes unnoticed. Let's have some fun, shall we? You like clues, try this. The flash isn't just for show. Let the music carry you to find it, and find it you must or else this whole evening is a bust. Or rather, in your case, a bomb. Good luck!"

A bomb? Crap!

I scanned the room for anything out of place. Every sweaty face, every blush, every gyrating body might hold some clue.

"Didi!" Christof gripped my elbow so hard I winced. "Let's discuss this somewhere else."

I yanked free and took off running for the DJ. A frost-tipped haired man in his forties, bedecked with jeweled reading glasses perched on the bridge of his nose, and perfectly in step with the music, looked down at me.

"Sir, have you been with your equipment all night?" No one heard me because of the music.

The man craned an ear in my direction and yelled, "Speak up!"

I cupped a hand over my mouth and tried again

The man cocked his head to the side and yelled back, "What?"

"Have you left your equipment at any point tonight?"

He pointed to the speakers and shook his head. "Lady, what do you want to hear? Write it down." He gestured to a clipboard with scribbled requests.

A tap on the elbow had me look around. Christof, hands on his hips, glared. "Why must you be difficult? I'll give you one more chance."

I turned back to the DJ and repeated my question, but he was more interested in the busty platinum blonde to his left bobbing up and down to the Criss Cross song, singing "Jump, Jump..."

I squatted, or bent as far as my slip dress allowed. I felt all along the equipment while Christof stayed on my heels, barking orders for me to leave with him. I reached the edge of the table. Nothing. I had run out of options save one.

"Callum?" I yelled into my phone, which I had hastily dialed. "There's a bomb somewhere in this ballroom I'm standing in!"

I relayed everything as quickly as possible and held my breath, checking my watch for the time.

Two minutes left.

"Lassie, look where the DJ stands."

I stepped around Christof spouting off another round of pleas for me to leave with him and started inspecting every square inch. I shoved the DJ away, then my fingers slid over a small box.

"Eureka! I found it." I tucked the phone between my chin and shoulder and stooped to see a black box with a blinking red light. "What now? I have less than a minute."

"Not enough time. Didi, run. Run! Get out of there!" Callum's graven voice filled me with dread and set my teeth chattering.

I looked down at my right wrist, which buzzed with an urgent vibration.

"You blew it. I said no outside help. Nighty night, Didi."

I grabbed Chris by the arm and took off. The blood drummed in my ears, and my heart slammed against my chest. One step, two, three… The closest office door was inches away.

When a blaring sound erupted over the music I jerked Christof in front of me and shouted, "Dive!"

We dove behind the desk. The *BANG* sucked the air from my lungs and all sound ceased. A jarring pain shot through my left side and hip as the blast blew my body sideways into the desk. I squeezed my lids shut and curled up under the desk. A searing heat lasted a few beats and then nothing.

I pried my eyelids open. Christof lay beside me, his body half hidden under the desk with me. I coughed, shaking him.

"Chris? Oh gosh, Christof? Wake up. Please…"

A high-pitched ringing sounded within my ears. I kept shaking him in between coughing fits. The room was hazy, and the smell of charred food, wood, and leather burned my nose and lungs.

"Chris! Chris, wake up!" I shook him more forcefully.

"Ugh," he grumbled and raised his hand to his bleeding forehead. He propped himself on his elbow and leaned his head against the bottom of the metal desk. Shards of glass sprinkled out of his hair and off his clothes. His lids drooped, his flesh ashen.

"No, stay awake." I tapped his cheeks until his eyes fluttered open, a glassy expression to them. "Can you stand?"

I tore my silk hem and dabbed at the cut over Christof's eye. He moaned but didn't fight me. I peeked over the desk and my stomach lurched. "It's on fire, Chris. We need to leave. Can you stand?"

I swiped at the glass shards surrounding us. Shoes lost in the tumble, I gritted my teeth and stepped out from the safety of the desk and gaped at the destruction. Where walls once stood, now only an expanse of glass was left, a few shards stuck to the window frames. Bodies lay across what once was the dance floor. At the threshold of the office were gem-lined reading glasses without corrective lenses.

Smoke swirled and fire licked up the walls and crawled toward us.

"Come on." I tugged at Christof's elbow. "Get up. Let's go."

He slowly rose and took an unsteady step forward. His feet slipping, I grabbed onto the back of his soot-stained shirt to steady him. I wrapped his heavy arm around my neck and propped him up, encouraging him on. Jagged edges of glass cut into my bare feet with each step. It's like an eternity had passed when we reached the elevator doors. Chris pressed the button, but I pulled him on toward the fire escape which was thankfully lit up in blazing red through the heavy smoke.

Both of us were wracked with coughing fits, and we stepped into the stairwell, which was devoid of glass or bodies. We hobbled down a few floors until I noticed the consistent buzzing on my wrist.

My smart watch! Callum had called over a dozen times.

I pressed a few buttons and heard the fateful words, *"911. What's your emergency?"*

CHAPTER 26

Detective Soo's keen eyes raked across my ripped, soot covered, blood-stained dress.

"Trouble seems to follow you, Ms. Day."

After a long hour of questioning I was huddled on the edge of an ambulance, partially covered by a thin foil emergency blanket, and I held a paper cup full of water within my trembling grasp. I hadn't heard from Mose, and I was itching to text him, but not in front of the police. If he'd somehow survived, I didn't dare give away his position.

"Detective, if you don't mind, I'd like to go home and take a shower. It's been a long day."

Soo narrowed his gaze. "Fine, but stay close, Ms. Day. I don't believe you're telling me everything, and one day soon, you will."

I simply nodded. He was right. I *was* keeping things from him. Important things. I couldn't risk one of Anice's moles finding out anything yet.

"Detective, may I trouble you for a phone? I've lost mine in the…" I waved a hand above us at the hovering skyscraper I'd climbed down with Christof, half blinded by a concussive headache and aching from the cuts on my feet. The paramedics had insisted on taking me to the hospital with Christof, but I declined since the cuts weren't too deep. Somehow, I'd avoided any major injuries.

"I'll do you one better. Get in." Soo gestured toward his nondescript black car. Not having the energy to refuse, I hobbled to it, climbed in, and sank into the cloth seats. I closed my eyes, figuring he'd leave me be, and luck was on my side. Of course he'd insisted on seeing me to my apartment door, even looking inside before leaving with a stern warning.

"Try not to attract any more trouble, Ms. Day."

"Fine, but uh... um... have you... What I mean is have you had any other disturbances tonight?"

Detective Soo tilted his head to the side, his face a total mask. "Why do you ask?"

"Um, no reason."

"Seriously?"

I shrugged unable to come up with anything better. Dang this concussion.

"Ms. Day, may I be honest with you? First, there's the murder of your boyfriend's teaching assist—"

"He's not my boyfriend."

"Then there's the janitor's murder, and now there's a bombing at a party you attended. If you connect the dots, they all lead to you, Ms. Day. Now you're asking about another bombing?"

My stomach flip-flopped at the word *bombing*.

"Bombing? I never said anything about another bomb."

Detective Soo sighed. "No, Ms. Day, there hasn't been another such disturbance in the city. Yet. But if there's something you'd like to divulge, then please save me the time and frustration and mention it now."

"No. If I find out anything, though, you'll be the first person I call."

After he left, I stripped down and soaked in my tub with no word yet from Mose.

When my wrist buzzed, I jolted upright, sloshing bubbles onto the bathroom floor.

Callum.

While it was great to hear from him, I couldn't help the sadness of not hearing from Mose yet.

"Hey, Callum."

"Lassie, if I could bend you over and spank you, I would."

I blushed at the prospect.

"Uh, thanks… I think." I turned on the hot water and filled it to the brim, warming the now cool water.

"Are you okay? Anything broken?"

"Other than a mild concussion and feet that resemble ground meat, I'm okay. There is something I want to discuss. Anice sent those messages, and she mentioned having people tailing me. Mose and I found bugs in our phones too. For all I know, she's listening to this right now. How else would she have known I was talking to you earlier tonight?" I explained the messages she'd sent.

"That's it. You're in way over your head," he said after a long moment of silence. *"Detective Soo needs more information than you're giving him, Didi."*

"There's a time and place for everything, and without definitive proof, we're only guessing, and it would be a waste of his time."

"The texts alone are proof, Didi, along with the information we have on her."

Although he had a point, I couldn't help thinking that the detective would wind up locking me up while searching for Anice, and I wanted to avoid that at all costs.

"Let's get our facts straight. First, why try to blow up Chris and Mose? What's to gain? They need those bones, Callum."

"They have them. You are all collateral damage and a bloody nuisance."

"But they don't. We stored the bones in the lab at work."

"Then they'll come back for them."

"Okay, but that was what Mose was supposed to deliver, right? Why blow him up, and the bones?"

We both agreed it was puzzling.

"Stay on guard, Didi. Get some rest, would you? I'll be on the first plane. Try not to get killed before then."

I wanted to argue with him about coming over, but the adrenaline rush dissipated well before I sank into the tub, and the concussion, along with my bruised and battered body left me with little reserve to argue.

"Fine," I conceded. "I'll contact you, alright?"

"*Got it.*"

We hung up and I sank into the bubbles up to my chin. The throbbing headache intensified with each passing hour. I needed to pack some clothes and slip the henchmen tasked with tailing me and reach the Ritz. After taking some painkillers the paramedics had given me, I dressed in sensible jeans, a blue t-shirt, and black dig boots still covered in dust from Scotland. I packed a few items, heaved the duffel bag onto my back, and went down the steps to a waiting car.

"Please, Mose, be there," I whispered. "I can't live without you."

CHAPTER 27

"Where to, lady?" the driver said brusquely over the hard rock music.

My fifth car tonight. I recited the address and sat back, rubbing my throbbing temples.

"...*another explosion tonight on the—*"

"Hey, turn that up."

The driver obliged and I sat in horror listening to the news report.

"*...again near the university where a teaching assistant and a janitor died earlier today. More later.*"

"Freaking ridiculous, all these killings," the driver said, switching the radio off. "Makes you not want to go out at all."

I stared wide-eyed out the window, tears streaming down my face. The blurring bright lights melded into one blob of yellow, purple, blue, and red as we raced down the street.

"Hey, lady. We're here. You need some help?"

I wiped my face and inhaled a shaky breath. "I'm fine."

"Uh, lady, you've got a bruise on your face. Sure you don't need some backup? I don't take kindly to men beatin' up women."

I offered a wavering smile. "Thanks, uh..."

"Antonio. My friends call me Tony."

I sniffled. "Tony, I appreciate the offer, but I got this from falling down at... work."

"Lady, I've heard it all." He rummaged around in his glove compartment, pulled out a business card, and handed it to me. "If you ever need some help, call this number and ask for Tony."

"Thanks, Tony. I will."

I walked up the steps of the Ritz, every fiber of my being on high alert. The doorman eyed me strangely, opening the door and ushering me in with a slight nod. I limped across the deserted lobby to the elevator that took me to the penthouse suite I'd shared with Mose.

I stifled the moan at the mere thought of Mosewan. The elevator attendant, repeatedly staring at my bruised face, thankfully stayed silent and didn't ask questions. From the reflection in the shiny elevator doors, I understood his curiosity. Red scratches lined my forehead and cheeks, a few dotted with blood over my brow. Wild tufts of hair stuck out at odd angles, and my ponytail looked like I had run through barbed wire. It was like a feral cat had attacked me.

When the doors opened, I hobbled inside and tossed my bag onto the floor, dragging myself to the couch. I sank down on it to and stared around the deathly quiet room.

"Mose?" I whimpered. "Mose, are you here?"

Nothing.

I wailed and stuffed a pillow over my face to muffle the cries. Unable to control myself any longer, I laid my head down, curled up into a fetal position, and balled my hands into fists, fearing the worst. A few minutes later—or hours, I had no idea—there was a soft click near the elevator doors.

Blood racing through my veins, I scanned the room. No movement. I was alone. Was it a hotel staff member? Who would even come at this hour? Wait, what time was it? It was still dark outside. I tapped my watch to light up its face. Four in the morning.

I grabbed the remote to turn on the early morning news. Sure enough, the explosions were front and center. Since my feet stung, I dressed them with the medicated cream the medic gave me and bandaged them up. I put on socks and thanked my lucky stars they hadn't been cut worse. They still hurt, but once I put on some running shoes, they felt fairly good.

I walked out to the TV room, where the clock now showed 5:00 AM.

After a phone call, a breakfast tray arrived within fifteen minutes. I sat alone at the table, took off the dome over my plate, and gaped.

A note.

Taking it by the corner, I held it up to the light. The familiar script jumped off the paper. Mystery Man J. I tore the envelope open.

You've had better nights. I'm sorry you're going through this and believe me when I say that I'm truly sorry. I've got a lead on Anice, but it's not over yet. Not even close. Take heart, Didi. We'll get them. Hold your head up. You did a great job tonight. They want you dead. For the time being, keep out of sight. I've included new phones, fake IDs, and another room if you need it. The Ritz is safe for the time being but be careful. Trust no one.

P.S. The IDs and phones are in the closet in the lingerie drawer.

Yours,

J

I raced to the closet and tore open all the drawers until I reached the one containing lingerie. Tossing one, then another, and another until the drawer was empty. Where were they?

I tapped against the drawer, the back of it, the sides, and then the bottom, eliciting a dull thud. I dug my fingernails into the bottom edges and it moved. I worked until I pulled the bottom out and sure enough there was a thick manila envelope full of multiple IDs, cash, phones, and a key to a motel on the outskirts of town. Christof and I had stayed there about a year ago when I got him to agree to take a nature walk. He'd grown weary of the bug bites and the wildlife and decided we weren't staying in a tent. We'd driven for hours before hitting the outskirts of town. By then, we could barely keep our eyes open and we'd rented a room at the motel.

I gripped the key in my hand and squeezed my lids shut. Too many memories. Bad and good. I inhaled a shaky breath and stood, tidying up the room before I left it. Wandering back to the food, I nibbled on the French toast and scrambled eggs while mulling sending yet another text to Mose from one of the new phones Mystery Man J had given me. He must have been responsible for the noise I'd heard at 4AM. Who the hell *was* he anyway?

Sitting here waiting for news was the worst form of torture for me. I was a person of action.

I dabbed a tissue at the corners of my teary eyes. If Mystery Man J was right, and I hadn't any reason to believe otherwise, then I was the target, though I wasn't sure why.

First, there was the shield maiden in Scotland, not to forget the visions of her I had in my dreams and her appearance in the tunnels under St. Magnus Cathedral. Then there were the Danish bones, male, dating to approximately the same timeframe as Hulda. He appeared to me beside Mose in my apartment barely twenty-four hours ago. Fast forward to Landon dying, along with Frankie. How did it all fit together? Frankie and Landon didn't even know each other, yet they were both killed. Lola mentioned Frankie had felt threatened; who at work would do such a thing? Shane? His was the first name that popped to mind. Plus, he'd sacked Dr. Gates. Was that just a coincidence? Probably not.

Speaking of…

I pressed the call button next to Dr. Gates's number and waited for his voicemail. He'd mentioned staying long hours at Roger's bedside, and I imagined he was resting at this early hour.

"Hello?"

I jerked, not expecting him to answer. "Dr. Gates, this is Didi."

"*Oh, my dear. Are you okay? I heard about the explosion and feared the worst.*"

He was whispering, which was odd, but as of late, everything was odd, I guess. Yet there was an urgency in his voice right now.

"I'm fine. Nothing but a few scrapes and bruises, although the shards of glass made mincemeat of my feet. That's another story for another time. Have you heard from Mose? Why are you whispering?"

I rubbed my temples, stifling a yawn. The pull of sleep nagged even with a couple of hours of rest.

"My dear, Roger passed away earlier this morning. I'm with his wife. She's been medicated, and I'm intercepting visitors."

I gulped, my voice barely over a whisper. "Dead? I thought he was improving?"

"Yes, we did too. It all looks a tad bit suspicious. The police swarmed in earlier and the room is off limits. Not even Moira can collect any belongings. What about Mose? Is something else wrong? Was he with you last night?"

"Uh, no. There's been... an incident. Mose received a message telling him to bring the bones with him to a drop-off site on the university grounds. They moved up the time to last night. It's Anice. She's here. She made me choose between them." I choked back the tears. "I had to pick between Christof or Mose."

Dr. Gates paused. *"My dear, that is an impossible position. I gather you went to Christof."*

"Yes. I haven't heard from Mose. Dr. Gates." I paused, sucking in air. "There was another explosion."

He inhaled on the other end. *"Time will tell. What you need to do now if stay safe. If Anice is here—"*

"Oh, she's here."

"—then you know the who. The why is still unclear."

"It's the bones. The ones from Denmark. Roger, Landon, Frankie, Mose... they're all dead because of those bones, and I can't help but think it's related to Hulda."

"The shield maiden?"

"The very one. The visions I'm having—"

"Visions? Of what?"

"Hulda and the warrior man. Though I haven't seen them in the last few hours. I would have loved Hulda's help earlier."

"I bet. I hear the police saying it's a homicide. I'm more certain now than ever that you're correct."

My phone buzzed.

"I sent you the pictures of the shield I sent Roger while you were in Scotland. See what you can decipher from them. I've included his notes on it too. If there's a connection between the Danish bones and Hulda's, then it's a good place to start."

"Thanks."

"Didi, no one mentioned a body at the university bombing. Let's hope Mosewan evaded them."

I gulped down a sob and thanked him before hanging up. For the next hour, I scoured the images and the ones of the bones I'd taken. When the elevator doors dinged I barely noticed, thinking it was the second breakfast I'd ordered.

"Daisy?"

I whipped my head around. My body tingled as I leapt off the couch and shot across the room.

"Mosewan!" I threw myself into him, wrapping my arms and legs around his waist.

He pulled me closer and rested his forehead against mine.

"Thank you," he whispered. "You saved me. That text..." He sighed and buried his head in my hair. "Thank you."

CHAPTER 28

I gestured to the couch and sat beside him, never dropping his hand. I took a deep breath and asked, "What happened?"

Mose looked down at our intertwined hands, running his fingers through mine. "When I got your text, I knew something was wrong. Nice touch. It took me a second to remember our made-up language. What I want to know is why you had to resort to that?"

I sighed. "Anice. She had me tailed. She said I had to choose between you and Christof. Since you and I had a code of sorts, I had... I had to... Oh, Mose." I brushed my fingers along his smooth jawline. "I thought you were dead."

"Hey, it's okay. You did the right thing. Christof wouldn't have left if you hadn't. By the way, where is he?"

"At home. They discharged him with only a few bruises and a concussion. His assistant's with him."

Mose arched a brow. "His assistant?"

"Yeah, well, I suspect she's a little more than that, or wants to be. I don't care. He's being looked after, and is out of harm's way."

Mose had escaped death, and for once I could breathe. I tucked a strand of hair behind his ear and grinned. "You're really here. You're not dead." Tears prickled the back of my eyes.

"Nope. I didn't want to risk getting caught. I figured with our code language that our line of communication was compromised. Anyway, when I got your text, I'd just arrived at the parking lot. I took off and drove around for hours trying to stay clear of them. It worked."

I hugged him again and refused to let go.

He patted the nape of my neck. "Hey, I'm okay." He gently pulled away. "You, on the other hand, look like you've been in a war zone."

I waved off his concerns. "I'm fine. My feet took the brunt of it. I'll survive. I found out a few things tonight. Things that are starting to add up."

"Like what?"

I told him about the elevator ride, the words with Christof, the DJ bomb, and the subsequent escape. When I finished, he sat for a few moments in dead silence.

"Geez, Didi. Dr. Gates is right. They want you dead. Why? They could've had the bones tonight if they hadn't blown up the trash bin."

"They were never after the trash bin, which means they didn't need the bones. Why attack Roger though? Why kill him in his hospital bed?"

Mose rubbed his neck. "One thing is certain. Those bones from Scotland and the ones from Denmark are linked, and Anice wants them badly enough to kill multiple people for them."

"Except Anice couldn't have killed Landon or Frankie, right? She didn't attack Roger either. She was still in a psychiatric ward at the time."

"True, but she's definitely behind it." I sat upright, a tingly sensation running across my flesh at a realization. "Anice *wasn't* in a psychiatric ward."

Mose stifled a yawn with the back of his hand.

"Why didn't I think of it before?" I groaned. "Anice was never in the psych ward. J mentioned she escaped on a boat to... where was it to again?" I snapped my fingers, trying to remember. "Spain!" I jabbed my finger at Mose's surprised face.

"J? You're calling him J now?"

"Gosh, how could I have been so stupid? Of course she would. That's where she and her husband went on their last vacation. She must have flown out from there and arrived in Boston in no time at all, giving her ample opportunity to track down Roger."

"That doesn't explain how she knew about the bones he had. How did she escape? Why Roger?"

I nibbled on my nail, lost in thought. Mose had valid points. However, Anice had proved herself resourceful before. Who's to say she didn't have an inside person in Denmark that alerted her to the bones? While how far this crime ring extended was anyone's guess, from the looks of it, it was quite far-reaching.

"Maybe she heard of it from one of her informants."

"Okay, but that would mean she was the ringleader, right?"

Something felt off. While I couldn't put my finger on it, the situation with Anice was disconcerting. She was high up in the organization, and with that came power and trust. Was she Boss Man? My hunch said no.

We agreed to sleep on it and order more food later. Both exhausted, we needed some respite. Once my head hit the pillow, I was off to the land of fjords and crystal blue waters, no longer worrying about the fear that had crept into my bones.

The salty air blew through my flimsy silk pajama top and filled me with strength and hope. I wrapped my arms about my torso against the chill, taking it all in. Why did this place feel so familiar?

"Datter, return the bones. Return them to their rightful owner."

I spun. Hulda stood, her feet hip width apart, her thick braid lying over her wooden shield, and she was armed with a bow and arrow. She boldly stared back. She took my breath away.

"Who? Who is the rightful owner?" I shouted, but the wind stole my voice.

"Return them. He is coming."

"Who?"

Her form wavered and then vanished, though not before she turned, exposing the shield hanging from a strap on her shoulder. It was in mint condition; a specific rune glowed orange-red as she walked off.

"Ragnar, datter," sounded in my head. "He is coming."

"Wait!"

She was gone, and I was left with more questions. Hulda was acquainted with this Danish man, Ragnar. If there was any doubt, it had been erased. Hulda bore the same rune we discovered on his ancient blade, and even though runes were commonly used on Norse Viking belongings, these were like no others I'd ever encountered. No, these two were linked, but how?

We awoke to blinding rays of sunshine peeking through the bedroom blinds. I'd insisted Mose sleep beside me since I wasn't keen on losing sight of him for the near future. He hadn't argued, which spoke to his fatigue. If his mother got wind of this, we'd be married off in a heartbeat. Traditional values ran deep in his family.

The breakfast we ordered arrived and we'd scarfed it down. Mose jotted down notes down while I nibbled on some bacon and searched the web for Hulda's birthplace. After half an hour, I stumbled upon some interesting documents about a place in southern Norway called Kaupang. Meaning "marketplace" in Norwegian, the place was a hub of activity for merchants and trade. It was established around 730 A.D. and all but vanished about 950 A.D. From earlier research, and with the help of Hulda in my dreams, this place felt right. If Kaupang was the correct location, then why the fjords though? Southeastern Norway didn't have the staggering fjords of western Norway. Why would she repeatedly choose to show me Norwegian fjords?

So absorbed in my research, I dropped my phone when it buzzed in my hand, landing with a thud on the table. The display showed a number I was all too familiar with.

"Hello, sis," I answered, holding my phone close to my ear. Mose stood up and absentmindedly walked off toward the bedroom. "What's up?

"Uh, nothing. Well... something. Do you remember last Christmas I

ordered a genealogy kit for fun? I thought it would answer some of our burning questions about our past."

Relieved nothing was seriously wrong, I leaned into the dining room chair, tucking my knees up to my chin. "Yeah... so?"

I heard the screech of a chair leg on tile and the hiccup of a sleeping baby. Laura whispered, *"Check this out. We're of British Isles descent. That's not the shocking part. Get this... we're Scandinavian. Why didn't Mom and Dad tell us this?"*

A billion bees buzzed in my ears. I fumbled for the speaker button on the phone and then brought up the internet. "What ancestry site did you say these findings were on?"

I immediately logged in with the info she provided. Hovering a finger over my DNA profile, Laura's chatter about United Kingdom towns and cities we were linked to faded into the background.

"Didi? Are you listening?"

"Huh?"

"Did you know that we're mostly from Scotland? How funny. Wonders never cease. Oh, and there's this other thing that'll blow your mind. We're over half Scandinavian. Can you believe it?"

I was on autopilot. My brain reeled from the numbers and places popping up on the screen. I clapped a hand over my mouth and forced myself to breathe.

"Laura," I interrupted her rush of words about haggis, scotch, and corgis. Mose had walked back into the room and held his phone up. The DNA results of the bones we'd received from Denmark had returned. "I've got to call you back. We'll talk about this later. I promise."

I went over to Mose, looking at his phone screen. "Well? Anything interesting?"

Mose bobbed his head. Unbeknownst to me, he'd had the forethought to extract DNA from the bones prior to their theft. Otherwise, we'd have to wait for the red tape and a few Hail Mary's to get the results from Denmark, which could take weeks.

"Oh, it's interesting alright, but not for the reasons you might think. It's male and of Scandinavian descent. From the carbon dating, this man lived between 800 and 1000 A.D."

I tipped my head back and let out a slow breath. "Viking."

"Didn't you say that Scotland had performed a DNA analysis of Hulda's bones?" Mose asked while scrolling through the results fast enough to make me nauseous.

"I'm on it." I checked my wristwatch for the time. It was a decent hour of the day for him.

The phone rang twice before Callum's burly accent grunted in my ear. *"Can I call you back? I'm kind of busy. Anice paid an impersonator to take her place in the psychiatric hospital and bribed a worker to switch them. There's an international search spearheaded by Scotland Yard."*

"Try the United States. Boston. It's about those bones. Do you have the DNA results from Hulda? We've got the Danish bones to compare them to."

"Related, you think?" asked Callum.

My phone dinged. "That's fast customer service, Detective Mortimer."

"We aim to please, lassie. But I'm afraid Mose beat you to it. He requested the DNA a while ago."

I uttered a curse. "They don't match."

Even though Hulda was Norwegian and the bones were Danish, they traveled a ton in those days.

Mose stood next to me comparing DNA profiles. His face turned two shades whiter. He gripped the phone closer to his nose, zooming in on one point.

I reached for the cell. He readily let me take it, stomping off, hands on either side of his head and staring off like a possessed man.

"What am I looking at?" I asked. He didn't respond. "Mose, what is this?" I shoved the cell in his face. "Whose DNA is this, Mose?"

Mose simply stared at me. Then I got it. My stomach dropped to the floor while I whistled through my teeth. "Oh my."

"Would someone please tell me what's going on?"

Callum! I'd forgotten he was on the line.

"Uh, so, Hulda's bones don't match the Dane's, but…" I rubbed my hands together, happy tears flowing down my cheeks.

"*But what?*"

"The Danish warrior's grave wasn't built for one." I shook Mose as he stood mute, a wide grin in place. "There were two sets of DNA. One from the man, and one from a child of approximately two or three years of age."

I stared at the DNA results, bouncing up and down in excitement.

"*I'm confused, lassie. Why the fuss? A child died.*"

"Yes." I inhaled deeply, trying in vain to calm down. "The child's bones match both Hulda and this Danish warrior Dane. Hulda had a child, Callum. Hulda had a child with the Dane."

CHAPTER 29

"*W*hoa." Unsteady, I reached out to the nearest chair and stumbled over my leaden feet to make it. Once seated, I leaned my elbows onto my thighs and stared at the phone. The bars and colors of Hulda's ancient DNA swirled around on the screen.

Hulda had a daughter? The thought prickled the hairs on my neck. Her own bones foretold the brutal history of a full life cut short at twenty-eight. Images of my parents came to mind. A child losing a parent was awful enough, but Hulda had known heartache in reverse. She'd lost a child.

I imagined a tow-headed toddler running around on chubby feet. She'd be gleefully squealing, chasing her father past crystalline blue water, through fields peppered by a cool summer drizzle, and crowned with cloudy skies. Her laughter would float across the settlement on the salty ocean breezes. Under Hulda's cautious watch, she'd chase bugs, learn to swim, cook, farm, and even fight. When she was more adept at hunting and fighting, Hulda or her father would train her until she was stronger, tougher, and lethal. Unlike today, swordplay and navigation were critical for their survival. The alternative was almost certain death.

My eyes glazed over. The room misted and tilted. I flung my arms wide, trying to grab hold of the table, but my fingers swiped through it. The chair tottered, and I fell. I flailed my arms and legs wide, but to no use. The floor had vanished. A swirl of bright colors rushed past. Bright blues turned to yellows, oranges, and then reds. Within another blink, they'd combined, forming a sparkling mishmash of the most beautiful rainbow I'd ever seen. The air warmed, and the scent of morning dew right after a spring storm hung in the air. The descent slowed. I reached out, touching the colorful streaks with my fingertips and leaving a rippling of hues in their wake. Without warning, I plummeted again, and it was all a blur. I gasped for air but couldn't breathe. My stomach lurched and my eyes rolled into the back of my head. I don't know how long I was out, but when I came to, I was lying on my back facing the bluest of skies, the sound of roaring water to my right. A wet, frigid spray landed on my face. I turned my head.

Fjords.

"Ragnar..." someone whispered. "Ragnar Lothbrok. He is coming, datter. He is coming!"

I shot up and it all disappeared. The phone was in my hand and I was standing by the dining room table. I looked down at the toppled chair behind me.

"Daisy?" Mose crept toward me. "Are you okay?"

I only nodded. Mose raced for the kitchen, filled a glass with cold water, and was back in no time.

"Here, sip."

The cool liquid slipped down my throat and sloshed into my squirming belly. The name Ragnar Lothbrok played itself over and over in my head. It was all too familiar, and if what Hulda implied was true, then those bones were worth a fortune.

"Um, Mose, do the Danes have any idea who those bones belong to?"

Mose shrugged. "There are rumors. We wouldn't know for certain. Other than a sign stating as such, we'd always be guessing."

"What rumors?"

He ran a hand through his thick mop of curly black hair. "There were other relics buried with the man that indicated he was of high status. A king perhaps. Along with them were remnants of shields, blades of the finest quality, and bits of jewelry. One of them had runes on it, and the Danish team feels they suggest a man called Ragnar. While the last name wasn't fully intact, they made out the letters L-O-T-H-B. The rest have rotted with time."

I gasped, feeling my breakfast burning my esophagus as it shot into my mouth. I scrambled for the kitchen trashcan, retching every morsel into it.

Mose lunged forward and grabbed my hair, keeping it out of the way.

"What is that? Is Didi okay?" Callum called from the speakerphone.

"She's fine," said Mose. "Nothing a bit of Pepto won't cure."

I dabbed at my mouth with the towel Mose offered and leaned my backside against the countertop. "Mose, I know the dead man's identity." My voice was scratchy and my throat was raw.

He cocked his head, a woeful warning in his guarded eyes. "Don't fall for it, Didi. We can't assume—"

"Don't tell me what to think. I've had about enough men in my life telling me what I can and cannot think, feel, or do."

He held up his palms in surrender and took two steps backward. The hurt washed over his face, and I immediately regretted my rashness.

"Mose—"

"No, Didi, you're right. Please, tell us who you think it is."

I puffed out my cheeks and blurted out, "Ragnar Lothbrok."

Even to me, it sounded bizarre.

"You mean the fabled Viking king they've made that show out of? The one everyone is crazy about?" Callum asked.

"Yep." I nodded. "The same."

Ragnar Lothbrok, also spelled Lodbrok, Lodbrog, Lodbrok, and the old Norse way, Ragnarr Loðbrók, was born sometime during the mid-700s AD and died during the early-to-mid part of the 800s AD. Thrown into a snake pit after an attempted raid in Anglo-Saxon England, his resting place is undetermined. Exact dates and accounts of his life are unknown, but his legendary existence, and that of his sons, are written for the ages. From wrestling dragons—hence his nickname signature hairy breeches or shaggy breeches, as they protected him from said dragons—to raids in Scandinavia, France, and Anglo-Saxon England, and even a battle with the Holy Roman Emperor Charlemagne. Ragnar, the son of King Sigurd Ring of Denmark and Sweden, was a merciless, fearsome, ale-guzzling warrior. His story, while possibly an amalgamation of other men of his time, is written in the Icelandic Sagas and the Gesta Danorum (a well-known work written by the famous Danish historian Saxo Grammaticus) has him the father of more historically accounted for men like Inward (Ivar the Boneless), Halfdan, and Hubby (Ubbe). These sons, all kings in their own rights of places ranging from France, the Baltic, England, and throughout Scandinavia, reportedly attacked East Anglia in Northumbria sometime around 865 AD to avenge their father's brutal death. Prior to killing the king, they sent a message to those who would retaliate, torturing the king by performing their infamous and barbaric blood eagle ritual.

I shuddered, thinking about what the Viking era did to people. The blood eagle in particular was horrific. If what Hulda was trying to tell me was that these bones belonged to none other than Danish King Ragnar Lothbrok, then the ramifications were huge. Historians documented little of Ragnar, but his sons' names were more known. If it were true, then no wonder Anice and her group wanted the bones.

I hotfooted it to the dining room table and grabbed my laptop, searching for any references to a real-life Viking named Ragnar Lothbrok.

"What's happening?" came Callum's deep voice. "What am I missing? Is this guy real or not? If he is, the bones hold more monetary value, right?"

"Yes." I stared at Mose while he paced from the kitchen to his bedroom and back. "Mose, tell me more about the missing artifacts. What exactly went missing? Is there anything else of value that you haven't mentioned?"

Mose paced a few more times before I lost my patience.

"Mose!" I snapped. "Talk to us."

He went to the refrigerator for a beer, popped the cap off, and knocked back half of it in five seconds. Wiping his face with his sleeve, he looked across the room at me. His features were drawn, and his skin was a sickly shade of pale green.

"There were the bones, of course, but... not only keys are missing. Someone took a ring with initials on it, and also part of a weapon."

He gulped down the rest of his beer, slammed the can on the countertop, and crunched it down. I jumped at the loud bang.

"What type of weapon?" I asked.

Mose ran a hand roughly through his hair. "An axe." He reached for another beer.

He drank half of it and threw the half-empty beer bottle across the kitchen. Yellowish liquid sprayed the kitchen counters, floors, and walls. He leaned his palms onto the countertop, head hanging in distress. "Uh, and remnants of a double-edged blade. It has a slightly rounded point on it. I took pictures..." He glanced sideways at me. There's an inscription. Runes. The inscription reads 'blade Sword of Kings.'"

I placed my hand over my abdomen, feeling woozy. "What?"

Callum remained quiet, except for the occasional keyboard stroke. It was as if the universe had perversely turned off. Even the refrigerator hum sounded like a train.

"Mose, what else did they take?" I pressed.

"A shield."

I gulped. "Describe it." My voice sounded a mile away.

"It was better preserved than Hulda's. They were similar, except for one thing—a rune I haven't encountered before. There were flecks of paint still present, which is remarkable considering its age."

I licked my dry lips. "What color?"

"Red. No..." He tilted his head to the side, forehead crunched in thought. "I'd say it's more of an orange color. Why?"

I sucked in a large amount of air and shook my head in disbelief. What did it mean? The unique rune emblazoned in an orange-reddish glow off the warrior man's shield popped to mind. This was no coincidence. Ragnar Lothbrok was coming, but for what? His bones? His child? His weapons? None of it made any sense.

I waved him off. "It doesn't matter. The real question is, if Anice isn't here to torture us, and she's got the bounty, then why stay? Callum, I assume Scotland Yard is working with the United States authorities on this?"

"Yes, but she's highly entrenched here. Who's to say she doesn't have henchmen in the United States?"

True. So why was Anice hanging around?

"Right. How do we get it back?"

Callum snickered. *"Oh, don't worry about that. I've got a plan."*

CHAPTER 30

I placed my hand on Mose's wrist. He'd sat beside me at the dinner table and was searching the internet for the rune he'd seen on the sword. We'd all agreed to a plan to draw out Anice, and that meant Callum would take a trip across the pond. While he was busy getting here, we were nose deep studying up on the runes, Ragnar, and anything else to do with Hulda and her lineage. I'd leaped at the opportunity to study both Hulda's and Ragnar's lines while Mose worked on the other part of our scheme.

"This Sword of Kings blade... why didn't you tell me about before, Mose? And the shield."

Mose stopped typing, interlaced his hands, and fixated on a piece of rice outside the Chinese takeout box. "I shouldn't have left my aide alone with the artifacts. That's a massive failure on my part, and when this is over, I'm telling Shane about all of it."

I looked up from my screen. "He'll fire you. Think this through."

"I have." He shrugged. "It's the right thing to do. It's bad enough my teaching assistant died over it. If I'd have stayed—"

"You'd be dead on the floor beside him."

"That's not true. I would've stopped them."

I snorted. "You and what army?"

Mose stared up at me. "I know martial arts."

I leaned my elbows on the table. "Martial arts is great if guns aren't involved. Plus there's three of them, Mose. Face it. You'd be dead right alongside with him. Promise me you won't do anything stupid."

Mose tapped his index finger on the table.

"Promise me," I snapped.

"I promise I'll think it over. That's all I can offer. What I've done..."

"What you've done? Please, Mose, you trusted your TA. Everybody does it. It's not a crime. There was nothing you could have done."

He sighed and hacked away at his computer keyboard again.

"Tell me about the blade. What type of steel was it?" I got a pen from my laptop bag and shoved a napkin over to him.

He stuck his tongue between his teeth and scrawled a crude sword. When he was finished, he shoved the napkin toward me. "Uh, it was crucible steel."

I studied it and tried to picture the shape in my vision that I'd seen on the shield. Everything matched, with only one difference. I stabbed the drawing with my jagged nail. "Wait. It was an Ulfberht sword?"

"YES, but there were other fragments. Part of a shield that I told you about already, a whetstone, daggers, and another longsword. They were all fragmented, but the designs matched those of the others from that time."

Wow! Only about 171 of them had ever been recovered. This was the most coveted sword of the time. The combination of lightness, flexibility, and strength made it every warrior's dream to own one. Few could rival a Viking with an Ulfberht sword. Charlatan sword-makers made many fakes to cash in on their popularity as only a few skilled men had learned the well-kept secret of their composition and make. Lots of warriors died because of it. If Ragnar owned an Ulfberht, then it proved he was a man of means, but it still didn't prove that our Ragnar was the Ragnar of Viking myth.

"Tell me again about the shield." I propped my chin on my hand. "Were there any other images or initials on it?"

"Yes."

"What?"

"Give me a sec," he grumbled, and tapped some more keys. He turned the screen toward me. "A raven," he said dryly.

My jaw dropped open.

He tapped the keyboard again, and a rune appeared. "There. I knew it existed. This is the rune on the shield. It means king."

I leaned close to the screen. Holy cow. It was the same rune on his shield. Ragnar Lothbrok. He wasn't a myth after all.

CHAPTER 31

"Alright. That about does it."

I clicked the top of the pen and tossed it on the dining table where Mose and I had various maps, pictures of relics, and ideas for drawing Anice out of hiding and back to Boston— if she'd even left, which I was beginning to believe. What relic would surpass the prestige of a shield maiden? Ragnar Lothbrok's bones, sword, and shield. She'd be a god in the black-market world.

I clasped my fingers together and looked at Mose. His unruly mop of hair needed a cut, and tiny crow's feet stood out at the edges of his eyes. In true fashion, however, he appeared cool and collected. Usually calm during a crisis, his demeanor at his office with Landon's death stood in stark contrast, and I feared something else was behind it.

"Mose?"

He'd been tapping his pen against a pad of paper containing the skeletal outline of our harebrained scheme, studying it with an intensity I imagined a neurosurgeon cracking open a human skull would have.

He rubbed his eyes, stifling a yawn. "It'll work." He reached over to place his warm hand over mine. "It's practically foolproof."

Though he grinned, the tightness to it was evident.

"It's not about that. I was wondering about the morning of Landon's death."

Mose yanked his hand back as if I'd stung him and gathered up the loose papers scattered across the table.

"Something else spooked you that morning."

Tight lipped, he piled the papers into one neat stack. On one with an Egyptian hieroglyph, he traced his finger over a bird that was in front of a hand. Besides the bird and hand, there was an eye and another bird. Cleopatra's cartouche, if I wasn't mistaken.

"It's not like you to panic, Mose," I pressed. "What aren't you telling me?"

Mose balled his hands into fists and covered the paper that had transfixed him with a crude map of a building and its various rooms we'd made for our plans with Anice. "It's not every day you find a dead body on your office floor, Didi." He stared at me. A look of anger flickered behind his dark brown eyes. "I'm human. I panicked."

I shook my head. "There's more to it. You once pulled an unconscious driver out of a burning car without so much as a blink."

"That's different. I didn't know him."

"You didn't know Landon well either, Mose. What aren't you telling me?"

"Nothing. Drop it." He scooted his chair back abruptly and stood, me hot on his heels.

"Un uh, Mose. What's wrong?"

He crossed the living area and ended up in the bedroom, stopping at the foot of the bed to take a deep breath. "The less you know, the better. Don't you see? I'm trying to protect you. That's all I've ever done, Didi. From the moment I laid eyes on you, I've only wanted to shield you. It's like a cloud of sadness hovers over you wherever you go, and when you went to Scotland, and all... this happened, I realized I can't save you anymore. Do you know how useless that makes me feel?" He sat on the edge of the bed and held his head between his hands.

I reached a hand to him, but he flinched at my touch. "Ugh," he groaned. "Why does this keep happening to you?"

I frowned, not understanding.

"Gosh, Didi. You seem to attract unfortunate events like a fly to sugar. You see, I think it's because you enjoy the pain. It's like you're dancing with the devil and narrowly avoiding calamity. But it's not just you that's affected. What about your nephew?"

"What about him?"

"He almost died. Twice. On top of that he's not the only one. It's Christof, it's Callum... it's me. We've almost been killed too." He slammed his hand against his chest. "Geez, even Dr. Gates got fired."

"Now hold on a minute." I held up my palm like it could somehow stem the hurt, anger, and sadness hurled at me. "Dr. Gates was fired because of Shane Bernard, not me. That guy has it out for anyone he perceives as threatening his status or who doesn't have loads of money."

"Now you're just fooling yourself. What about Roger?"

I paused, crossing my arms against my chest. "Roger was attacked because of the bones."

"Yes!" Mose snapped. "Those bones which are connected to Hulda's, connected to a baby they shared, and connected to *you*. Face it, Didi. Everyone around you either pays financially, emotionally, or physically. Look at your sister."

"What? Are you blaming her infertility on *me*?" Heat flushed my skin.

"Laura took care of you like a mother from the first years of her marriage. Don't you think that took a toll on her? On her marriage?"

I blinked back tears. "Don't. Don't you throw that at me. I didn't have a choice. She didn't have a choice. Our parents died, Mose. Am I to blame for that too?"

I grabbed my wallet, keycard, and phone from the dining table, but the second I headed for the kitchen, he stood in my path, arms wide, barring my exit.

"Didi, your parents' death wasn't your fault, however, all your unresolved trauma from their car accident has affected those closest to you. It's time you face it."

I snorted. "Nice try, Mose. Dr. Gates' firing and Landon's death had nothing to do with me. As for Ross and Dr. Pinnick, that's on Anice. Back to Landon, though, you still haven't answered my question. What are you protecting me from? What had you so panicked that morning?"

Mose gritted his teeth, pulling out two bloodstained cards from his pocket with a set of keys. "These were on Landon. I saw him arguing with Shane the night before his death. They were outside the bone lab. I overheard them saying something about 'it better work' and then he gave Landon this card."

I took the card. It was blank except for a phone number. "What's this?"

Mose shrugged. "I tried calling it, but it only beeps. It's relaying a message of some kind."

"What about the other card you're holding?"

Mose handed it over with the set of keys. I blinked and wobbled a bit. "But... but these are... how did he get these?"

Mose's face was like a ghost in the pale light of a winter morning.

I stared at the keys on my shaky palm. It was an identical set to my apartment, office, and my sister's home. As if that wasn't horrifying enough, I blanched when I looked at the other card. "Why did Landon have Christof's business card?"

Again, Mose shrugged. "Everyone around you is at risk, Didi." He looked at the floor and shook his head. "I found them after Landon's murder. They were sticking out of his pocket. I realized this was way bigger than anything I could help you with. I panicked because I realized that your life might be on the line and turning these cards into the authorities would implicate you in the investigations. Someone is trying to frame you, or to delay you, or even trying to kill you. You'd better hurry and figure out it out. How many more innocent people must die because of you?"

He walked away, leaving my path to the door unblocked. I remained where I stood, reeling from what he'd said. What hurt the most was that some of it was true. I did love the thrill of danger, and one day it would likely get me killed. Or worse, my loved ones.

CHAPTER 32

On the Uber ride, I mulled over all that had happened from Scotland to today. Hulda's appearance, Ragnar's, and now the baby bones... it was all connected. Was Mose right? Was Dr. Gates fired because of his mentorship with me? Likely. Was it something more than peer rivalry? What about Shane? Why was he arguing with Landon the night before his death? Could Shane be in on this? Anice had admitted trying a week ago to recruit him as a pawn in her black-market scheme. Did she get her claws into him?

I paid for the ride and hopped out in a suburban neighborhood of Boston. Bright, sunny rays warmed the top of my head, and the sweet scents of summer flowers rushed towards me as I walked up the brick pathway to Dr. Gates' front door. I stopped for a moment to admire the pinks, purples, and yellows in the flowerbeds lining the front of the old Georgian home. Spruce green shrubs, planted hundreds of years before, acted as a fence marking the land's boundaries while at the same time inviting people in. The earthy yellow exterior of the home struck a warmth in me I hadn't felt since my parents' death. It was a ray of sunshine in my otherwise dreary existence. A three-story home, it followed the pattern of old Georgian houses of the 1700s era, and fortunately for Dr. Gates, he'd inherited it from his parents, who'd inherited it from theirs, all the way back to the founding of our nation.

I bounded up the few brick steps and knocked on the door, hoping I didn't disturb the grandbaby, whose nursery was right above on the second floor. Since his firing, Dr. Gates reveled in the ability to take care of his first grandchild, and he'd taken it on practically full time. His daughter didn't mind because they overworked her at her firm, though she only worked part time now that the baby was born.

The thick oak door creaked open like doors on old houses do, and the puff of dampness and dust drifted into the air.

"Hello, Dr. Gates. Thanks for seeing me on such short notice."

After a brief hug, he ushered me into his foyer. On the immediate left, there was a stairwell to the second floor, which was lined with family portraits, some oil canvases, and other more modern photographs, and dated back to the 1700s. Beside the stairwell was a walkway that led straight to the kitchen. The 1950s white stove, still gleaming like it was brand new, was presently heating an electric blue tea kettle while the sweet scents of cinnamon and brown sugar tickled my nose from the cookies Dr. Gates' wife was famous for. On the right of the foyer, which housed a wooden bench and coat rack, sat the parlor. Its federalist blue walls and shoulder-high white wainscoting were dotted with shelves filled with history books and anthropologic finds forever preserved in picture form of his last forty years of work. From the pyramids of Giza to the tomb of Tutankhamun, Dr. Gates lived, breathed, and dreamed ancient Egyptian culture. Rightly so. He was one of the foremost Egyptian scholars in the world and good friends with Mosewan's parents. While he appreciated my love for all things Norse, his heart rested in the sands of Alexandria and the Valley of the Kings.

Dr. Gates led me into the old parlor used as his office instead of the ladies' parlor they had built it for. Gone were the feminine touches of generations past, and in its place were huge cream-colored velveteen drapes, a cigar cabinet, rich blue and gold area rugs, with his chunky boat desk smack dab in the center of it all. I eyed the few family relics stashed in between the pictures and his life's work and marveled at it all. His ancestry could be traced back to the founding of this country, and walking into this home was like time traveling into a different era full of angst, promise, and hope.

Dr. Gates sat his plump frame behind the desk. The squeak of his desk drawer was loud. He pulled out a bottle of his finest bourbon, clinking two glasses together from yet another drawer, filled the bottoms of the cups, and beckoned me over. I sat in the overstuffed chair in front of the desk and happily took the glass of spirits. Knocking it back in one fell swoop. He poured in more of the brownish liquid.

"Take it easy on this stuff. It'll knock your socks off."

The chair creaked as he leaned against the chair back and swirled his drink with one hand, properly taking me in.

Eager to be free from his intense scrutiny, I asked, "How's Moira?" Truth be told, I'd been thinking about her ever since Dr. Gates had mentioned Roger's death. "Is she holding up okay?"

Dr. Gates nodded. "She's upstairs right now with my grandson. If that little boy isn't a good luck charm, I don't know what is. She wasn't eating, drinking, or sleeping until I insisted she come over. Roger was her only family." He paused and sipped his bourbon. "The second she laid eyes on our Henry," he grinned, "the grief lessened, and she became more herself again. My daughter doesn't mind. It's a relief to be honest. She can rest and even tie up loose ends at work. Plus Moira... she's taken on Henry like a grandson, and it suits her. He might have saved her life."

He raised his glass up in salute.

"I'm sorry about Roger."

He waved off my sympathies. "Roger loved adventure, and this last one left him acting younger than I'd seen him in decades. In all honesty, he's the one who warned me about the danger you were in. He made me promise to watch out for you like he knew something would happen to him."

Dr. Gates sipped on his drink while I fought against all the whys.

Though Roger dabbled in Norse runes, he wasn't the only one with knowledge on the subject. Why attack him?

"Was it murder?" I asked.

He bowed his head in thought and stared down at the swirling brown liquid in his glass. "Yes. Someone suffocated him with a pillow. Detective Soo is on the case. I'd be careful with that one. He asked loads of questions about you."

I grunted. Detective Soo was intelligent, of that I had no doubt. I also suspected my name was at the top of his suspect list from the beginning. The morning of Landon's death I'd stumbled over his line of questioning, especially the timing of events, but in my defense, I was only protecting Mose. As for Mosewan, he was hiding something. Something other than keeping the business cards and the set of my keys. Why Landon had them to begin with still vexed me. It didn't take a rocket scientist to pinpoint Shane's involvement in this. Mose had been upset with Landon over him asking Shane for clearance on who knew what. Was Shane acting out on the people closest to me? Though he was linked to Landon, that was easily brushed off now being the chair of the Archaeology and Anthropology Department. But the whole lot smelled fishy. Shane's position was bought, or my name wasn't Daisy Day. To pinpoint murder on him though, to me, was a step too far. Although stranger things had happened, and even well-intentioned people ended up killing in certain situations.

I set the glass on the desk and crossed my legs, bracing myself. This plan of Callum's, Mose's, and mine not only placed our own lives at risk but Dr. Gates' too.

"I have a huge favor to ask."

He stared boldly across the desk at me. "Does it help find Roger's killer and capture Anice Foster?"

"Yes."

Dr. Gates drained the contents of his glass and slammed it onto the desk. His rosy cheeks were redder than usual. "Count me in."

In less than half an hour, Dr. Gates had rounded up funding for an auction to be held later that evening. What better way to draw Anice out on such short notice? We both suspected she'd hung around in the

US. If not her, then she had one of her henchmen hanging about. We'd give her something worth showing up for, and what better than a coveted papyrus written by Cleopatra herself? Anice had her hands in many pots, one of which was ancient Egypt. Those antiquities would go for millions on the black market, and who wouldn't want to get their greedy grubs on a document written by Cleopatra? How Dr. Gates accomplished this was mind blowing. He certainly had connections in high places. Now that the trap was set, we needed to blow up the airwaves and internet with a last-minute auction.

"Will people come on such short notice?" I ask Dr. Gates.

"Oh, they'll come. Among the auction items is a night at Le Ruse. There's a two-year waiting period to eat there. Trust me. People will come."

I arched my brow. "How did you come by that?"

Dr. Gates wiggled his nose. "That's for me to know, my dear. I will only say that I must lecture several classes at Harvard for the next few years."

I grinned. Dr. Gates relished in teaching, and Harvard was as good a place as any to teach. Besides, I couldn't imagine him sitting here the rest of his life twirling his thumbs even if he was the occasional babysitter for his beloved grandson.

"Well, it seems you've made out in the deal."

He winked. "What's next? What more can I help you with? If it means catching Roger's killer…" he eyed the ceiling where we heard the creak of footsteps, "…count me in. Moira needs answers."

I leaned forward. "There is this one thing. What do you know about Francisco?"

"Ah, Frankie. He was a dapper man. Proud of his family and a hard worker. He'll be missed. What are you asking specifically?"

"He'd told me about a second job."

"Not surprising, though I'm afraid I know very little. We talked about his family. He never brought up work. Have you talked with Manny?"

I perked up. "Manny?"

"Yes, the manager. If anyone knew Frankie, it would be Manny."

I thanked Dr. Gates for all the help and left. Next stop was the university. We had a few hours before the auction, and this couldn't wait. Someone had to talk with Manny, and since Callum was somewhere over the Atlantic Ocean, and Mose was busy tying up other loose ends for tonight, it was me or nobody. I hoped he held a piece of the puzzle that would make all of this make sense.

CHAPTER 33

*W*andering the university hallways had never been scary before. Today was different. My imagination had taken over, turning the hallways into mazes of henchmen, each with a gun and a mission to kill me and everyone else I loved.

At the squeak of a shoe and murmurs of a heated conversation, I stood flush against the wall, hugging it, and peeked around the corner.

"Stop questioning me," Shane snapped into his phone. "I'm on it. You can count on me."

His gaze darted around the hallway and I jumped back, holding my breath.

"Tonight?" He swore. "Fine. I'll be there. I wouldn't miss it for the world. She'll get what's coming to her."

The steps echoed louder, and I frantically glanced up and down the hall for a place to hide when a door I'd been standing in front of opened, and I fell into it.

"Dr. Day, can I help you with something?"

I turned around to stand face to face with the very man I'd come to see.

"Manny, right?" His name was embroidered on the lapel of his navy jumpsuit. Dr. Gates was right, I'd seen him around before, though he'd kept to himself, never once returning my greeting. Today, as he stood before me, shifting on his feet, hands gripping his mop with white knuckles, he managed a tight smile.

"Uh... yes."

I straightened my shirt, trying not to cringe with each approaching footfall. Manny's expression changed from frosty to flushed pink.

"Sir," Manny mumbled through gritted teeth.

Hot air brushed against my neck. I turned, pasting a smile on my face, as it was now impossible to ignore him.

"Shane Bernard." I clapped my hands together. "Are you out terrorizing the neighborhood again?"

Tact flew out the window with Shane. He'd taken delight in pestering me throughout school, and he'd made it perfectly clear what he thought of me long ago. Time and again, he'd thwarted my treaties with a donation here, a donation there, at just the right time. In the end, he'd advanced with little work, and his lack of published papers proved it. There weren't any. No one took him seriously. No one professionally, that was, and not even his rich parents could bribe the approval boards of the finest publications in our industry. His only option for advancement was here at Massachusetts College, and he'd made every attempt to have me fired along the way. It didn't start as colleagues; he'd tried getting me expelled from the university when we were students. The happiest day of my life was when the university had offered me a position as associate professor of anthropology. The scathing look on his face lasted me quite a while.

"*Dean Bernard* to you." He crossed his arms and tried peering down his nose at me, but instead of shaking in my proverbial boots, I laughed. He barely stood an inch taller than me, and it only made him look more pompous, if that was even possible. Even Manny chuckled.

"Get back to work!" Shane barked.

Manny shoved his cart beside us, flopping the wet mop in the bucket full of water, some of which splashed onto the floor and Shane's high-dollar shoes.

"I'll dock your pay for that stunt." He stepped forward and jabbed a finger on Manny's chest. "Try it again and I'll fire you. How will you pay for sweet Selena's physical therapy if I do, huh? What about that pretty little wife? Her brother works here. From what I can tell, they're close. I bet she'd need a shoulder to cry on… what with him in prison again, right? I mean, this job is a stipulation of his parole."

Shane snickered while Manny stared down at Shane's finger jabbing at his sternum. "Know your place or else I'll have to comfort your wife. What do I leave… a five? Or is she more of a dollar type of girl?"

Manny's nose flared while he ground his teeth. To his credit, he kept his mouth shut. He shoved the cart around Shane and walked off while Shane laughed. "Don't worry, Manny. I wouldn't dare. She's liable to have something catchy."

I balled my fists and stood nose to nose with Shane. "You don't scare people, Shane. Fire as many people as you'd like, but we all know what a pathetic loser you are. No amount of money can buy you a reputation."

Shane's mouth twisted in anger. "I'd be careful if I were you. Things might… happen to you or someone you care about."

I crossed my arms. "I'll know where to look. If you're in bed with Anice Foster, there will be trouble, and you don't have a clue what you're up against. Anice isn't to be trusted, so watch your back. Daddy won't be able to bail you out."

I stepped beside him and followed Manny down the hallway and around the corner where I leaned against the wall, my heart pounding in my chest. I knew poking the beast wasn't a good idea, but *man* that felt good. Maybe Mose was right. Maybe I liked an adrenaline rush a little too much.

Someone whistled and called, "Hey."

I scanned the corridor but saw no one. Then another whistle. To my right, at the end of the hallway before the stairwell entrance, I saw the top of Manny's head poking out. He waved at me.

I jogged over. He ushered me inside, shutting the door behind us, peeking out the slim window before turning to me.

"That was either a brave thing you did there or genuinely stupid," he said, sizing me up. "I haven't decided which yet."

I sighed. "I couldn't let him bully you."

Manny shrugged. "I can take care of myself. Why were you hiding, anyway?"

"Not important. About Frankie…"

Manny's face turned grave. "What about him?" He dumped the dirty water into the steel sink in the corner of the janitor's closet that looked like it had been there for decades. Streaks of blue, white, and red paint lined the outside, which must have been left over from the multiple painting attempts the university spent money on over the years. Although the inside was immaculately clean, as were the storage shelves. All the cleaner bottles were lined up one behind the other, labels facing forward, and the towels were neatly folded. Not a speck of trash or dirt to be found.

"Um, was there any kind of rivalry between him and the other janitorial staff or university staff members?"

Manny stacked the now empty yellow bucket after washing it out with a Clorox solution and water into another empty bucket. "What janitorial staff?" He huffed. "There's me, my brother-in-law, and Frankie. I guess there's only me and my brother-in-law now."

I nibbled on the inside of my cheek. "Okay. What about his other job? Did he mention any problems with it?"

"Frankie kept to himself about stuff like that."

I slowly shook my head. Another dead end.

"He *was* acting differently these last couple of weeks."

A break. At last! "Did you question him about it?"

Manny nodded. "He said he'd had it with Dr. Bernard. That man laid into him. The day before he died, I saw them arguing. It got loud. Frankie said it was over the trashcans or something, but that can't be right. Dr. Bernard jerked him around a bit before saying he'd better follow through."

"With what?"

Manny shrugged. "I don't know. Oh, and he mentioned he'd gotten in over his head with the new job."

"The one at the lawyer's firm?"

"Yeah. He said he'd seen stuff."

"Like what?"

"He refused to say. The next day, though… he died."

I thanked Manny for his help and asked him to stay far away from Shane.

The time until the auction was quickly approaching, but there was one more person I needed to interrogate. This one wouldn't be pretty.

I walked out of the janitor's closet, free from the noxious smells of cleaner, down the hallway, and around the corner to an enormous office. A man was outside affixing a nameplate to the recently vacated office. With a steadying breath, I opened the door and walked inside.

"Shane… we have to talk."

CHAPTER 34

Shane stared out his expansive window overlooking the fountain his family donated money to build. His fraught features belied a man deluged with worry, and the constant pecking at his phone and returning pings of texts underlined a preoccupied man in over his head.

"What do you want?" He cast a sideways glance at me before refocusing on his phone, which lit up for the fifth time since I'd entered.

I ran my hand against his soft leather chair in front of his desk and admired the coolness of it. Money wasn't everything, but it bought things I'd only dreamed about.

"Why were you arguing with Landon Fisher the night before he died?" I asked bluntly.

Shane stared at me from behind his chunky office desk. No picture frames, no papers, nothing to suggest he cared about anyone or even his work. The near empty desktop held only his laptop and a landline phone.

"Landon who?"

He wasn't fooling anyone. The pinched lines around his eyes said a lot.

"Oh, come on, Shane." I tilted my head, taking in his rigid posture.

"Spill it. What were you arguing with Landon about? Why did he have your business card? He's Mose's teaching assistant, right?"

Another idea popped to mind. From what both Charity Chase, Dr. Gates' teaching assistant, and the young doorman at Christof's last party said, Landon was a bit of a loner. One who chaos followed. Was it because he was involved in shady business? Was Landon actually working for Shane and *not* Mose?

Shane had answered the last text and shoved his phone into the front pocket of his pressed khakis. "Landon Fisher was Mosewan Aten's assistant. He, and only he, interviewed him and hired him as a teaching assistant. I had nothing to do with it."

"Why did he have your business card?"

Shane shrugged. "I don't have business cards. Why would I need them? I can count on one hand the number of times I've used one for work. Most people call me for… other things."

I noticed the thumping pulse at the base of his neck. Whenever he was anxious, upset, or angry in the years since I'd met him, his telltale sign was the prominent thudding heartbeat.

"Sure you do. Maybe this will change your mind." I pulled out the blood-splattered white card and held it out far enough away to prevent him from taking it. One side held his scribbled name, while on the other was a printed phone number.

Shane glanced at the card. Jaw set, he continued, "That's not mine. Like I said. I don't have business cards."

He was definitely lying. But why? Was he capable of murder? I looked into his eyes and saw them drifting away from mine.

"Alright, what about the argument?"

Shane's phone beeped, and he was again busily tapping on the screen. "I barely noticed the man, Daisy. Could you be more specific?"

"The night before Landon's death, you argued with him in Mose's office."

After sending the message, Shane scratched the side of his head. "Do you have a point?"

Why I expected him to say anything relevant was beyond me. Still, I'd hoped he'd protest or slip up, or maybe I hoped his better angels would make him do the right thing for once. He stood there cool as a cucumber and calling my bluff.

"Fine, let's talk about this project you're so excited about."

Changing the line of questioning made Shane visibly jerk. He glared with barely disguised contempt.

"This will be my defining moment." He jutted his chin high and proud, like a peacock spreading its feathers. "No one will deny my contribution to anthropology and archaeology."

"I doubt that."

"You think you know it all, don't you?" He snorted. "You don't know the half of it."

I perched on the side of his chair with that new leather smell and interlaced my fingers on my thigh.

Shane arched a brow. "Don't look so smug. You've got nothing on me. Soon, the world will see me for who I truly am."

I rolled my eyes. "A conceited, arrogant prick?"

He clenched his fists and fixed a chilling smile on me that would peel paint off a wall. "Don't say I didn't warn you. When this is announced, your little project in Scotland will be yesterday's news and I'll be front page. Oh, and I'll be rid of your goody-two-shoes act once and for all."

"Where is this project taking you?"

He grinned. "Egypt." He walked around his desk and stepped beside me, hovering a little too close for my comfort. I forced myself not to budge even as he bent, his lips poised close to my ear. In the past, I'd have been convinced he'd never lower himself to killing anyone. Now I wasn't so sure.

"Daisy," he whispered, "turn back now before it's too late. I know you're planning something, and the people I'm working for will kill your loved ones to keep you from interfering with their plans." He straightened. "Go home, Daisy. Paint your toenails, drink margaritas, dance in the rain, do anything else besides get in my way. Because if you do, you may not live to regret it."

"Is that a threat?" I snapped.

"Take it as you will."

His pant pocket lit up, followed by a ding. Shane stepped away while I resisted the urge to flee out of the office, out of the building, and away from all the chaos that had slammed into my life a little over a week ago.

Shane blanched, swore under his breath, and shoved his phone into his pocket again. He headed for the door. "If you'll excuse me, I have business to attend to."

He held the door open, waving me out. I hopped up and scampered down the hallway toward my office. Once around a corner, I stopped and peeked at Shane's retreating form. He raced out of the building toward his new parking place. Every ounce of me wanted to follow him, but with his lingering threat, all the faces of my loved ones popped into mind.

A rumble of an engine cut through the empty halls. I ran to the door and saw Shane scanning the area for prying eyes. He slammed his foot on the accelerator, tires squealing in protest against the pavement and kicking up smoke, and zoomed toward the gated parking lot exit.

If I didn't follow him, I'd also lose the biggest lead we had. Plus, my loved ones were already in danger.

I craned my neck around the university parking lot and spotted Manny between some cars.

"Manny!" I waved my arms frantically above my head, not caring if Shane saw me or not. The gate attendant scrambled into his hut and fumbled around. It wasn't fast enough. Shane's waspish voice flung another tirade at the poor man in a campus police uniform, who repeatedly hit a button. His blotchy red face stuck out of the hut door, and he gawked at the still lowered gate.

Manny spotted me as he was climbing into his car. Not wasting time, I ran over, keeping Shane in view. "Hey, I need a huge favor. It's risky."

Manny pressed his lips together and followed my repeated glances over at Shane's fancy Beemer. "Get in."

I raced over to the passenger side and buckled up just as the gate attendant raised the bar. With a screech of rubber, Shane shot out of the parking lot and veered right.

"Follow him. I need to see where he's going."

Manny whipped the car around and zoomed after him, barely missing the falling gate. "Promise me one thing, Ms. Didi."

Manny expertly zigzagged through traffic, keeping two cars between us and Shane in a dangerous game of cat and mouse.

"What?" I asked, praying I wouldn't throw up on his sleek interior. For a janitor's salary, Manny's car rivaled Shane's.

"Promise me you'll nail him. Make sure he pays for what he's done."

CHAPTER 35

Shane's cherry-red Beemer squealed into the car garage attached to Christof's law firm. After we circled the block, Manny dropped me off at the front entrance. Although he'd offered to stay, I thanked him for his help and sent him on his way. No sense getting him killed like Frankie.

I entered the swivel-door entrance with my head down and headed to the elevators, hoping the reception attendant didn't see me. As it was, moments before, I'd watched Shane sneaking peeks behind him, scanning the area like a man up to no good before he stepped into an elevator. I scurried in when the elevator doors slid shut and watched the numbers rise from the first floor until it stopped.

I gulped. Christof's floor.

Stepping inside the next elevator, which thankfully didn't have an attendant, I pushed the button for the penthouse. My stomach dropped into my shoes when it rose. What if they were standing there when the doors opened?

On second thought, I hit the button for the floor directly below it and hopped off a few seconds later and located the stairwell. Charred streaks still lined the walls from the explosion, and I marveled at how quickly the police had allowed the offices to reopen.

I stepped onto the landing, crouching low and moving swiftly. Left and right, I scoured the area. No one seemed to be around. I cracked the door open, holding my breath when it creaked, and my eyes widened in surprise. There was no one in sight, not even a janitor cleaning up debris. In fact, there was no debris at all! How did they clean up so quickly? What type of money passed through these walls, anyway?

A murmur of voices caught my attention. I stepped into the shadows and leaned against the wall, keeping the door cracked. From this new angle, I saw Shane wringing his hands and pacing before the elevator doors. Good thing I'd gotten off when I did. His lips moved rapidly, but he was too far away to make out any words beyond a few phrases such as "please don't."

Who was he talking to?

"Please don't let it be Christof," I whispered.

I cracked the door farther open, stuffing a rubber door holder between the door and the wall. I plastered my ear to the opening, hoping to hear the animated conversation.

"What... do now? She's... police are... what's... plan?"

His words were spotty, but he was clearly agitated. Who was this *she*? Me or another woman? Anice Foster?

New furniture decorated the room and it smelled of paint fumes mixed with bleach.

I crouched on all fours and crept forward, scurrying behind the new leather couch and potted Ficus trees.

"Don't be a fool," came an acerbic retort.

Between two Ficus branches, I witnessed a sandy-haired man stride up to Shane. He jabbed a finger into Shane's breastbone and sneered. "Your father can't help you now. She owns you. Do you understand? Do as you're told, and everything will be fine."

"What if I don't?" Shane snapped.

"That promotion you received can easily be taken away."

Shane grunted. "That job means nothing."

"Oh, yeah?"

The sandy-haired man walked toward the leather couch and I saw his face. Brian Smith?!

"How about your home?" Brian hissed. "What about your cars? Would that upset you?"

"You wouldn't dare. My father—"

"Will do nothing. It doesn't matter. Shane, don't you know who you're dealing with? Boss Man will destroy you and anyone you care about. Do as you're told. Trust me."

They moved off toward the offices, and I crawled to the door and tiptoed down the stairs. I descended all twenty-something floors and traipsed out of the lobby into the frenzied early evening crowd of millennials rushing to leave work behind. The scent of gasoline, greasy burgers, and smoke filled my nostrils. I remained silent the entire way back to the Ritz even though the driver droned on about the latest baseball game on his radio. It wasn't until we reached the hotel that I emerged from the fog that had taken over my brain as I pieced together a life-sized puzzle that would help solve this case. The second I stepped out of the car, a flutter of movement caught my eye by the hotel's entrance. Was it...?

I skimmed the crowded sidewalk. Nothing. I sidestepped a family, nearly knocking over an elderly white-haired woman, who looked more plastic than the Barbie dolls I'd played with as a child. Dressed in the finest of furs, silks, and drowning in a gallon of French perfume, she mouthed off a few epithets unbecoming of a lady. I rushed on and jogged into the Ritz lobby, searching the crowd. A woman with red hair pulled into a bun breezed by the reception desk. It wasn't her hair or style that caught my attention; it was the way she walked.

Anice Foster.

I ran after her as she disappeared around the corner. When I turned into the hall, she'd vanished. I walked down the hallway and pushed on every door, and none budged. After a fruitless search I trudged back to the lobby and headed for the elevators. Halfway there I stopped, bent down, and picked up a white business-sized card. No print, pictures, or anything else save for a phone number on one side.

Scanning the area to no avail, I gave up and entered the elevator. I whipped out my cell and messaged Mose, warning him to keep a low profile and that our cover may have been blown. Noting the time, we didn't have any time to change course. The plan must go on whether we'd been spotted or not. The good news was she'd taken the bait. Game on.

I breezed past the kitchen and into the closet. After rummaging through multiple ensembles, I held a black slip dress up beside a fitted red dress with a scooped neckline meant to showcase an ample chest. Since time was of the essence, I rehung the red dress, not because it was bad though. Quite the contrary, the red dress was gorgeous. The shiny material practically danced under the light, and the bodice was embellished with sparkly jewel-like stones. However, tonight wasn't about beauty or fun, it was about catching Anice Foster. So practicality won out.

I slipped the black dress off the hanger, laying it on a mauve ottoman stool, and pulled my top over my head. My cell buzzed. Arms bound by the tight shirt, I struggled to disentangle the shirt. Tugging it out of my front pant pocket, I noticed a message from mystery man J.

"She's gone for now. Go back to Mose, he needs you. Oh, and the red dress fits you better. J."

I clutched the shirt to my chest and cast a glance around the closet. Were there cameras in here? Slightly creeped out, I dressed way more modestly, keeping most of my clothes on and covering the important parts while sliding into the dress. Finally, I put on a pair of black pumps and swept my hair up into a bun.

I grabbed the card key for the room and headed for the door after one last look in the mirror. Satisfied with my appearance, I pressed the button for the elevator and waited. My phone chimed.

I moaned and pressed the answer button. "Hello, Christof." I hated how stilted I sounded, yet it was unavoidable. Our relationship was in tatters and I didn't have time to fix it. Besides, at this point I didn't want to.

· · ·

I RAISED A BROW. "Aren't you recovering from a concussion?"

"I'm fine. Only a few cuts and scrapes, honestly."

"What about your assistant? Won't she be disgruntled?"

It wasn't a big secret. The chemistry between the two was palpable. Before the explosion, I'd seen her dancing with him, and she couldn't stop touching him. Like a moth to flame, that woman was smitten, and I couldn't blame her. Christof exuded confidence, charm, and he was exceptionally attractive. Add in a successful career, and he was the total package. Except... I wanted more.

"Didi, she's my assistant. That's all."

"Right." Arguing with him now was futile. Besides, I needed to focus. Anice had to be caught before anyone else ended up wounded or worse. Then it hit me. If he was a part of Anice's organization, now would be the perfect time to suss him out. Keep your enemies close, right? "You wouldn't want to come to an auction tonight, would you? There's this function Dr. Gates is putting on to raise funds for Moira, Roger's widow. You can bring your colleagues. The more the merrier. There are some pretty exclusive pieces to bid on."

Without hesitation, Christof agreed. *"I'm in. What time do I pick you up?"*

"I'm on my way right now. How about meeting me there in an hour? I'm sure what you're wearing is more than suitable."

Christof normally dressed to the nines. He'd always said to dress for the job you wanted, not the job you were interviewing for. Appearances mattered to him, which was another vast difference between us.

I hung up, hoping he'd invite Brian Smith. It was time to kill two birds with one stone.

CHAPTER 36

Speeding away in the back seat of another Uber, I texted Mose. We'd been over the plan numerous times, but his life and so many others hung in the balance, and I wanted to get it absolutely right. It had been thirty minutes since the last text I'd sent, and he had not responded. Nibbling on my lip, I imagined all the worst-case scenarios. When the phone rang, I jumped, bumping my head on the roof of the car. I winced when one of the bobby pins I'd used for the bun jabbed into my scalp.

"Hello?" I whispered, peering at the driver, who paid no attention to my conversation, focused on the scantily clad platinum blonde strutting up and down the sidewalk, her ample bottom and chest mesmerizing to drivers and pedestrians alike.

"*Didi... uh... you need to get to the school. Right now.*" It was Dr. Gates and his voice was terse.

"What? Why are you at the school?"

"*Long story. Get here as soon as possible. They have ransacked your office along with Mosewan's.*"

My gut dropped to the floor. I barked a change of address to the driver and held on for dear life at his swerve to correct our course.

Scotland changed everything for me . It was a mental and physical wake-up call that left me quaking in my boots. Around every corner lurked the possibility of danger. Gone were the safety nets I'd clung to. Corrupt police officers, morally bankrupt professionals turning a blind eye for a buck, innocent people slaughtered without remorse, and what was worse, I had unwittingly swept my loved ones up into it.

The driver stomped on his brake in front of the gaudy Zeus fountain, sending my phone skittering to the floor. I unbuckled and went to get out. The driver's sour look told me I wasn't getting a stellar review.

I scurried up the steps, my heels echoing on the concrete. In a flash, I had made it to my office. Dr. Gates stood like a graven statue, holding out his hand and shaking his head in warning. I craned my neck to glimpse inside, and what I saw filled me with dread. I clutched my fluttering stomach.

"Dr. Day," said the deadpan voice I'd only heard a couple of times before. Detective Soo stepped outside my office. Notepad in hand, he scribbled a few notes before looking up at me. Calculating, stern brown eyes searched mine. "We meet again. Notably this time there aren't any bodies."

I let out a sigh of relief. However, it was short-lived, as the detective's stare put me on edge, like I was under a microscope and he didn't like what he saw.

I nodded politely enough. "Detective." What I actually wanted was to search my office and see what the culprit had taken and find Mose. His office had also been raided. Why wasn't he answering his phone?

I stepped forward, then stopped when Shane's shirking face appeared at the door. My stomach turned queasy.

I wanted to turn tail and run, but with the Detective standing two feet away, I didn't stand a chance. Shane was up to something. Probably Anice's doing, but what?

"Dr. Day," Detective Soo waved me toward my office, "would you kindly step into your office? I'd like to ask you a few questions."

Detective Soo stepped aside, giving me no option but to comply. Checking my watch, I saw I had an hour at best before they expected me at the auction. When I stepped into my office, my heart leaped into my throat. On the floor next to the desk lay a serrated knife. This was a special gift I received when they offered me tenure at the university. Why was it on the floor and not in my locked desk drawer?

I circled my desk and settled into my chair, quickly checking all the nooks and crannies for their contents. The only thing out of place was the mess of paper everywhere and the broken lamp on the floor to the right of the desk.

Detective Soo loomed large in front of the desk.

"Dr. Day, why do you suppose your office and Dr. Aten's were burglarized tonight?"

I stared from him to Shane, who hadn't left. Dr. Gates was looming in the hallway behind them, his white head visible from his towering height over the other two men. He'd come to gather a few last-minute items we'd planned to showcase.

I shrugged. "I have no idea."

Detective Soo cocked his head and narrowed his gaze. "First the teacher's assistant, then the janitor, then the bomb at the law firm, and now this. Dr. Day, I'd say someone has a vendetta against you, or—"

"Or what?" I snapped. The longer we spent here, the more danger Mosewan, Dr. Gates, my family, and Christof were in.

"Dr. Day, we've examined both your office and that of your boyfriend. They took nothing from his other than ransacking it."

"He's not my boyfriend. We're colleagues."

Detective Soo stared unblinkingly at me. He bent, and with blue gloved hands, picked up the bloodied knife and deposited it in an evidence bag, sealing it with a flourish. "This blade, however, matches the description of the wounds we found on Francisco Ramirez Garcia. Don't you think it's odd that we would find it in your office?"

Shane snickered behind the detective while I rose to my full height, still having to look up at Detective Soo. "I do not know how that knife got in here. This morning, it was safely locked away in my drawer."

I rummaged through my clutch and pulled out the key for the locked drawer where I kept all my valuables. Thefts, while not common, certainly happened on a college campus, so I was careful to keep my belongings safe. The drawer unlocked with a soft click, and I searched it, hoping my dagger remained safely tucked away, thereby clearing my name.

My cheeks burned.

The drawer was empty. Not even the picture of my parents, nor the postcard they'd sent on one of their many world trips was there.

"I don't understand," I said, slamming the drawer.

Detective Soo blankly stared. "May I?"

He slid beside me and inspected the drawer, running his fingers over the outside and bottom of it. "What did this contain?"

I wondered why anyone would go through so much trouble for a postcard and a picture. "Um, nothing of significance. Sentimental items."

He fingered the keyhole of the lock and grunted. "It's been forced."

He beckoned to an officer in the hallway, who promptly entered. "Fingerprint the drawer and take the knife with you when you're done," he instructed the officer. To Dr. Shaw and I, he said, "Follow me into the hallway, please."

When we exited, I stared from Dr. Gates' worried expression to the detective's pensive one.

"Dr. Day, I won't mince words. There's a bloodied knife like the one used on both Mr. Roger Phillips and Francisco Ramirez Garcia. What was your relationship with either of the men?"

I paused. It wasn't because he was accusing me of murder, but the spinning details within my head that kept me mute. I needed a few more pieces of the puzzle to make them fit, to solve this once and for all, and Shane's smug face set another piece firmly into place.

"Dr. Day?" Detective Soo prompted, slapping his notepad against his palm in agitation.

"They killed Roger and Frankie for the same reason." Though Roger had been suffocated to death, it was news to me they had stabbed him in the original attack. That meant someone had been in my office before I'd returned from Scotland. But who? How?

"And that is?" Detective Soo stood stock still, not moving his notepad.

"They used one for his job, and the other simply was in the wrong place at the wrong time, either witnessing or knowing something he shouldn't have."

"Such as?"

Both Dr. Gates and Shane inched closer in anticipation.

"Detective Soo, I believe they were killed by someone that traffics in illegal goods. Just last week, numerous items went missing from a Scottish dig I was helping on, and my colleague, Dr. Pinnick, as well as the excavation manager, Ross Foster, were murdered. Those under the employ of Kimberly LeClaire pillaged the goods and then sold them to the highest bidder."

Detective Soo pursed his lips, fixing his dark brown eyes on me. "This Kimberly... you believe she's the one who murdered Mr. Phillips and Mr. Garcia?"

He shifted his stance, seemingly uncertain yet slightly intrigued. Hopefully, I'd be spared a trip to the police station.

"No, Kimberly was murdered. It's Anice Foster who's behind it. Or, strictly speaking, that's what I think. There's someone they call Boss Man who orchestrates it all. I haven't figured out who that is yet. It's possible Anice and Boss Man are the same person."

"Ah." Detective Soo flipped open his notepad and sifted through multiple sheets of paper before landing on one. His chicken scratch was difficult to decipher, but one circled word jumped out. *Daisy.*

I gulped, heat rising on my face and neck.

Lines extended out from the circle with both Frankie's and Landon's names, the law office bombing, and even the word auction was underlined. How did he find out about the benefit tonight?

"Come on," I raised my voice and flung my arms wide. "Using a replica Viking dagger with my initials on it to commit murder and then leaving it in my office to be found? You must admit that's pretty silly."

The detective drew a deep breath and nodded slightly. "If—and that's a big if—you're being framed, Dr. Day, then I'd say they're doing an incredible job. I have every reason to handcuff you and take you down to the station. But assuming you're innocent, someone has it out for you. Is this Anice Foster presently in the United States?"

"Yes!"

"Why hasn't she been arrested yet?" Detective Soo challenged.

"They arrested her," I replied. "But she's got some high-powered allies."

"A rogue cop?"

"Try multiple. Anice Foster escaped Scotland and admitted to controlling police officers, government workers, you name it. Her influence spans all time zones and countries."

Detective Soo flipped his notepad shut and stuffed it in his interior jacket pocket. "I'll check into it," he said gruffly. "Scotland, you say? If it's true, you'd better watch out, Dr. Day." He walked off down the hallway toward the front exit, calling out, "Don't leave town. You're now a prime suspect in the murders of Roger Phillips and Francisco Ramirez Garcia."

"Wouldn't dream of it," I shot back, rocking on my heels.

The three of us watched his raven-black head bob out of sight around a corner.

"Now you're done." Shane's delighted tone made Dr. Gates and me turn our attention to him. "As of this moment, Dr. Day, you're officially suspended. Pack up your stuff. Your days at Massachusetts College are over."

CHAPTER 37

The man practically foamed at the mouth saying it, though, which positively twisted my knickers. Still, he'd warned me.

Collecting my wits, I tugged Dr. Gates' elbow and set off after Shane's receding form. I kicked off my shoes at the front doors and waited while he paced in front of the fountain. His focus wasn't on the replica worth a fortune that bought him the chair of the department. Instead, he stared at the road leading up to the university building.

"What are we looking for?" whispered Dr. Gates, who was bunched beside me, trying in vain to reduce his formidable stature and failing miserably. His cottony white head, burgeoning belly, and tall frame were like a beacon to anyone paying the slightest bit of attention.

"Shane's in on it. The pieces are falling into place."

I explained to Dr. Gates about Shane's argument with Landon the night of his death, the one with Freddie. I spewed all the details connecting Shane to Anice.

"That's why he fired you," I said. "That's why they offered him the position at the university."

Dr. Gates scratched his immaculate white beard and stared out the window at Shane marching like a soldier waiting for orders.

"Interesting. So Anice contacted him, and his poor parents probably do not know how in over his head he is. You say this Brian Smith person threatened Shane?"

"Yes. He threatened to ruin Shane's parents if he backed out now."

Dr. Gates' bushy white eyebrows resembled wiggly gerbils as he pondered what I'd told him.

"The dots are indeed connected. Anice, this Brian fellow, and Shane are up to something, making tonight critical to solving this whole mess. If true, then Roger, Landon, and Freddie were all victims of these heinous black-market dealings."

Dr. Gates' mouth twisted into a grimace like he'd tasted a sour lemon.

"There's another thing," I said.

Dr. Gates stared at me intently. I was too busy watching Shane get inside a car. I squinted through the smudged glass doors of the university building I had grown so fond of over the last few years and my mouth dropped open.

"What?" Dr. Gates whispered.

I pointed at the red Mercedes driving away from the university. "That woman driving the car. She's Mosewan's girlfriend."

We gaped at each other in astonishment.

WE HAD no time to spare in looking for Shane, so we jumped into Dr. Gates' rust-covered pickup truck and tore down the road. It seemed impossible to get to the auction within ten minutes, but he expertly navigated us around traffic jams, turning down side roads and alleys until we were parked in a garage close to the Huntington Avenue entrance to the Museum of Fine Arts. The Remis Auditorium seated roughly 350 plus guests. The perfect place to host the local wealthy patrons from whom we hoped to gather funds for university research, college scholarships, and academic endeavors for the next decade or more.

My phone lit up. I fumbled, nearly dropping it.

"Mose? What's wrong?"

Dr. Gates held the door to the auditorium open for me, and I walked in ready to explode at Mosewan for keeping me in the dark.

"I'm fine. Olivia called and we argued. It's nothing. I'll deal with her later. Where are you? I'm over at the cafe."

Olivia called him? Shane riding away from the university with her was suspicious, yet I didn't have any proof of her involvement in any of this. For now, I'd keep quiet. That is until I uncovered more solid information about her. For all I knew, she was an innocent bystander.

I hung up with Mose and followed Dr. Gates to Taste, the quaint cafe close to the Remis Auditorium where tonight's auction would be held. We needed to review our plan, making certain everything was covered. We couldn't afford for Anice to escape like last time.

As we walked up to the cafe, I caught my breath.

Mose was dressed in a black suit and tie. His silky black hair was combed back, highlighting his tawny skin, much like liquid gold. He extended a glass of red wine to me. I could only gape like an idiot. Beside him was a petite brunette in a low-cut red velvet dress. Her skin shone much like Mosewan's. She spun to face me. Long, straight black hair glimmered under the cafe's lighting, and her dazzling smile left me speechless. She pawed Mose's arm, and the flicker of ink on her inner wrist drew my eye. Of course she had a tattoo. Not only was she gorgeous, but she was daring enough to tat herself for eternity. A floral motif was around a serpent. Geez, even her tats were cool. She was the picture of perfection as far as Mose was concerned, and if I didn't already know it, his approving gaze was the final nail in that coffin.

I clumsily thrust out my hand in greeting, almost causing the wineglass to slip from Mose's grip. "Olivia, right? Mosewan's told me lots about you." I dropped her dainty grasp and took the glass, gulping down the wine in one drink.

"Wow." Mose grinned. "Slow down, girl. We've got a program to run."

Olivia playfully patted his arm. "Lady or woman, but never girl, my love. We've talked about this before, remember?" she purred up at him, at 5"3", almost melting into his side.

Mose stayed lost in her admiration. Why wouldn't he? She was stunning. Few women could hold a candle to her.

Dr. Gates was already intervening. He grabbed my wrist and gently squeezed a warning sideways glance to top off the telepathic demand that I keep my mouth shut.

"Isn't he lovely?" Olivia cooed.

"Just." The edged bitterness wasn't intentional. It slipped out. Fortunately for me, the gods were on my side because Olivia kept beaming up at Mose, oblivious to the world.

Dr. Gates cupped his hands. "Young love. I dare say it's been a while for these old bones, but it does my soul good to see such a thing. Dr. Aten, would you be kind enough to show me the lavatory? I'd like to clean up before eating."

He wiggled his chubby fingers, a twinkle in his eye. Mose kissed the tip of Olivia's nose and walked off, Dr. Gates two steps behind. He winked at me, which meant he'd question Mose, and that was good enough for me.

"Olivia…" I started then my phone rang.

I cursed under my breath, plucking my phone out of my clutch and holding up a finger to the gorgeous woman dating my best friend.

"Can it wait Laura? I'm kind of busy right now."

The choked sob on the other end made me rigid as a statue. The pounding of blood rushed through my head like AC/DC on steroids. A million and one thoughts wrestled for control, but it all ended on one face. Anice Foster. My hands shook so badly I nearly dropped the phone.

Laura sucked in a breath. *"It's over. It's all over, Didi. You've got to help me. Fix this. Please, Didi, I can't lose them."*

Her soft whimpers mixed with incoherent sounds as the whirl of a thousand bees exploded within my ears. Balling my free hand into a fist, I clutched my arm around my belly, frantically looking toward the bathrooms where Mose and Dr. Gates had gone, but saw nothing. I grabbed the nearest chair when my wobbly knees gave out and flopped unceremoniously into it. Dang it! Why had I worn heels, of all things?

My odd behavior brought more than a few eyes on me. I bowed my head and turned away from them all, including Olivia, who was eyeing me curiously.

"Laura," I dropped my voice, "what's happened? Is she there? What does she want?"

"Everything's ruined. Didi... it's over."

"Ruined?" I blinked rapidly, catching quick shallow breaths, trying not to envision a gun held to Laura's head. "Laura, put her on the phone. No one needs to get hurt."

"What?" Laura sniffled. *"She's only a week old. It's not like you'd get more than a cry or suckle."*

"Wait, what? Anice isn't there? She's not holding a gun to your head?"

"A gun?" Laura squawked. *"Daisy Day, what on earth are you talking about? Don't tell me you've run into that psychopath again? Haven't I warned you?"*

I sagged against the chair and puffed out my cheeks. "So you're all safe? No henchmen? No guns?"

Laura snorted. *"Yes, we're fine. Now spill it. What's going on?"*

After I brought Laura up to speed as quietly as I could, her grunt of disapproval deflated me.

"I told you medicine, law, heck, even veterinary medicine would be better than this. In some measure you'd be doing something useful."

"My work *is* useful, and I've never understood why you tried to steer me away from it. What? It's not lucrative enough for you?" I snorted. "You're as bad as Christof."

"Young lady, you've got some nerve. I've only wanted the best for you."

"Then why not support my decisions? Why are you always second guessing me? Huh? Mom and Dad supported me."

"Yeah?" she snapped. *"Look where that got them!"*

"What?"

"Never mind."

"No, Laura. Say it. I killed our parents. Go ahead. Blame me. If I hadn't taken the quartz angel from Mom that night, they'd be alive, right?"

"You don't know what you're saying."

"Don't I?"

"Listen, forget I even said anything. You know how I get. Please, Didi, I don't blame you for our parents' death. Really. Sweetie, I'm sorry. It's been crazy around here, and I took it out on you."

The heavy sadness in her voice sucked all the wind out of my sails. Laura was a hotheaded demon when provoked, and Mom had always brushed it aside as a family trait. Something about her grandmother being the same. According to her, our lineage was clan leaders, ready to right the wrongs of the world, and some of the feisty blood trickled down into our generation.

"It's okay," I mumbled, closing my eyes against the tiredness that wrought my body into knots. "I shouldn't have lost my temper. I haven't exactly processed their deaths."

Laura chuckled. *"You think? Oh, Didi, I'm truly sorry. You're a great anthropologist, and our parents would be exceptionally proud."*

I smiled weakly. Fortunately, we made up quickly. I hated being at odds with Laura. She was the last bit of sanity I had left.

"So what's going on? What's over?"

Laura groaned. *"My marriage."*

I wasn't completely surprised. From what Nick told me in Scotland, Laura's marriage had been teetering on the path to divorce for some time. I suppose inheriting me, a thirteen-year-old child, after marriage wasn't a good start for wedded bliss. which Mose was quick to remind me. Add on Laura's strong will, determination, perfectionism, and her knee jerk reaction to drown herself in work instead of dealing with problems and it was a recipe for disaster. While we'd always focused on my avoidance, she never once considered that she did the same thing. Sure, it catapulted her as a surgeon, but virtually squashed a family life.

"Ah, so it's truly over? Nick mentioned something about it in Scotland."

"Ugh, Nick's not talking to me right now. I don't blame him. What's worse is that Mitch isn't even speaking to me. He'd have to be home to do that. I haven't seen my husband in weeks except for a quick shower and change of clothes. In fairness, with the baby crying, me sobbing, and my workload, it doesn't surprise me he'd turn to some tart at work."

"Whoa. Back up. What tart?"

"Sabrina. She's someone that works in his office."

Dr. Gates and Mose had made it back, and from the looks of it, Olivia had been filling them in because all three stared at me with varying levels of concern.

"How do you know he's cheating?"

"Oh! I found a pair of her thongs in my bed. Add that to receipts of flowers, chocolates, and meals at that new restaurant everyone raves about. You know, the one people wait for months to get a reservation for? Anyway, he's taken her there. It was the honeymoon meal. Ugh. Can you believe it? How stupid can I be? While I was working hard on marriage counseling, taking time off work, even adopting a child because he lamented not having more children, I've done it. I've stepped down from my board position at work in order to save my marriage, and all this time..." The audible intake of breath cut my heart into pieces. *"All this time, he's been messing around with someone else."*

"How long has it been going on? Have you confronted him about it?"

"Yes, I've talked with him. Two years. Two years that woman has been in my house, my bed, right under Nick's nose." Laura groaned. *"Poor Nick. I haven't had the nerve to ask him if he knew. Not that it matters. He's been through so much, and I don't have the heart to break it to him if he doesn't already know."*

I looked over at my companions sipping wine and eating the odd bit of cheese, each casting glances in my direction. As much as I wanted to run to my sister, take care of her and the baby, Nick if he needed it, I also knew time was running down. Anice would soon be here, and while my sister's marital problems were indeed severe, all of our lives were on the line.

"Hey Laura, can I call you back later?"

"I suppose you've got to stop another bomb or some sort, am I right? Go. But be safe, Didi. You're..." She paused for a long moment. *"There's stuff we need to talk about. Things about Mom and Dad. That can wait though. Stay alive."*

After we hung up, I stared at my companions again for a few seconds, pondering the events of my life until this point. It seemed tragedy struck throughout. Even before my parents' deaths, my maternal grandmother died suddenly when I was about eight years old. The circumstances of her death were never revealed. Not to me. Her death was the first of many that rattled me to the core and kept the nightmares coming. Now this.

I stood up, feeling a ton of invisible weight that I couldn't shake, and walked toward Mosewan, Dr. Gates, and Olivia.

My phone vibrated in my hand, and Taylor Swift's "I Knew You Were Trouble" played. I put it to my ear and grinned at the familiar brogue voice on the other end.

"I'm here. Can I get a lift?"

CHAPTER 38

J ignored the honks, glares, and obscene gestures I received as I poorly navigated the Boston streets toward the airport in Dr. Gates's clunker pickup truck. The crunch and groan each time I wrestled with the gear shaft in the stick shift made me wonder how much damage I'd inflicted on the old thing. Dr. Gates prided himself on keeping it in "like new" status, but on the umpteenth shift and thrashing of the gears, I feared a toddler would have driven better.

When I pulled into a parking space and turned off the engine, it sounded like the truck sighed. In my pointy designer heels raising me to new heights, I wobbled my way to baggage claim as instructed and waited by the carousels already vomiting luggage. Punchy passengers, eager to play the roulette of the did-my-bag-make-it game, impatiently waited by the swirling beast.

I found the carousel for Callum's flight and stood, neck straining among the throngs of passengers, in search of the tall, freckled, auburn-haired man who'd sauntered into my life a week ago. Until then, I'd fooled myself into believing that I'd achieved my life's goals. Perfect job, perfect friends, and perfect boyfriend. Then, *poof*, it all evaporated. Much like an oasis mirage amid a desert, it vanished, leaving me untethered and anxious.

I scanned the crowd for his telltale features, texting Chris for the fourth time that I'd meet him at the auction. Not one for brush-offs, he was insistent that we arrive together. His antics would have to wait. For now, I had only one thing on my mind. Well, maybe two. If it went off without a hitch, the plan would soon have Anice behind bars, leaving Dr. Gates, Roger's widow Moira, Mose, Laura, and I feeling heaps better. If it failed, then more than one person would die tonight. The other weighted topic wreaking havoc was soon to appear, and what did that mean for Mose? What had happened to my safely constructed life? A boyfriend, a dream job, a loving family... it was all I ever wanted, and now...

I skimmed through the crowd. Families hustled their children to the carousel. Harried, clothes wrinkled, some sporting food stains from a turbulent flight, they trudged to the baggage claim to snatch their luggage like a granny in a white panty sale.

I checked my watch for the billionth time. Where was he?

I stared at the arrival boards for what seemed like the millionth time. Callum's plane had landed twenty minutes earlier. At any minute, he'd appear among the throng of flyers and we could race back to the auction.

The crowd parted, and the rusty reddish-brown hair stood above the others. I hid a grin as people mindlessly ogled, stumbling over themselves as he strode forward, oblivious to his effect on them.

I waved my hand high in the air. Even with heels, I was still swallowed up by the crowd. When he was within fifteen feet, Callum spotted me. I pushed through the remaining baggage claimers standing between us, stood on my tippy toes, and threw my arms around his thick neck, nearly squeezing the life out of him.

It wasn't until that moment that I'd realized how tense I'd been, missing his calming presence.

"Is this how you normally greet people in America?" he quipped. "I'll have to come more often."

The salty scent of his skin tickled my nose. I unwrapped myself, hoping the hot flush of my cheeks wasn't too evident. It wasn't like me to accost men I barely knew.

"The carousel is over there." I pointed to the one closest to us and frowned. There were at a minimum a hundred people, three deep, swarming the carousel.

"Right. This will only take a second."

I watched in wonder as Callum's bulky, over six feet frame maneuvered through the crowd, nudging others aside. He snatched a bag off the carousel and was soon beside me again.

"You were saying?"

The deep green woolen sweater against his ruddy skin enhanced his piercing eyes, and I found myself lost for words. "Uh, yep. Let's go," I emitted.

He followed me out into the garage while my ankles wobbled under the duress of unfamiliar heels.

"If I didn't know better, I'd say you were slightly tipsy, lass."

"Yeah, well, it's a formal event. Heels are a prerequisite."

Callum ventured a furtive glance as I unlocked the passenger side. I tugged at the bodice of my dress as I rounded the truck and hopped in. It took three tries to insert the key into the ignition while he looked on. When the engine roared to life, I carefully pulled out.

"Like anything in your life, Didi, you'll defeat those torture devices or die trying." Callum hadn't taken his eyes off me since I'd practically accosted him in the airport. "I must say, though, you look stunning."

A car horn honked. I swerved.

"Watch where you're going, lady!" a taxi driver yelled, flipping me off.

I gripped the wheel, grit my teeth, and pushed on.

"Friendly," Callum cracked.

From the moment I'd met him in Scotland, we'd gelled. He helped solve Dr. Pinnick's murder, rescue Nick, and he'd risked his life for me. I owed him. He wouldn't see it that way. He was the exact opposite of Christof.

A text dinged on my phone.

"Can you get that?" I bobbed my head to my purse, maintaining focus on the congested road.

The gears groaned as I yanked the gear shift yet again.

"It's Mosewan. He's wondering where we are. The event is starting. No sign of Anice, but he says Shane's there."

From get go, Shane Bernard had been on my list of suspects. I was virtually sure of it. Roger's own blood-written clue: "S." It all made sense. Anice wanted a malleable person, someone who would do her bidding no matter the cost. Shane fit the bill perfectly, and she'd even admitted it. Still, something felt off. Would he murder someone? Several someones? I had my doubts.

I swerved in front of a candy apple green Porsche and slammed on the brakes, eliciting a few unsavory words from the driver.

Callum slammed a hand on the dash, bracing himself from the abrupt stop. "No wonder you all come to Scotland. This is insanity times a million."

I grinned. "What? Are you scared?"

Callum tugged at his sweater, and it was then that I noticed the beads of sweat on his brow and upper lip.

"You can't wear that to the function. Did you bring something more formal? And cooler?"

A few blaring horns and angry grimaces flashed my way as I stalled for the second time since the light turned green. We weren't going anywhere. Another logjam had formed. A construction crew was working in the middle of rush hour, and it would probably take us another fifteen minutes to travel the last quarter mile.

"Aye, keep the heid!"

Callum unzipped his rather large backpack. He pulled a white button-down shirt out first, followed by a black jacket, tie, and then black pants.

I gawked. "What kind of bag is that, anyway?"

Callum's eyes sparkled mischievously. "A mystical one. Don't you know? We're the land of magic. Wands and wizards, Didi. Wands and wizards."

"Fine. As long as they're not wrinkled."

"Ah, but that's the thing. Modern technology." He gripped the shirt and tugged. "Wrinkle resistant clothing."

"What about the wizards? If you pull someone out of that bag, I promise, Callum, I'll have to report you for human trafficking."

"Ye of little faith." He winked. "If it's a wizard, then it's not. They're technically a hybrid. If it wasn't against their will, then there's nothing to report."

Callum tugged off the woolen sweater. I quickly focused on the road.

"Um… uh, wh-what are you doing? You're changing here? Now?"

"No time like the present, lassie. Don't tell me you're modest. Haven't you seen a man without a shirt?" There was a playful tone to his voice.

I slid down into my seat, stealing glances at the surrounding vehicles. Sure enough, all honking and curses ceased. Who knew Callum had such generous biceps?

I inhaled deeply, feeling the blood rush to my cheeks, and stared out the windshield, looking anywhere but at him. Did they all lift weights in Scotland or just the police? Jeez!

Ogling matrons, spinsters, admiring men, young and old alike, zeroed in on him. I stole a glance when he pulled on the crisp white dress shirt, the red tie, and the black jacket. When his pants came off, I turned away again, fanning my face.

He wrangled the rearview mirror, tweaking his tie, and nodded in approval. "How's that for formal attire?"

I feigned interest in a hot dog vendor, my tummy flip-flopping at the sight of him. What was wrong with me? I was beginning to think I was a woman in heat for all the pitter patters of my heart these days. Laura was right. I was losing my freaking mind.

"Uh, it's great. Just great." I gripped the steering wheel and refused to make eye contact. I focused on the non-moving traffic and waving away all the hoots and hollers from the surrounding vehicles.

"They're friendly here." Callum waved and smiled at the onlookers.

"Yeah, a free strip show will do it."

Callum smirked. "It's the least I can do."

* * *

WE MADE it to the auction. Dr. Gates, Mosewan, and Olivia were still at the café. The two men shifted in place like men facing a firing squad, and I likened their complexions to a bleached white sheet.

Mosewan kissed Olivia's cheek. "Why don't you go inside? I'll meet you in a moment."

Olivia seductively wiped the remnants of her lipstick left on Mose's lips. "Alright, but don't take too long. I might buy too much." She kissed the tip of his nose and sauntered off, hips swaying to and fro, hypnotizing all three men.

I snapped my fingers. "Hey, minds on the task. Are we ready? Any questions?"

All three men zeroed in on something behind me. I snapped my fingers a couple more times in a vain attempt at drawing their attention, but none obliged.

"I'll bite," came from behind me.

I briefly clenched my hands, and then slowly turned, mentally slapping myself.

"Christof." I pasted on a smile and wrung my sweaty hands together. "How marvelous to see you here. I-I was wondering if you'd show up."

Christof planted his hands on his hips. "Out with it, Didi. What's going on?"

Before I could stammer a lame response, someone called his name. When I saw who it was, my stomach tightened.

"Brian, happy you made it on such short notice." Christof straightened his tie while my three companions busily ordered and sipped more drinks, making themselves invisible. "You've met Brian Shaw. Brian, this is my fiancé, Daisy Day."

CHAPTER 39

I stiffly held out my hand. "Nice to see you again."

While I'd certainly hoped Brain showed up, the whole fiancé thing twisted me into knots, which made it difficult to think, let alone do anything else.

Brian shook my hand, and when I tried pulling it away, he held onto it. Lowering his head, eyes fixed on mine, he kissed it.

Christof beamed like a kid on holiday. He gripped his silken black lapels and grinned. "I'll be moving into that corner office you promised."

Brian cocked his head toward Chris, dropping my clammy palm. "Cart before the horse, Chris. Aren't you forgetting something?"

Christof's forehead wrinkled in confusion. "What?"

Brian laid his hand on Christof's back. "The wedding. Don't forget the honeymoon. Am I right, Didi?"

Brian's cold smile landed squarely on me, and my stomach ell to the pit of Hades.

Chris chuckled nervously. "What kind of husband would I be if I didn't give my bride a proper wedding and honeymoon?" He flicked his wrist. "The honeymoon is a surprise, though. We wouldn't want to spoil the fun, would we?" He winked at Brian while I stared from one to the other.

"Didi?"

Christof nearly popped a vein on his temple. His head swiveled toward the bar behind me.

Callum eased up beside me. I was a dwarf compared to his soaring height and broad frame. I imagined him effortlessly lifting bales of hay, ripped muscles glistening from a hard day's sweat. The image was too bright, and I physically shook myself to erase it.

"Pure dead brilliant." Callum's lilt broke over the guys like a bucket of frigid water. "We've an auction to catch, and you're dallying." He extended his elbow, not minding Christof's beet-red face, and I latched on, willing my wobbly legs to move toward Dr. Gates and Mose, who were guzzling down a second glass of ale, averting their attentions.

Callum bent close to my ear and whispered, "Are you alright? Time's running out, and there's no sight of Anice. I figure she'll make an appearance shortly. I'm sorry if I manhandled the situation, but you looked like a sheared lamb, and I couldn't help it."

After a quick glance back at Christof's brooding face, I leaned against him, squeezing his arm for dear life, and drained the beer Dr. Gates offered upon our arrival in three seconds flat. The bitter liquid burned my throat and the bubbles brought tears to my eyes. I sputtered, and with a swift thunk on the back, Callum offered his pressed white handkerchief. I dabbed at my eyes and thanked him. Christof wouldn't dare interrupt. He had to uphold the falsity that we were engaged, and it wouldn't do to storm up and break into an argument in front of all his coworkers and the wealthy patrons that employed their firm.

"Well..." I gulped, not ready for what we were about to do, "I guess it's time."

Almost immediately, I started shivering. The air thinned, and I licked my lips excessively, fumbling for what to say. There was a solid chance that one or all of us may never see each other again if this turned sideways.

I sucked in a breath and jutted my chin out. "Callum, take me to the coatroom attendant. Mose, you and Dr. Gates oversee the auction. I'll look out for Anice since I'm the only one who's seen her recently. Callum, hang in the back of the theatre, and when I give the signal, we go to our respective places. Dr. Gates, have you secured the gallery for our artifacts? Is there a private area only for the main shield and dagger?"

Dr. Gates nodded. "It's done, my dear. We all meet in the auditorium first. There's a PowerPoint presentation of the artifacts plus the auction items up for bid. It'll take about twenty minutes. After that, we'll disperse into the gallery where the auction items are laid out on a few tables. The artifacts are all similarly spread out, except for the shield and dagger. Those are in a more secluded area. They didn't bat an eye when I asked. High-priced items are their specialty. Anyway, everything is ready."

"Great," I said, not feeling anywhere near so. Anxious and dreadful were more like it, but now wasn't the time to dwell. We'd meticulously planned the bait and trap scenario as much as one could over a couple hours, and it had to work.

I peered up at Callum and forced a grin. "Care to disrobe me?"

Callum smirked. "Lassie, I am a gentleman."

I was unsure if he was joking or serious. He was impossible to read. "Meaning?"

"I will gladly disrobe you." A warm grin enhanced the wrinkles on his forehead and around his eyes.

Arm-in-arm, we walked to the coatroom attendant. Since I was the only one with an overcoat, I exchanged mine for a number and tucked it into my clutch. A cool breeze brushed against my arms and I shivered.

"Are you cold?" Callum caressed my bare skin with his finger, leaving goosebumps in its wake.

My pulse quickened at his touch. He bowed his head further toward mine and the soft scent of fresh soap and a hint of whiskey lingered about him. He gently brushed his hands up and down my arms, setting them on fire. He stepped closer. I leaned in, legs like jelly. Eyes shining, he fixed his gaze on me while cupping one arm around my waist. When I didn't resist, he inhaled and gently tugged me closer. I threw my arms around his neck and raised up on my tippy toes when someone cleared their throat behind me.

"Excuse me."

Callum and I immediately separated. My hands flew up to tidy my hair as Mosewan gave me a hard stare.

"The auction's starting," he said.

"Right." Callum ran a hand through his wavy auburn hair and moved toward the stairwell leading up to the auditorium, calling out, "See you all later."

"Care to escort me to the ball, Dr. Day?" Mosewan stuck out his elbow and half bowed, a twinkle present in his eye. All was forgiven.

We followed Callum along with all the other wealthy patrons. A black tuxedoed waiter announced the beginning of the auction, and we all headed to the auditorium.

"Why, Miss Day, we haven't even had a first proper date yet."

I playfully smacked him. His candor pleasantly surprised me. Mose wasn't one to joke. Or rather, his jokes usually resulted in him being the butt of them.

When we arrived on the landing outside the theatre, Mosewan sidetracked us into an open area of walls covered in artwork. I viewed each one, appreciating the red, orange, and pink hues as we walked past.

"It's your life, but—"

"But what? Callum's too old? He's too Scottish? He lives across the pond?" I scoffed, tired of dealing with feelings. Generally, I buried them, secretly hoping a later conversation would never come. These new emotions for not one but two men were making me loony. Then there was Christof. Although I thought we'd ended our relationship on the flight home from Scotland, he'd apparently decided otherwise. He always loved a challenge.

Mose stopped and stared down at his feet, hands on his hips. The lighting accented his shiny black hair, which formed a kind of halo around him. "What about us? I thought we had something happening. Was it the heat of the moment? Is it all in my head?"

"No." I placed my palm against his chest. "There's… something."

Mose's frown spread into a wide grin. He went to wrap his arms around me and I pushed gently against his chest.

He halted; arms frozen in mid-air. The sullen look nearly ripped my soul in two.

"I can't get into another relationship, Mose. It's too complicated. Too much for me to process. Besides, you've got Olivia. What about her?" I firmly shook my head and stepped away from him. "I can't do this. Not now. There's a killer on the loose and we must stop her. We address that first. Anything else will have to wait."

Mose stuffed his hands in his black tuxedo pants pockets. A sad shadow masked his tight features. "Fine. But don't fool yourself, Daisy. I saw you with Callum. What's between you two?"

Right as usual. Mose was a champion at deciphering my moods, and he'd hit the proverbial nail on the head. Callum brought the best and worst out in me. I loathed the way he awakened emotions in me I'd never thought possible. He was a magnet, and I was the metal, pulled toward him whether I wanted to be or not.

"Nothing." The moment the word left my mouth, a part of me died. One thing I'd always promised Mose was to be honest. Brutally so. And I'd lied. Worse yet was he knew it. The hurt on his face left me breathless.

He raised a finger and pointed over at Callum, who now stood on the other side of the auditorium entrance, watching the patrons enter and scanning the crowd for any sign of Anice.

"He'll end up hurting you."

"Mose—"

"Daisy, you pick the absolute worst men."

I snorted. "There's only been Christof."

"Exactly! Listen to me…" He stepped forward and grabbed my upper arms, "…whatever you feel for him, whatever you think, it'll pass. He's transient, Didi. Don't you see? I'm here. I always have been. Lying to yourself will only bring you and Callum pain. We're meant to be. You know it, and one day, you'll realize it. I just hope I'm still around when it happens."

Mose dropped his hands and plodded off toward the auditorium, disappearing into the crowd.

The air felt thin and heavy. I stared at the auditorium entrance, somehow expecting him to return. His words rang loud in my jumbled brain.

My knees wavered under me. I thrust out a steadying hand on the wall, leaning against it for support. In the next instant Callum was by my side. His callused hands landed on my bare skin while he lowered his head to mine. His lips moved, but only a jumbled mess was audible. The room spun, and I was at a loss to stop it.

Callum motioned to a black-tied waiter who jogged over with a glass of brown liquid. I shut my eyes, praying the room would stop spinning, but the nausea escalated. Hand over my abdomen, a jet plane roaring within my ears, I clamped a hand over my stomach when I felt the pressure of a glass upon my lips and a hand at the base of my neck. The cool liquid burned a trail of fire down to my stomach. I sputtered and coughed, opening my eyes wide. It was like flames were shooting from my mouth, nose, eyes, and ears simultaneously.

"Better?" Callum slapped me none too gently between the shoulder blades.

"Yes."

The waiter offered a napkin and walked off with a nod to Callum.

"What was that stuff?"

"Whiskey. Drink some more."

I waved him off and leaned my bare back against the cool wall, thankful for its support.

"Care to tell me what that was all about?" Callum held the whiskey glass in one hand while surveying the crowd. A simple smile to all the concerned patrons to acknowledge he was handling the damsel in distress.

"Nope."

I smoothed the bodice of my gown, unable to meet his intense stare burning a hole into my soul. I skimmed through the crowd, ready to return to tonight's task. That was when I saw her. The black dress, the red hair... it was her.

I wrapped my fingers around Callum's arm and squeezed.

"What?"

He followed my gaze and saw her step into the auditorium, but right before she did, she cast a sideways glance towards me, a smirk on her red lips.

"She's here. Game on."

CHAPTER 40

*C*allum swallowed the remaining whiskey after I refused it. "Right. I'll follow her."

I shook my head. "We must spread the word. The trap, remember? Let's set it up. We mingle among the crowd first. I'll tell Mose, and you tell Dr. Gates."

Callum pulled away and marched over to the auditorium. Meanwhile, I straightened my dress, shook off the last hint of nerves, and set off for the art exhibit. The shield and dagger were the principal attraction, but it was intended for one pair of eyes only. Anice Foster's.

I ducked around a corner, out of sight of the main crowd, and carefully made my way through the tables with benefit items to bid on, past the drink and appetizer tables, and turned a corner into the main exhibit hall. Dr. Gates had called in a ton of favors in such a short time to display items from the eras of ancient Egypt all the way to the artifacts from Amelia Earhart's flying days. Of course, all of it was under lock and key with glass cases supplied by Roger's widow, Moira. Even she wanted to come tonight, but Dr. Gates thought it too much for her, and honestly, it would most likely alert Anice to our plan.

I slipped behind another corner marked "Off Limits," kicked off my heels, and went over to the waist-high glass box with the coveted shield and dagger, casting a quick glance to make sure I hadn't been followed. With a heavy sigh I observed the rectangular glass box. The case sparkled under the exhibition lights, and I itched to whisk the contents away to safety. The sheer size of it prohibited the action, then there was also the trip wire installed by museum staff for security purposes. So I merely looked at it. Gosh, it must have taken over an hour to assemble Ragnar's bones into a skeleton. Though many pieces were missing, it took little effort to see it was human. I laid my fist on the glass over his skull and chewed on my inner cheek. As a special bonus, we'd included the charred bones, or rather, what remained of them, figuring it would entice Anice. It couldn't hurt considering she'd blown up a law firm over them. Or in part, that's who I figured was behind all of this. If I was wrong... I shuddered to think.

Dr. Gates' last-minute suggestion was brilliant. What better way to draw her out? Still, those bones held the key to solving what scientists considered an ancient myth and turning it into a reality, and the thought of them being stolen set my nerves on edge. Dr. Gates had insisted though. He even added them to the PowerPoint presentation. "It's the nail in the proverbial coffin," he'd said. He'd even sent an alert to every wealthy patron, anthropology, and archaeology enthusiast in a two-hundred-mile radius, highlighting the bones as "possible Danish royalty." We'd set the bait. Would she see right through it?

Another set of overhead lights shone on a similar glass case to the left of the charred bones, containing the remnants of a wooden shield, bits of an ancient sword, and the teeny pile of a child's bones which were buried with Ragnar. Sadness tugged at my heartstrings. If the test was true, then Ragnar and Hulda had at a minimum one child. Why wasn't she buried with them?

Hovering over the glass where Ragnar's bones laid bare for all to see, the glass fogged up with each exhalation. I nervously glanced right and left, making sure I was alone, and whispered, "Fear not, warrior. If you can hear me..." The hairs stood up on my arms and a shiver snaked down my spine with a sense of being watched. I searched the room and found I was utterly alone. "This is something I read online. I'm uncertain if it means anything to you or not, or if it really was said, but here goes..." The thundering of my heart beat so fast and loud I thought it might explode. "Hail to you, old warrior. May Thor protect you and Odin watch over you."

After one last look at the bones, I prayed for strength and courage to do what must be done, and then made my way to the auditorium. Head down, heels in place, I rounded the corner and exited the roped off area only to slam to a halt.

"Oh!" I bounced backward a step. "Sorry!" When I lifted my head, I was staring at Christof.

"What are you doing here?" I snapped. I looked behind him, but he was alone.

"Looking for you. Why did you walk off earlier? How could you embarrass me in front of Shane Bernard like that? Don't you know how influential he is?"

I folded my hands, still clutching my purse, and puckered my lips. "I'm fine, thanks for asking."

I started off past him, but a sharp jab shot through my shoulder when Christof wrenched my arm.

"Ow!" I rubbed the reddened spot and glared. "Let. Me. Go."

"No, you'll answer me."

What did I *ever* see in him? Besides his good looks, he was a miserable, controlling, arrogant jerk. "I'm not your fiancé." I yanked free and frowned, watching a fiery storm of emotions cross his face.

"Is that what this was about?" he huffed. "A technicality?"

"A technicality?" My voice was rising, the adrenaline, anger, and bitterness propelling me on. I jabbed him in the sternum. "You don't own me, Chris. We are not, nor will we *ever* be engaged. How's that for a technicality?"

I set off again, only to have him bound around me. He spread his arms wide and blocked my exit.

"Move." I gritted my teeth and watched the last patron enter the auditorium. We were completely alone. The program must have started.

"Not until you put all this nonsense aside." He gestured to the artifacts room behind me. To him, this was only a hobby. He'd made that perfectly clear.

"This is my job. My career. No one, not even you, will take it from me. Now get out of my way."

Christof lunged forward, grabbed a hold, and shook me. My teeth chattered with the force. I blindly lashed out, pounding his chest. It was about as useful as an umbrella in a hurricane.

"You are mine, Daisy Day," he hissed. "I won't lose that promotion because of some stupid hobby."

He crushed me to his chest. When he bent his head, his lips crushing mine, I froze. What was happening?

He shoved his hand against my breast and yanked so hard I heard the faint rip of fabric. I kicked, squirmed, beat my fists against him, and he only laughed. He pinned me against a wall and seized my velvet skirt, jerking it upward.

I wrenched my head sideways, avoiding another feral kiss.

"Stop! Chris, *stop*! This isn't happening! This isn't happening!" He covered my mouth with his and I did the only thing I could. I bit hard on his lip. The bitter taste of blood seeped into my mouth, but it worked. He yelped.

"Help!" I called out to an empty room.

"Har du ingen ære? La henne gå."

The hiss of unintelligible words chilled us both.

Christof's head snapped to the left. "Who's there?"

He kept his forearm pinning me to the wall. I frantically scanned the area. Even though I didn't understand the words, the intensity of them spoke volumes. Further yet, the voice sounded familiar.

"Show yourself," Christof hissed.

I futilely scratched at his arm, beat my fists against him. With the full force of his body on mine, I had barely any way to move. The effort to fight him, added with his bodyweight against mine, made my breathing labored. The wild look in his eyes clarified Christof wasn't in his right mind.

Chest heaving, vision growing dim, I strained to gain some space.

Tap, tap, tap...

The faint beat of drums. Was I imagining it? No... Christof turned his head toward the artifact room where the beats came from.

"What the hell?" he muttered, squinting into the room.

Ominous grunts, and before long they were near shouting level. It was a foreign tongue. An ancient one.

"What's going on?" Christof lodged his forearm against my throat, cutting off my air. "Tell me who's behind there." His mouth twisted into a sneer while I gagged and sputtered, futilely clawing at his arm.

The beat pulsed off the walls, more menacing, and the shouts overwhelmed us. My eardrums vibrated painfully Christof squeezed his eyes shut and yelled, "Stop it!"

Dropping his arm, he stormed toward the artifact room.

I hacked and sputtered, rubbing my sore and swollen neck, sucking in precious air. I staggered forward and eyed the auditorium doors. Then, like a moth to flame, I bounded toward the artifacts room, rounded the corner, and stopped short. A wavering image of the warrior man rose in front of the artifact case. His savage countenance flicked to mine. I fell against the wall in surprise and reached toward him.

"Ragnar?" I croaked, my voice raw from the pressure on my windpipe.

The man dipped his head briefly and then locked onto Christof.

Chris pointed at Ragnar, his forehead furrowed in confusion. "You know this man? What the hell is happening?"

Ragnar's light blue eyes sparkled like diamonds under a desert sun. Jagged scars lined his exposed leathered skin, one dipping into his beard. While Chris gaped, trying to process what we were witnessing, Ragnar gripped his spear and affixed his shield in a defensive posture. Flashing back to the underground tunnels at St. Magnus Cathedral in Kirkwall, Scotland, I remembered all too well what he could be capable of. It was like the veil between death and life was temporarily lifted. With a crippling effect, Hulda had stopped Anice in her efforts to kill me. Then, like now, I was merely an observer. Only this time it was with the Viking King, Ragnar Lothbrok. And he wasn't playing.

"I'd leave if I were you," I warned Christof.

Ragnar wore the same trousers, footwear, and tunic as before when he'd appeared in my apartment. The longer we stood, the clearer Ragnar became. No longer a wispy ghost, he was of solid flesh and bone.

Chris cast a worried glance at me. I saw the wheels rapidly turning within him, trying to process what I was saying and the man that had appeared before him out of thin air.

The chanting roared to a feverish pitch, and the drumbeats reverberated within my body. Chris stiffened, dropped his hands to his sides, and stared at Ragnar.

"Who are you? Is this some kind of joke?"

"*Nei. Jeg heter Ragnar. Du vil forlate og aldri se henne igjen, eller du vil møte Valhallas vrede.*"

Ragnar beat the blunt end of his spear against the ground and shook his shield violently. He blasted a violent yell that would strip paint, and then he struck. Wide-eyed, I stared. Heart frozen in midbeat, I gaped as Chris flinched. Everything moved in slow motion. Chris flung his arms in front of him as the violent blow arced down and he stumbled backwards. Ragnar's relentless blow crashed down. A crack split the air, and then the scream. Chris's arm was bent at an awkward angle as he scurried on his butt, inching back to the exit. Ragnar unrelentingly flipped his spear, sharp point facing Chris, and raised it high in the air. I attempted to scream but nothing came out. I scurried on my knees over to Chris just as Ragnar thrust downward. Throwing myself over Chris, I tucked my head and awaited the pain. Chris's moans heightened, and after a few seconds I looked up. My mouth hung open. The spear hovered within millimeters of my back. I raised my palms in surrender, crouched low over Christof.

"Ragnar... I'm okay now. I'm okay. Do you understand?" I gently touched his spear tip. "Ragnar? Do you understand?" I repeated.

Ragnar narrowed his eyes and slowly withdrew his spear. "Hulda?" he grunted.

"Yes, yes… Hulda. I've seen her. She's okay."

Ragnar regarded me briefly before turning his attention to Chris's moaning form. I rocked onto my heels and studied his arm. Yep, it was broken.

Chris opened his eyes. Pale and drenched in sweat, he clutched his injured arm against his body and braced himself on his other elbow. He turned his poisonous glare at me.

"You'll pay for this, Didi," he sneered. "You will pay."

Ragnar growled and raised his spear. After only one step, a voice rang out.

"Christof? Christof, are you in here? The auction is starting, and we don't want to miss—" Brian jogged around the corner and looked at Chris's crumpled form beside me and stopped cold. From my slightly torn bodice to Christof's angry countenance, it didn't take a brain surgeon to figure out what had happened.

"I-I can explain," I stammered, holding up my hands in surrender and flicking my head toward Ragnar, but he'd vanished.

Brian cleared his throat. "Christof, can you get up?"

Chris had already righted himself and now stood glowering down at me.

"Come with me," ordered Brian.

Chris shook his head. Hate rolled off him.

I stood, elbows tightly at my sides, and hands balled into fists.

"Now," snapped Brian. "Let cooler heads prevail. Come. You need a hospital." He waved an arm at Chris, beckoning him out.

Christof took one last look at me and then marched out, leaving Brian alone with me. He perused the room, noting the glass cabinet with a dagger, shield, and bones. His eyes lingered over them for a moment, a flash of recognition in his eyes, then his tight smile reappeared.

"Dr. Day, he's under a lot of stress at work," he said. "Please don't hold this against him. Whatever happened between the two of you, I'm sure you can work it out."

I folded my trembling arms around my waist and focused on a piece of paper on the floor. It appeared to be a gum wrapper of some sort.

"No. We're finished." I leveled my cold, hard stare at him.

Brian opened his mouth and shut it again. He peered at the corner that led to the gathering room where all the auction items were to be bid on. I imagined Christof listening to every word. The low growl that erupted was confirmation, along with Brian's slight shake of his head. He faced me again, hands splayed in appeasement.

"I hope this doesn't deter you from partnering with me in the future, Dr. Day. I've already lined up a lecture for you. It's between some amateur archaeology enthusiasts that have a lot of money burning in their pockets and savings accounts. You have my card. Call me."

With a curt nod, Brian left. I sagged against the wall, legs giving way, and leaned my head back, closing my eyes for a split second. Dr. Gates mentioned it was a twenty-minute presentation, which meant patrons would soon arrive. That left little time for me to pull myself together.

Stepping away from the wall, I straightened my bodice to the best of my ability and walked toward the auditorium, taking a last glance at where Ragnar had stood.

"Thank you," I squawked. My throat stung from the gratitude I felt for a man over 1,200 years old. I had no idea why he helped me, but I wasn't one to kick a gift horse in the mouth.

As I approached the auditorium, I spied a black shawl and snatched it, promising myself I'd return it before the night was over. Truth be told, if I hadn't done it, my appearance would without a doubt draw more attention than I needed.

I slipped inside to catch the last slides of Dr. Gates's presentation. A quick survey of the theatre, and I spotted Mose seated next to the ravishing Olivia in the front row. She was resting her silken head on his. Since he wasn't facing me, it was difficult to tell if he enjoyed it, but what man wouldn't love a gorgeous woman's affections?

I looked away from the cuddly twosome and watched Callum

stride out the auditorium door a few feet away. Though I waved, he didn't see me. With his head down, he barreled out. I didn't give it much thought, considering we'd planned to meet. Ironically, it was to be in the same room I'd just come from. How I hoped one of the men had noticed Anice. While searching the crowd, I hadn't spotted a redhead anywhere.

A round of warm applause followed Dr. Gates' presentation, and a ten-minute round of questioning followed. The wealthy patrons filed out. There was to be a one-on-one session with Dr. Gates at the cafe below now, designed to give Callum, Mose, and me enough time to corner Anice and adequate time for the police to arrive.

Mose was the last to leave. He kissed Olivia, encouraging her to attend the session with Dr. Gates. Her pout was one for the record books. If it had been back in ancient times, she'd have launched a thousand ships like Helen of Troy.

"Ready?" Mose whispered. He fingered the shawl. "What's this?"

I tried smacking his hand but was too late. The scarf slipped and revealed the ripped seam of my velvet dress.

Mose turned a violent shade of red. He took one look at me and spun, pacing toward the exit.

"Mose, no. We're running out of time."

He slammed his fist into the wall. "Did he hurt you? Did he—"

"No, Mose. Someone stopped him."

Mose snapped his head in my direction. "Who?"

"Ragnar."

"Who?"

"Too long to explain. Let's go."

I linked my arm through his, thankful for his warmth and support, and we headed to the artifact room.

CHAPTER 41

The moment we set foot in the room the temperature dropped twenty degrees. I absentmindedly brushed my fingertips against my bruised throat. After readjusting the shawl, I followed Mose toward the locked glass case of items. He bent forward, palms pressed against the top glass, and studied the human remains and artifacts.

"It's gone."

"What?" I stared at the empty spot where the bones had been.

How was it possible? I'd left only minutes ago.

"Look!" Mosewan stepped behind the waist-high cabinet and fingered the lock on the cabinet. "It's been busted." He slid the cabinet door open only to slam it shut again.

"Damn it!" He dashed for the entry.

"Where are you going?" I asked, barely keeping up with him.

"Callum was supposed to be here. Where is he?"

Struggling to keep up with him, I panted, "He left minutes before we did. I was sure he was headed here."

We neared the auditorium entrance and zoomed past it as patrons made their way up from the cafe and entered the gallery.

Mose pushed his cuff up and checked his watch.

"What?"

"Something's wrong." His tawny forehead crinkled in concern. "Was anyone with Callum when he left?"

I mentally replayed the scene. "No, he was by himself. Do you think Anice followed him?"

Mose clutched my hand and squeezed. "Maybe. That or she had someone follow him. Either way, we need to look for her *and* him."

We stopped by the bathrooms, which Mose searched. From one gallery to another, we turned the building upside down. No Callum.

We ended up outside the auditorium. The shawl had fallen off my neck in our haste, but I didn't care anymore. It wasn't possible for Callum to simply up and leave. Something terrible had happened to him.

I rubbed my hands up and down my arms and looked right, left, and back.

BEEP.

Mose glanced at my clutch tucked under my arm. I stared down at it, unmoving for a moment. It was only when it beeped again that I pulled my phone out.

"It's Anice." I blinked back tears. "She's in the auditorium."

We both slowly turned to face the closed door.

Tucking my purse under my arm I inhaled a steadying breath. "Let's go." I flung the door wide, flitting inside. It only took seconds to find her. That red hair was a beacon. She stood behind the lectern. To her right was Callum.

I bolted down the steps.

"Come any closer and he's a dead man."

I halted, one foot on the bottom step and the other level with the podium. The overhead light shone down on them both. She shoved a gun into his ribs, aimed at his heart.

A baseball-sized bruise bloomed on Callum's right cheekbone, and there were a few minor scratches on his forearms and neck. He'd somehow lost his jacket, but that was the least of our concerns.

I held my hands up as a show of truce. "Whatever it is you want, take it. There's no need for this."

Anice threw her head back and roared with laughter. "Oh, I plan to. But first, let's play a game, shall we?" She picked up a white linen bag and shoved it in front of Callum. "Take it," she ordered him.

When he refused, she dug the gun more deeply into his side and cocked it. "Do it or I'll pull the trigger."

Callum begrudgingly took the bag.

"That's a good boy. Now here's the fun part." Although her eyes danced with mischief, nothing about this was anywhere near funny or fun. "You have a decision to make. Who will it be, Daisy Day? Callum Mortimer or Mosewan Aten."

I frowned. "What? I don't understand."

"Of course you do. Pick one. Callum or Mosewan. Who will live and who will die? Time's a'ticking." She looked down at her imaginary watch and giggled.

"Are you *mad?*"

"Neither here nor there, Dr. Day. You must pay a penance for that stunt you pulled in Scotland. I lost millions of dollars thanks to you, and you owe me. What do they say in the Bible? An eye for an eye? I'd say a life for a life. That money was my new life. You stole it, and now you'll pay the price."

I gawked at her. The idea was simply archaic and cruel. However, if past experience proved true, she wasn't bluffing. I looked from one man to the other. Surely there was another way.

Think, Didi.

I glanced from Callum to Mose, surreptitiously searching the auditorium for some type of weapon... some way to save all of us.

"You're taking too long. Pick," Anice huffed, a cruel sneer on her crimson lips. "If you don't decide soon, I'll take both."

From behind the lectern, her left hand swung up. She aimed another gun directly at Mose. "I'm a perfect shot. So who will it be? Hunky Scotsman or the brilliant Egyptian? Tick tock."

Callum still stood several inches taller than Anice, and the bag he held was more than a weapon. Yet even if I relayed what I was thinking, He wouldn't be faster than Anice's trigger finger. Then there was Mose. He stood with his hands at his sides, face drawn.

Where were my warrior friends now?

"Take the bones. Hell, take all of it. I don't care. Just leave them alone."

Anice laughed. "Tsk tsk. Such a conundrum, isn't it? How does that make you feel, Mosewan? All your drivel," she chuckled. "You need a better hiding spot for your journal."

Mose's ruby-red face glowered back at her. Though he stayed rooted to his spot, he eyed the bag and then the gun.

"Why?" The word hung in the air, but I already knew the answer. I'd humiliated her. Not only that, I'd apprehended a valuable piece of wall art for some ultra-wealthy man somewhere in this world who cared less for the historical significance or its priceless worth to the Scandinavian culture. Most of these people who'd bought antiquities through the black market didn't consider the implications of their actions. They simply desired to possess what others dreamed of, and they didn't perceive any wrongdoing. Money triumphed over everything in this world.

Anice sneered. "If you have to ask, then you're more foolish than I thought. No matter, you'll meet your end soon enough. There's a surprise around every corner for you, Ms. Day, but I dare not let the cat out of the bag. All in good time. Now stop stalling. Which one dies? Hurry, I've got a plane to catch."

I licked my dry lips, searching both Callum's and Mosewan's faces. The grim realization of their set jaws almost brought me to my knees.

"Oh, and none of that voodoo from before in the tunnels," Anice snapped, waving the gun pointed at Mose. "I don't understand how you did it, but it won't help you."

I remembered Hulda's sudden appearance in the dusty tunnels underneath St. Magnus Cathedral. She'd saved the day, no doubt. Even though I'd been shot, she'd saved Nick, and for that, I was indefinitely indebted to her. Though if she hadn't shown by now, it wasn't likely she would.

Then we all heard a creak. Our heads swiveled in slow motion toward the door behind the podium. At once, the nightmare unfolded at an agonizing pace.

"Drop your weapon!" It reverberated in the empty hall.

My white-haired mentor stepped out from behind the door that exposed a storage room full of brooms, mops, weathered shipping containers, and cleaning supplies.

Eyes bulging, Anice swung the gun away from Mose. He dove behind a row of the red velvet folding seats while I sprinted for the stage. Callum swung with all his might, hitting her square in the temple. The gun barrel flashed orange.

"NO!" I screamed.

Callum's eyes widened. Crimson spots spread on his white dress shirt and he crumpled to the floor. The bag dropped beside him, splattered in blood.

I leapt onto the stage, fell to my knees, and cradled his head in my lap. "No..." I searched his side and felt the entry wound with my fingertips. Yanking at the hem of my dress, I tried tearing off a piece of fabric. "Help!" A hard knot formed in my throat as I frantically searched for something to stop the flow of blood.

Gone was any concern for Anice, my well-being—I was only focused on stopping the bleeding.

Dr. Gates was slammed into the wall beside the door. Anice had slammed the butt of the gun onto the top of his head. A river of blood drained from the crown of his head. She lunged for the bag and snatched it. With a wicked grin, she blew me a kiss and ran out the door, her rubber soles echoing off the wooden steps. Mose took off after her, casting me a concerned glance as he disappeared.

"Callum? Callum, can you hear me?" I tapped his ashen cheeks. His eyelids fluttered open, then quickly closed again.

I tugged and yanked on the hem of my dress, ripping the cloth. Once I'd gotten a wad of it loose, I jammed it over the bleeding wound and pressed.

Callum moaned, his eyes flittering open for a brief second.

"Dr. Gates?" I called. He was leaning against the wall, hand to his bleeding forehead, in shock. "Dr. Gates, call 911 and ask for an ambulance. Nod if you understand?"

The door leading to the lobby opened and Shane Bernard stuck his head in. "Wh-what's happened? We heard gunshots."

I nodded to Dr. Gates, who was still standing with his hand against the side of his head, blood seeping down his face and dripping onto the floor of the stage. "Help him. He's been hit. Call the cops. We need an ambulance. Callum's been shot."

Shane gaped at the pool of blood on the stage floor growing by the minute next to Callum. My hands, now christened in his blood, kept the pressure on his wound, but his respirations slowed.

"Hurry. Please."

I didn't dare take pressure off the wound for fear of losing Callum. I whispered a prayer that somehow he'd pull through.

Shane whipped out his phone and called the police, then he was at Dr. Gates' side, stanching the blood with a handkerchief.

"This wasn't supposed to happen. This wasn't part of the plan," he mumbled.

I slowly turned my head toward him. "What exactly was the plan, Shane? What type of person steals artifacts, huh?"

"Nobody was supposed to get hurt." He dabbed at the deep wound on Dr. Gates's head.

"Hurt?" I snorted. "Come on, Shane. How stupid can you be? Landon and Freddie *died* because of her."

He closed his eyes for a few seconds. "She promised me it was over."

The sound of distant sirens entered the enormous hall and soon the thumping of shoes surrounded us, and hands tugged me away from Callum's side. He'd gone completely still. I'd started CPR, waving off those who urged me to step aside and pumped my hands rhythmically down on his chest, hoping beyond hope that he'd breathe again.

"Lady! Hey, lady, let us work!"

I kept pumping.

Strong arms pulled me away kicking and screaming. "Let us do our jobs, lady. Stand over there."

I choked back sobs and wiped a bloody hand against my forehead.

The EMTs swarmed Callum. Shiny metal scissors appeared out of thin air, slitting his shirt down the middle. One EMT positioned the paddles over his chest and glanced back at his partner, who nodded.

ZAP!

Callum's back arched and his head lolled. The glassy stare of death was illuminated under the stage lights.

My vision blurred as they pumped his chest in between rounds of shocks.

"Callum…" I whimpered.

"Didi… step away. Don't watch." Christof's ran his hand up and down my arm; his other was in a sling.

I jerked, my skin crawling from his touch. "Get away from me."

"Clear!" Another round of shocks. Callum's torso arced. I gawked, unable to breathe.

"We've got a pulse!"

I rushed forward.

The keen-eyed EMT and his partner lifted Callum onto a gurney and strapped him on.

"Miss," asked the first one, "what's his name?"

"Um… Callum Mortimer, and he's from Scotland. He arrived today." My voiced wavered.

The medic's brow furrowed. "Are you hurt?" He reached for my hand, but I shook my head.

"It's Callum's blood. I'm fine."

"Let's go," said the other EMT. The EMTs lifted the rolling gurney with ease down the stairs and onto the floor. I stayed close on their heels and followed them outside, where they secured him in the ambulance, still unconscious.

"Where do you think you're going?"

I'd almost forgotten about Christof. His bruising grip on my elbow stopped me from entering the ambulance.

He spotted Callum's lifeless frame and half-grinned.

I yanked my arm away, but he remained glued to my elbow. Anger radiated off him.

The EMTs readied to leave, but there was one medic hyper

focused on the two of us.

"Leave now, and it's over this time, Didi. Are you willing to give up everything we have?" While his tone was low, the intent made my blood curdle.

My hand tingled from lack of blood flow. When I flinched, he squeezed harder. I spun into him. With the shock of it, he lessened his grip and I twisted free, jogging backward a few steps. He lunged forward, then the medic called out.

"Miss... I have a few more questions for you."

Christof stuffed his fists into his pockets and glared. Rubbing my aching elbow I trotted to the van, hopping inside to sit beside Callum's still body. They hooked him up to an IV line and an oxygen cannula was stuck in his nose.

"Miss?" I lifted my gaze to the medics standing by the ambulance doors, one hand on the handle. "Are you okay?"

I settled a cold, hard gaze on Christof and nodded.

The medic looked from me to Christof's rigid frame. He hadn't moved. "Good. Are you family?"

Focused on Christof, I saw him shake his head almost imperceptibly under the flashing red and blue lights of the ambulance and police cars.

I met the kind medic's eyes. "Yes... I'm his fiancé."

The metal doors slammed shut and we pulled out into traffic. As I slid my hand under Callum's thick and calloused hand, my phone buzzed inside my clutch. It was a wonder I'd had the wherewithal to grab it off the auditorium floor when the medics rolled Callum out.

I gently replaced Callum's hand and retrieved the phone. The text was from Dr. Gates: *Mose is missing. His smashed phone was found by the stage exit. The police are searching now, but Didi, there was blood. A lot. I'll keep you posted.*

I dropped the phone on my lap. "Oh God."

The medic gave me a sideways glance but was too busy working on Callum to say anything. In between injections of medicine and applying pressure to his wound, she handed me a tissue. I remained rigid like a wooden toy, transfixed by the rapid rise and fall of

Callum's chest. I scooped up his hand and gently dabbed some of the congealed blood away with the tissue. I brought his hand up to my lips and feathered kisses along his chalky-white knuckles.

"Callum," I whispered, "don't leave me. Do you hear me?" I squeezed his lifeless hand over and over. The medic eyed me with pity. "Fight, Callum. Please, fight."

Body shaking, I bowed my head onto his hand. The images of Dr. Gates' stunned expression as he leaned against the wall of the auditorium stage, forehead bleeding, Mose rushing without hesitation after Anice, and Callum crumpling to the floor all jumbled together. The three of them in peril, and for what?

I raised my head and peered down at Callum. My eyes glistened as I took in his pasty skin. I sagged against the cool wall of the ambulance. Anice had to be stopped. And I was the only one left to do it.

CHAPTER 42

The EMTs wheeled Callum off at a jog into the hospital ER. One nurse hopped onto the moving gurney, straddled Callum, and performed chest compressions. The high-pitched whine of medical equipment rang loud in my ears.

"Callum Mortimer," said the medic, handing off a slip of paper to an ER nurse. He kept in step with the throng of medical professionals that surrounded the gurney. Someone stuck a rectangular white object over Callum's right index finger while others took over, applying heavy pressure to his abdomen.

"White male, between 30 to 35. Gunshot wound to the abdomen. BP is 75 over 50. He's tachypneic and unresponsive. Abdomen is distended, no sign of an exit wound."

The doctor nodded once and jogged around to the head of the gurney, pulling on purple latex gloves.

When the doors swung open to the belly of the ER, I focused on Callum's pale face. An oxygen mask covered most of it. The nurse on top of him stopped pumping his chest right before the doors shut. I ran forward, but firm arms wrapped around me.

"Miss... Miss, you can't go in there." It was the kind EMT. He motioned me to a nearby chair. "Sit here. A nurse will be out when they can to update you."

I nodded numbly and let him lead me to the chair. The sound of rushing waves beat against my eardrums for what seemed like hours. Tingly pricks worked through my fingers and toes while the rest of me trembled.

I opened my clutch, which was on my lap, found my phone, and dialed.

"*Hi, Aunt Didi. What's up?*"

"Nick, hi." I cleared my throat. "Um, I need you to do something for me."

"*Are you okay? Is that... moaning?*"

"Oh, uh…" I smiled weakly at the gray-haired man across from me. "I'm fine. I'm at the hospital. There's been... an accident."

"*What? Did you call Mom?*"

"No!" I snapped, drawing more than a dozen curious stares. "Uh, I mean, let's not bother her. She's busy, and I'm sure everything will be fine."

Nick paused. "*Alright, then, what can I do for you? Do I want to know what trouble you've gotten into? It's like it follows you.*"

I clutched the phone to my ear so hard that my fingers lost feeling. "That's not true."

"*Uh, yeah. Lately.*" He chuckled. "*Don't worry about it. I like our new relationship. It's nice to be of use. I'll shut my door, put my noise canceling headphones on, and dream I'm back in Scotland. Hey, speaking of... have you spoken to Callum yet? That man's in to you.*"

I shuddered at the mention of his name. "Ah, Callum is... he's... I've not... Uh, the real reason I called was to use your special skills."

I skimmed the crowded room and, except for the man who sat across from me, no one else noticed me, which was slightly reassuring. The man was reading a tattered magazine, which in and of itself wasn't an issue, but there was just one problem. The magazine was upside down.

"Um... give me a second."

I walked across the ER lobby and out into the main reception of the hospital. I craned my neck to see the skylights far above. Enormous fake seagulls soared among the puffy white clouds and colorful kites the architect had elegantly designed. For a dreaded destination, the designer had brilliantly created a haven, a refuge, full of whimsical objects, soothing color palettes, making it as inviting as one could be at a hospital.

I scooted past the reception desk and waved at the clerk, Henrietta. She'd been like a favorite nanny ever since I'd frequented these halls at the ripe age of thirteen. It was right after my parents died, and the staff had welcomed me like a family member, watching out for me ever since. One of my favorite hiding places was thanks to Henrietta, and I sure needed one right now.

"Okay, now I can talk." I snuggled into the circular hole in the wall designed for a potted plant or decorative object, but since they'd erected a wall, deciding to make these back spaces offices, it was left empty and relatively obscured.

"Wait. Are you in trouble?"

The glee in his voice gave me pause.

"Hey, mister. Danger isn't something to seek out. Laura told me about the bungee jumping trip you took with your friends."

He snorted. *"That's nothing. I'm fine. What's the problem with a little fun?"*

"The problem, Nick, is that it wasn't done by a professional. You take too many risks. It's bungee jumping now, and what's next? Skydiving?"

"That's a great idea! Thanks, Aunt Didi."

"Not funny. Anyway, back to your special gift."

"What do you need hacked?"

"Shh!" Even though I was secure in my hidey hole, I scanned the area, only relaxing when I was certain of no prying ears.

"Nick, I need you to hack into Mosewan's phone. Bring up his photos and any of his texts."

"Whoa, stalk much?"

"Nick, now's not the time. Can you do it?"

"Okay, okay, just give me a minute."

I heard his fingers fly across a keyboard and imagined him in his bedroom. His light blue walls still displayed the vivid blue, red, and yellow striped airplanes Laura and I had painted seventeen years ago when her belly stuck out like a bowling ball.

"Here we go. Where do I send it?"

"To me."

Within seconds the phone beeped.

"I sent his search history too because, well... um... in case you were stalking him."

His cheeky laugh drowned out my protest. "One last thing. Can you hack another number? Last time. Promise."

A few minutes later, he grunted. *"This one's tougher. Give me an hour and I'll send everything available."*

We hung up after I promised to fill him in on everything that was happening. I already regretted calling, yet who else hacked into systems without giving me the third degree? It *was* illegal. Ugh! What did that say about me? I was corrupting a minor. My own nephew. Laura would have my hide.

I scrolled through his messages. There were only a few to Olivia and the ones to me. A nasty twinge of jealousy seized me seeing her name. I'd give anything to see him, even if it meant losing him to Olivia, though her role was suspicious. Was she a wolf in sheep's clothing? Seeing her with two people linked to Anice made me even more determined to find Mose, Anice, and fix this once and for all.

I came to the last texts he'd received and gawked.

Wait a minute. I blinked once, twice, a third time. I even rubbed my eyes. It didn't change the texts, nor the person who sent them.

Mose had a series of messages from none other than Shane Bernard, and on more than one occasion. Most of them were stuff about work and deadlines. Shane loved to hold things over us, especially now that he was dean, but the last messages escalated into veiled threats. I stared at the last text. The dread I'd been holding at bay let loose and crashed down in a thunderous jolt.

It was only an hour ago, and it wasn't from Shane. Why would

Brian Smith text Mose to meet him using Shane's phone? What the hell was going on?

I switched to his search history, thinking it might hold some clues. All that came up were things like Norse runes, Ragnar Lothbrok, and shield maidens. However, there was one thing that struck me as curious. He'd found a black-market dealer, and as I looked underneath the smiling photo that shined up at me, I cringed.

"Bryce Smyth?"

Unless Bryce had a twin, then Brian Smith wasn't who he claimed to be. Everything suddenly made more sense. He probably worked for Anice, but how did he infiltrate the law firm where Chris worked? There was only one way to find out. Time to swallow my pride. If I was ever getting Mose back safe and sound, I'd willingly do it.

I sat marinating on everything I'd learned when the phone beeped again. Laura's text flashed upon the screen.

"Fascinating DNA results. Check them out and call me."

CHAPTER 43

*T*he university lot was practically empty when I reached the back entrance to the anthropology building. It *was* late, but happily the campus lights were in working order. I'd parked Dr. Gates' pickup truck a half mile away because of a repaving project. More than once, I'd heard the shuffle of feet behind me or a twig breaking. Each time I stopped and scanned the area, there was nothing. Not a single soul was on campus, but that's not what stood my hair on end. It was the birds. Not one of them chirped. Which meant either a storm was coming, or they sensed danger. Peering up into the cloudless, warm night sky full of stars, I suspected the latter.

A rush of cold air burst out when I pulled the door open. I rubbed my uncovered arms and hustled down the hallway and around a few corners before landing on the threshold of the dean's office. Someone was flitting about the room.

I knocked on the doorframe and eyed the scattered papers and overturned furniture. Plumes of smoke wafted around the trashcan. I waved a hand to fend off the noxious fumes.

"Shane, what's going on?"

Arms piled high with papers, he crossed the room from his floor-to-ceiling bookcase jammed with expensive, state-of-the-art books and dumped them into the smoky trashcan by his obnoxiously expensive desk. Flames leapt up to greet the newest additions.

Shane zipped back to his wooden file cabinets, grabbed a heap more of the papers, then flitted back to the fire to dump them on the others turning black and disappearing in a mountain of smoke.

I coughed into my arm. The smoke filled and swirled about the room. Eyes stinging from the soot, I shouted, "How is the fire alarm not going off?"

Shane repeated the process a couple more times before gesturing to the ceiling where the fire alarm should have been. In its place was a gaping hole.

"Shane, what are you doing? The alarms in the hallway will go off in a few minutes, and then you'll have a lot of firemen and police storming the building."

When he ignored me I latched hold of his arms and pushed against him. "Stop. Tell me what's happening. Why are you so frantic?"

Shane stepped back and swiped a sooty hand against his forehead, leaving a blackened streak. He looked down at the burning inferno and stamped it down with his foot. Picking up a liter bottle of water, he dumped it on top of the flames. While it doused the fire, more smoke billowed up. He stormed over to the windows, opened several, and positioned a large fan at the door. Within a few minutes, the smoke dissipated a bit, but Shane shoved another pile of papers that had been on the edge of his desk into his burgeoning army green duffel bag.

"Leave. Or face whatever is coming." He shoved everything but his stapler into the bag. In a swift motion, he secured it on his shoulder and stopped long enough to face me. "I didn't mean for it to get like this. I'm sorry, Didi. If I'd have…"

"What? You'd have what?"

Shane grunted. "You don't understand."

"Try me."

He glanced at his watch. "I'm a gopher. Sort of. I relayed the details of where the bones were hidden, who worked for whom, where you were, basically anything they wanted. They swore nobody would get hurt, and besides, it was only some bones."

"Stop. What did you do with the bones?"

Shane shoved his fists into his khaki pant pockets and frowned. "I replicated them. When Landon turned up dead, I panicked." He readjusted the weighty bag and eyed the door.

I held up my palms, impeding his exit. "Where are the bones? The real ones?"

He shrugged. "Last I saw them they were in a white linen bag." He tried stepping past me, but I blocked him.

"Where?"

"If I knew that, we wouldn't be having this conversation. I need those bones, Didi."

I pursed my lips. "Why?"

Shane brushed past me, checking my advances with his duffel bag. I was knocked sideways and thrust a hand out, grasping a hold of his leather couch, but he had made it a foot from the door. Sidestepping the fan, he jogged into the hallway. I scrambled after him, swearing at the blasted heels. It was worse than roller skating. When I rounded the corner, he pivoted. I skidded to a halt and stifled a curse.

"Didi, if you find them, the real ones, get them far from here. Two people have already died over them."

"Three."

Shane held up a hand. "Don't tell me. The less I know the better." He removed his hands from his pockets and interlaced his fingers. "Look, I threatened them, Didi. I did. Said I'd go to the police with all this. I tried doing the *right* thing," he air quoted. "But it's too far gone. I'm a dead man."

He turned on his heel to leave, but I flitted over and grabbed his arm, swinging him around. "Where will you go?"

He chuckled humorlessly. "See, Didi, that's your weakness. You care too much. After all I've done to you?" He shook his head. "Oh, and that bloody knife in your office… it wasn't me. I misjudged him. He promised…" He swallowed hard, his face pained. "All I wanted was the job in Spain. It was the boost I craved for. It would shut up the old man. This is what I get for having ambition. Stay safe, Didi. So long."

Shane jogged for the exit.

"Wait! What about Freddie?"

He looked back at me, brow scrunched. "The janitor? What about him?"

"Someone saw you arguing with him."

Shane paused, a dawn of reckoning turning his pursed mouth into an O. "I didn't kill him either, Didi. He saw me making the copies. I threatened to inform the authorities about him. Since his wife is sick, I figured he'd shut up about it."

"What about Olivia?"

Shane grinned. "Yeah, I hoped you'd pick up on her. She's bad news for your boyfriend."

"He's not my boyfriend."

"Whatever he is to you, Didi, his life isn't safe around that one."

"Why?"

"Because she's a world renowned thief. Ruthless, too. If she doesn't get what she wants, people go missing."

I lifted my chin, attempting to appear confident, but my knees wobbled. Mose was missing, chasing after Anice. If Olivia was in on it, then this thing had been in the works for a while. But how was that possible? I'd only just returned from Scotland. From what Mose had said, he'd been dating Olivia for a couple of months.

"I see the wheels turning, Didi, and you're right. Olivia's assignment was to infiltrate the university. Get intel on Dr. Pinnick, see if he had a weakness."

"A bribe?"

Shane grinned.

"She didn't find one, did she?"

He perked up. "Dr. Pinnick was a pillar of ethics and morals, it turns out, much to my disgust. But I could have told them that if they'd have contacted me before a week ago. Instead, Olivia latched onto Mose."

"Before or after they determined Dr. Pinnick wouldn't play?"

"Before. Olivia always works multiple angles. Mose was easy." He snorted. "The way he stared at her... it didn't take a rocket scientist to work out he was interested. After that, she pumped him for all sorts of stuff on you, me, the department. He even gave her a tour of the bone lab. She's rotten to the core, and if I were you, I'd run. Hide. A bullseye is on your back, and if Anice isn't coming for you, then Olivia will. She tapped your phones, your office, even your sister's phones."

I felt the blood drain from my face. Laura? Nick? But if their phones were tapped, how could I warn them?

"Yeah, she'll kill them. My parents are currently on a private jet headed somewhere. Not even they are safe. I've never heard him so angry." He sighed. "I'm also leaving tonight. Oh, and those bones," he tapped his finger against his chin, "they were meant for someone named Boss Man. If he doesn't have them by now, I'd be surprised. You can't win, Didi. Best to cut your losses and run." The fire alarms began to blare and he hurried away. I ran the opposite direction. There was one last thing I had to check.

CHAPTER 44

I slowed to a walk. The red blinking lights and sirens eventually stopped. Ears ringing, I checked the area for anyone, but thankfully I was alone.

DING!

My phone.

DING!

Mystery man J contacted me.

"I've intercepted the package. The bones are safe. Don't worry about Anice. But Didi, Boss Man is in town. Be careful. I'll distract them while you get somewhere safe. Yours, J."

A slight chill seeped into my bones. Drawing my arms about my waist, I sank against the wall. In spite of everything she'd done, Anice wasn't Boss Man. My hunch was right, but this scheme was bigger than I'd imagined.

I pulled out the office keys and hoofed it the two hallways over. When I stuck it in the lock, my heart nearly stopped. The door creaked forward an inch and I squinted into the darkened room. Scant light peeked through the tiny rectangular window, casting eerie shadows about the teeny room. I pushed until the door clanged against the file cabinet. A rumbling chuckle floated in the darkness. A flicker of light hovered over my desk. It illuminated the menacing grin seated in my chair. Flecks of orange and yellow glinted off a gun leveled directly at me.

"Take a seat."

The man waved the gun toward the guest chair left in the office. I slowly approached the chair and sat. Sadly, there wasn't a single object I could use in defense, save for the lamp on the desk. Clenching my purse in my lap, I ran through several escape scenarios, but none turned up with me walking out of here alive.

+"Mr. Smith. Are you here to clean up the mess?"

Brian Smith, Christof's law partner and apparent henchman, smirked. "Clever. Shame Christof never appreciated your wild spirit. Though, I suspect his type is more the dumb, adulating blonde. It's of no consequence now, though, is it? You've got spunk, I'll give you that, but he's incapable of rescuing you now. Not that he would."

"I'm no damsel, Mr. Smith."

"Brian, please. I think we've grown past formalities."

"Fine. Brian, why did you murder Landon Fisher?"

He tipped his head, his eyes sparkling with amusement. "When did you figure it out?"

"I didn't. Until now. Shane insisted he wasn't to blame."

"That left only me? Please, Didi, don't be so naïve."

"I'm not. Anice wouldn't reduce herself to actual murder. Not like this. She likes others to do her dirty work, unless, of course, someone's screwed up. That keeps the authorities off her."

"Who's Anice?" His eyes sparkled, but the gun never wavered.

"Don't insult my intelligence."

He shook his head. "I never underestimate my foe."

I narrowed my eyes. "Anice Foster"

He shrugged. "Not ringing a bell."

I paused. Was he telling the truth? If he didn't work for Anice, then was it for Boss Man? Worse yet, was *he* Boss Man?

"Why did you kill Landon?"

The old chair creaked under his weight as he leaned back. "Landon was too nosy for his own good. All he had to do was copy the bones and deliver them at the designated time, because Shane lacked the balls to do it. No one was supposed to get hurt." He banged his fist onto the desktop. "I hate it when people don't listen, don't you?"

I fidgeted in the chair, aware of the gun still aimed at me, and wondered at his rising temper. He was a hired hitman who didn't like killing? I'd have suggested a change of career if I stood a chance at living through it.

"Landon was to replicate the bones and give them to you?"

Brian leaned his elbows onto the desktop and bobbed the gun at me for added emphasis. "He couldn't resist. That little busybody wanted more money. Rich kids make the best gophers. They're always trying to prove themselves to their daddies."

"Out of curiosity, how much does something like the bones go for?"

"Are you in the market?" Brian chuckled. "Let's say it pays well and leave it at that."

"Not for Landon. How much more did he want?"

"One million."

I sat back in the chair. "Total?"

Brian shook his head. "On top of the two million we'd agreed on. Still not interested? With your credentials, we could make a fortune, Ms. Day."

I glanced at the gun. "Not with that pointed at me. So you killed Landon because he was greedy."

"No. Landon was killed because he was threatening to tell the authorities."

There it was. From Shane to Landon, alerting the authorities was grounds for a death sentence. What about Freddie?

"Who do you work for, Mr. Smith?"

"Not important. Move." He motioned for me to stand, and I wasn't in any situation to disagree. I slowly rose and stepped toward the side of my desk closest to the trashcan. "Here." He held out a cord of rope. "Tie your feet and make sure it's tight."

I squatted and circled the thick, scratchy rope around my ankles, leaving a smidge of room, hoping he wouldn't notice. If I was to stay alive, I'd have to outwit him. Would the ghosts show up? Better not rely on them too much.

"What about the janitor? Did you kill him too?"

Brian lowered the gun by his side and exhaled noisily. "That was unfortunate. He found me rummaging through your office. I was holding your knife when he traipsed in. He had a look of someone who would talk. I couldn't have that."

"He had a family. Two kids. His wife is sick."

"Again... it was unfortunate."

"What about the bomb?"

He threw his head back, exposing his white teeth. "That was genius. If Mose had only dropped off the bag, then that trashcan would still be alive today. Don't tell me you care about inanimate objects, Ms. Day?"

The trashcan? What about Christof's office party? And Shane's quarrel with Brian in the law offices after the bomb? Things weren't lining up. Was he telling the truth? Did he not know Anice?

"What about Shane? Are you after him too? Is he next to die?"

He checked my handiwork around my ankles and stood. I examined the scant objects on the desk big enough or hard enough to overtake a man the size of Brian. He was a good foot taller than me, and also, he had a gun.

"Why would I kill Shane? He's on a flight headed for the Caymans right about now."

"But... I don't understand. You argued. At the office. After the explosion?"

"Oh that. He messed with the wrong person. Pitting two sides against each other. Not a good look. He's more valuable alive than dead, so he's high in the sky flying to safety. Now hold out your hands."

Blood pumped wildly in my veins. It was now or never. I lurched forward and grabbed for the sturdy lamp. It tipped. Brian lunged forward. At the last second, I wrapped my fingers around the base and struck upwards. His head flipped back with a thunderous crack. Body rigid, his eyes rolled into his head and he crumpled to the floor. I wriggled out of the ankle restraints. Pausing only long enough to find a strong pulse, I stepped over the growing pool of crimson. The lamp had left a jagged cut on his chin. I picked up the gun and took off. Each hallway loomed larger as I slid on tiled floors, rounded corners, and each ragged breath burned my lungs. My legs ached, but I pushed harder until the last corner came within steps. I leapt for joy when the doors came into sight. Only a few more feet. I reached for the handle when a light flicked on down a side hallway.

Skidding to a halt, I pointed the gun at it. Hands trembling, I squinted down the hallway. Mose's office? I tiptoed over. I got closer, muttering "please please please" until I finally made the agonizing distance to his office door. Gripping the gun, I nudged the door open.

"Oh God."

"Well, hello there," came the velvety smooth voice. "Did you miss me?"

CHAPTER 45

"Where's Mose?" The gun bobbed as I gripped it double handed and aimed chest high. Anice was rummaging through his desk drawers, unbothered by my presence.

"Mosewan Aten." She smirked. "A god he is not. Though he's Egyptian, right? A shame. How will his *ba* find him without the sarcophagus and mummification process? Doesn't he, or rather his *ba*, have to reunite with his corpse to navigate the afterlife? No burial chamber, no hieroglyphs to help him to the afterlife for rebirth." She sighed. "Such a shame. Akhenaten, no… scratch that. Osiris will be disappointed."

Her knowledge of Egyptian afterlife, while notable, made my blood boil.

I held the gun with one hand and plucked out the cell phone I'd hastily stashed in my bra.

"Dialing a friend? Trust me, he won't answer." She perched on the corner of the desk, legs crossed, her face shrouded in a murderous glow. "Tell me, were you two a thing? It's fine. I see the attraction. Trust me, if he hadn't tried choking the life out of me I'd have kept him around." She tugged at her collar. Dark blue and purple finger marks dotted her creamy white neck. "I like a good tussle, but he tried to kill me." Anice hopped off the desk, knocking over a picture frame. She picked it up, traced a finger down the image and grinned. She placed the frame on the desk and stared at me. "You didn't care for him like that, did you? From outward appearances, he loved you." She shook her manicured nail at me. "But you liked the adulation, am I right? I completely understand. I myself have to beat them off with a stick. Although, this time it was more of a tire iron. But I digress."

I inched into the dimly lit room, the moon's illumination providing the only light. Anice made no move when I crept toward the desk. Keeping it between us, I glanced at my phone and hit the emergency number. We stood in silence as the phone rang three times.

"911. What's your emergency?"

"Yes," I cleared my throat. "There's been a break-in at Massachusetts College in the anthropology building. I've neutralized the intruder. Send an ambulance."

I clicked off the phone and stuffed it back into my bra.

Anice grinned, holding her hands loosely behind her back. "Confident. Good. But you lose. Tell Mose hello for me, won't you?"

"Two things." I gripped the gun harder. I squinted into the darkness but saw no weapon, however, that didn't mean something wasn't tucked into her waistline or back pocket. "First, is Olivia yours?"

Her booming laugh bounced off the walls. "Of course."

Anice sauntered to the office chair meant for students, turned it toward me, and sat. She leaned forward, placing her elbows on her thighs, and rested her chin on her clasped hands. I noticed a snaked serpent tattooed on her inside wrist. Like Olivia's, it was of a serpent eating its tail, but that's where the similarities stopped. Anice didn't have any blue flowers around hers, nor did she have a dagger in the heart of the design like her henchman.

"How did you plant the bomb?" I asked. "In the law office."

Anice lifted her chin. "It's easy when people stumble over themselves to serve me. Money talks, and what better place than a law office?"

"But they uphold the law," I retorted.

. . .

ANICE LEANED INTO THE CHAIR, pumping her crossed leg up and down like a metronome. "You baffle me, Daisy. Anyone is corruptible. Find their price tag or pressure point and it's that easy."

"Who?" It came out so softly I wondered if she'd heard me.

"I'M NOT USUALLY A GIVING person, especially to someone who's been a thorn in my side since day one, but for you, Daisy, I'll make an exception. It's been right under your nose the whole time, and you failed to see it. I'm disappointed. You're such an intelligent woman. One who has been on top of every clue. Yet everybody has a weakness."

My finger twitched over the trigger as she stared triumphantly up at me.

"Come on, Didi. Think. What's your weakness?"

I ran through all the faces, all my friends, family, and colleagues, struggling to process her implication. People were my weakness. Anyone with half a brain would know that. Then Shane's words echoed from earlier.

"Not playing? Okay, I'll spell it out for you." She stood and circled around me, stepping for the door, her palms held up in mock surrender. I kept the gun aimed at her, hearing faint sirens in the background. The police. I licked my dry lips.

She held up her index finger. "He's about six feet tall, blond, a seasoned lawyer..." She kept raising fingers with each clue. "Oh, and someone desperate for success. All it took was convincing him that if he did this one thing, he'd be guaranteed that partnership."

"No," I croaked. It couldn't be.

Anice's steadfast grin drove home the point. "Denial is a slippery slope, Didi."

"You lie," I barked, shaking my head. But the reality of what she'd said was like a torpedo to the heart.

Nope. He couldn't have. He wouldn't have.

"Didi, he's your weakness. Face it."

She was perched on the threshold, inches from fleeing.

"Stop or I'll shoot." The words sounded hollow and far off.

Anice cocked her head. "No, I think not. You're not a killer, Didi. It's not in your DNA. Plus, you need answers, but alas, I must be off. Plane to catch, and I can't have these pesky cops getting in my way. Oh," she stopped and flicked her hair, "thanks for the bones, by the way. There's fifty million riding on them. Although there was a minor hitch, but we sorted him out. It's crazy how many people want their hands on these old things. Then again, it's not every day that the bones of a Viking king are unearthed."

I lowered the gun but kept my finger over the trigger. "This isn't over."

"It is for now. Tell Christof hello for me, will you?" She blew me a kiss. Then, in one fluid movement, a flash of orange blinded me. I stumbled back, crashing into the desk. A deafening bang roared from the barrel of the gun. Her gun. A searing heat burned my wrist. I dropped my firearm and dove behind the desk, landing like a sack of potatoes. I sucked in air and pressed my eyes shut, cradling my bleeding wrist against my abdomen. Three, four, five more bangs, and I scooted on my bottom underneath the desk in the semi-safety of the 1940s industrial gray desk. Back pressed against the cool steel drawers, I bit down on my lip and stifled a yelp.

"Bitch!" Anice roared. "You're mine."

Pop, pop, pop!

The tinny roar of bullets hitting steel sent shockwaves down my spine. Round indentations two inches from my head appeared where bullets lodged. The air grew thick and hot. My body convulsed with each pop. Teeth chattering and jaw aching to the breaking point, I tucked my knees under my chin and cupped my trembling hands over my ears.

"No one to save you now." Anice's throaty laugh turned the room upside down. I panted, gasping for air, and watched her feet move slowly around the sides of the desk.

Bam!

Stars flitted within my vision. I blinked rapidly, gaping down at the dark stain growing on my abdomen. I swiped at it, biting off a moan, and stared at my blood-soaked fingertips. The glint of steel caught my eye. My gun! A ray of moonlight glinted off the muzzle. In the sliver of space beneath the desk, there was enough room for me to slip a hand under and maybe reach it.

"Found you!"

The smoking barrel pointed down at me.

I coughed, spitting out blood, and reached behind me, fingers extended, searching in vain.

"A pity. Why won't you play along? We could've been rich, you and me. Now, sadly, it'll be just me." Anice pulled a silencer out of her pant pocket and screwed it on.

I thrust my hand further under the metal drawers toward Brian's gun, fingertips fumbling for the handle.

BLIP. I jerked. Another stab of pain and a crimson stain, on my right thigh. Eyelids heavy, my fingertips closed around the cool steel.

"Not so fast, girlie. Stay awake. I'm not done with you yet."

She dug her boot into my thigh. I screeched, temporarily breathless. My vision turned spotty until there were only wisps of light. I laid my heavy head against the metal desk as she let up on my thigh.

The sweet relief inflated my lungs. My chest heaved. The stars floating within my vision cleared. I stared into her cold, dead eyes and... laughed.

"What's so funny?" she jeered.

"You're not the only one after those bones." My numb limbs felt like lead. The frozen tendrils of death seeped in where no pain penetrated. I wiped blood spatter off my mouth with the back of my hand. "Boss Man... has sent... someone else to... clean up your mess, Anice," I gasped, each word a 100-pound weight. "It's only a matter... of time before... they catch up with you."

"That's ridiculous." However, the panic on her face said otherwise.

"Is it?" I squeezed my lids closed, praying to stay conscious for a moment more. "Brian Smith ring a bell?"

I opened my eyes to see Anice's face blanch.

"I see... you're familiar. He's been here... already," I wheezed. "Seems Shane's working for him... now. I doubt... you'll find him."

"Who told you about Boss Man?" She leveled the gun at my other thigh, but I merely grinned. Death was close and what was another bullet? I couldn't even feel my legs anymore.

"It's not hard. But... it appears... he doesn't like messes. Brian's... his backup, isn't he? Not what... you planned, huh?"

Coughs wracked my body as Anice paced in the tiny space behind the desk, unscrewing and re-screwing the silencer.

"No," she shook her head. "No, this can't be. He can't be here. The Order—"

"Who's... Boss Man, Anice?"

She curled her lips back. "It's time to shut you up for good."

The orange flashed and ripping pain set my torso ablaze. I sank sideways, my head falling against the inner part of the desk. The pungent smell of exploded gunpowder floated in the air. I groped for oxygen. Lungs spasming, pulse racing, I frantically fumbled for the gun one last time. That was when I saw her. Like out of the mist, she appeared behind Anice, a wispy form turned solid. Her thick blonde braid hung over her colorful tunic. The gleaming blade was poised in her hand, ready to strike.

I gawked.

"Datter, rest. I handle this now." It was a whisper. A faint thread of words, but the meaning hit home.

I lolled my head back, fighting my leaden lids to stay open, squinting into the dim light.

Anice's face had turned white. She shrank against the wall behind my desk, right under the only window in the room, cowering. "No... you don't exist. You can't exist. Ghosts aren't real."

I fell sideways and propped on an elbow to witness the impossible. Anice pointed the gun and fired, but the whirling bullet lodged into the dusty cinderblock walls, leaving only a puff of dust in its wake.

"Hu-ul-da?" I stammered, struggling against the weight of my eyelids.

The fiercest blue eyes bore into mine as Anice opened fire again.

Hulda stood steadily, never flinching. Feet hip width apart, she studied Anice much like a cat would a mouse right before they struck. Hulda tilted her head, a hint of a smile on her lips, and stared down at me halfway underneath the desk. "Rest now, datter. Rest... you are safe."

My heavy lids drooped, leaving me with the fragments of Hulda's shape burned into memory as I sunk to the floor in defeat. Cold tendrils of darkness pulled me toward unconsciousness. As the icy oblivion overtook me, I heard a piercing howl, followed by a dull thud. Then there was only blackness.

CHAPTER 46

*A*s I wavered between consciousness and a dark abyss, multiple conversations went on around me.

Detective Soo hadn't changed demeanor since the first time we met. His brusque voice at one time blurted, "She's lucky. Where's the other woman? Have we called for a psych eval?"

The other thing that left an impression were the squeaks and stomps of multiple boots on the floor, which must have been the cops. At one point I was light as air, and then a salty smell filled my nostrils.

My eyelids fluttered open and bright light stung my eyes. I weakly held up a hand to block it. "Where am I?" I croaked.

A hand patted my arm and I winced.

There was a consistent beep every second or so, and my arm throbbed. Eventually adjusting to the light, I stared down at my arm and noticed a blood pressure cuff inflating. From the IV bags hanging overhead, the lines going into both arms, I'd say I hadn't died.

"You're in an ambulance." The squatty woman smiled from overhead. She pushed her glasses up on her crooked nose. "We're on our way to the hospital. Thought we lost you there for a minute. I'm Darlene, by the way."

A faint ringing had me flailing my arms around, patting down my bra.

Darlene huffed. "Lady, please don't make me use the restraints."

"The phone." I pointed at my chest.

Darlene peeked under the thin white sheet covering me and retrieved the buzzing phone. Miraculously, it hadn't broken in the confrontation. "I can't let you answer this."

I reached for the phone and recoiled in pain. Bullets hurt worse than I could have imagined. And I'd imagined the worst. "Please? My friend's in danger."

Darlene begrudgingly handed it over. "If anyone asks, I didn't give it to you."

I nodded gratefully. It was an unknown number. My heart thumped wildly.

"Hello?" I whispered.

"Didi? Are you okay?"

Tears welled up and brimmed over my lashes. "Mose? Mosewan? You're safe? Oh my..." I choked up and was met with another of Darlene's reproachful gazes. She strapped on an oxygen mask, saying something about my oxygen levels.

I didn't bother refusing. From her developed biceps, I'd say she could curl sixty pounds minimum, which meant I didn't stand a chance. I had to pick my battles, and this one wasn't it.

"Yes, I'm alright."

I pulled up the mask to speak. "But the blood...They said there was... Oh, Mose." The awful scene played out in my mind. Mose strangling Anice and her pummeling him with a tire iron. I'd always had a vivid imagination.

"Hey, I'm okay. I promise. When I chased Anice, she shot a dog. Poor thing. I didn't have any time to think. I just ran after her."

I wanted to dance for joy, but every part of me hurt. "Mose, I'm so sorry. We need to talk. I've figured it out. Well, I've figured out part of it, and—"

"Didi," he interrupted. *"I-I need some space."*

"What?" I tried sitting up on my elbow and flinched. "I don't understand."

"*Olivia—*"

"Mose, she's a thief. Stay away from her."

"*A thief? She's after the bones?*"

"She works for Anice."

Mose grunted. "*Great. That settles it then.*"

"Settles what?"

Mose sighed. "*I'm leaving.*"

"Good. Go to the hotel, and we'll regroup later."

"*No, Didi. I'm leaving town. I can't do this right now. I need some space.*"

I held the phone away from my ear, staring at it for a second. "O-okay," I stuttered. "Where will you go?"

"*I don't know. I'll call when I get back. Take care, Didi.*"

The phone went dead. I handed the cell over to Darlene's outstretched palm and replaced the oxygen mask.

"Take some deep breaths and let's get that blood pressure down. We're almost at the hospital. Can I call someone for you?"

I was too absorbed in Mosewan's tortured words. He was leaving. I'd lost, regained, and lost him again. It was too much. As the hospital's golden lights came into view through the ambulance window, I let grief overtake me.

CHAPTER 47

The bullet wounds, remarkably, hadn't hit any major arteries. While I was full of holes and pumped with antibiotics and pain meds, I was in pretty good shape. The staff were friendly, and they even delivered notes to Callum for me once I found out he was recuperating in the same hospital. I itched to leave, to flee from the incessant wound cleaning, temperature checks, and Laura's watchful eyes. At the very least, I wanted to return to the hotel where Mose and I were staying, but the hospital staff were under strict orders to keep me in bed. The doctor was a real stickler for protocol. I should know. It was my sister.

"Don't ever scare me like that again." Laura swatted my thigh.

"Ow," I groaned.

She planted her hands on her tiny hips, a sign she hadn't eaten in weeks. How had I failed to notice? She'd always carried around a few extra pounds since Nick had been born, even with her crazy work schedule. "Don't chase after psychopathic killers."

She had a point, and even with all her fussiness, it felt good to be looked after.

"I agree." Detective Soo's stern voice floated in from the doorway. He held up his badge before Laura's hot reply left her mouth.

I sat up a little higher in bed with her help.

He hauled out his pocket notepad and tapped the sharpened pencil tip on it. "Ms. Day, care to explain why there is a trail of bodies wherever you go?"

"It's a long story."

"I've got time. Let's start with the teacher's assistant." He thumbed through a few pages of notes. "Landon Fisher."

Landon, Freddie, Brian Smith, Shane Bernard, and Anice Foster. I relayed the past days' events leading up to the deaths, capture, and departures.

"Okay." He tapped the pencil on his notebook. "But there's no report of this Anice Foster."

"What do you mean?"

"She doesn't exist."

I clutched the linen sheet to my chest and felt the blood rushing to my palms. "Callum." I bobbed my head. "Ask Callum Mortimer. He's in room—"

"Mr. Mortimer has already been interviewed, and I told him the same thing. No one by that name exists in Scotland, the US, or anywhere else in the world. Your lady is a ghost."

I rubbed the goosebumps that had popped up along my arms. "It's an alias," I mumbled, staring at the bundle of vases filled with colorful flowers on every available counter surface. I settled on a vibrant blue flower crowded by dozens of rose vases on either side. The blue stood in stark contrast, and with its spindly petals, its petite elegance drew my attention.

"This black market dealing has been going on for ages, and those attached to it rarely use their real names."

"But you can still find her?" Laura rubbed my back in smooth circular motions. A mom first and a surgeon second.

Detective Soo inhaled slowly, like he was pondering what to say. "It's possible." He regarded Laura with interest.

A blush warmed her cheeks as he lingered a little too long.

"But don't get your hopes up. They have endless supplies of money and reach."

I snorted. "Like the police force."

Detective Soo inclined his head. "Meaning?"

"She admitted having people all over the world, including police." I reconsidered the blue flowers again, taking a special interest in the dainty petals. There was something peculiar about them, but for the life of me, I couldn't place it.

"Consider yourself lucky, Ms. Day. A few minutes longer and..." He glanced at Laura. "Will she be staying here for a while?"

"For the next few days."

"Alright. We'll need her to visit the station and sign her witness statement when she's released."

The detective stepped to the door and turned, his hard-soled shoes squeaking against the bland tiled floor. "Good job, Dr. Day. But leave the detective work up to the professionals next time."

When the door clicked shut, I glanced at Laura. The pink hue lingered on her otherwise drawn complexion, and there was a lightness to her, a bounce in her step that I hadn't seen for a long time.

"What?" she asked, emptying the dirty water out of a few vases and refilling them.

"You tell me. Flirt much?"

Laura stepped over to the bed and fussed over the blankets, tucking them under my chin.

"Laura, I can't breathe." I resembled a rolled-up sausage inside a bundle of sheets.

"Sorry." She loosened the sheet corners and flitted about the room, on to her next task of rearranging medical supplies for my dressings.

"Laura? What's going on?"

She walked over to the windows and, with a quick flick, opened the blinds. Golden sunlight streamed in and highlighted the dark brown circles she'd had ever since she entered med school.

I waited patiently until she flopped into a chair close to the bed. She picked at a fingernail and mumbled, "My marriage is over."

Several responses that came to mind; I kept silent.

"He's moving out. Nick found out this morning." She twisted her wedding ring over and over on her gaunt finger. "He wasn't surprised. I guess it's only me. I'm always the last to notice."

I laid my hand over hers and gently squeezed. "I'm sorry, Laura."

Her lower lip quivered. "She sniffed, withdrew her hand, and slapped her palms on her thighs, standing. "It is what it is." She took both of my hands between hers. "He's right."

"Who?" I glanced around the room, confused.

She puffed out her cheeks and exhaled. "Detective Soo." She was irritated, but not at me. Her life had turned upside down, and this was her usual way of handling things. Avoidance. She dove into me, Nick, or work.

"Ah, yes. The detective." I grinned impishly. "It's not like I asked for any of this. Kimberly Foster hired me, remember?"

"Yeah. See where that got her? Six feet under."

From what the doctors had told me, Detective Soo was dead on. If the bullet had been centimeters to the right in my leg, I'd have bled out.

Instead, I was alive with four bullet wounds, one in each thigh, one shoulder, and my abdomen. One had only grazed my wrist.

"If you don't listen to him, I'll do much worse." She wrinkled her nose at me.

"I'm an adult, Laura."

"Really? Act like one." Her voice wavered and then her hands fluttered up to her face, covering a sob as she raced to the sink.

"Oh, Laura... Sis, I'm so sorry. I'm okay. Please don't cry. I'll be fine."

Drat these wounds! I was on bed rest for the time being, and no telling how long it would take to heal.

Laura hiccupped. "You almost died. I can't..." She whisked a tissue out of the box on the wall and dabbed at her nose. "I can't lose you too."

She turned and leaned against the Formica cabinet, facing me.

"You won't. Come here." I opened my arms wide with some effort. She stepped over and hugged me.

"See? I'm here. Look on the bright side. You have me under lock and key for another day or two. Pick my meals if it makes you feel better. Plus, we'll go to lunch every Saturday and have movie nights again. You've said yourself that you've missed those nights. Tell Nick. The more the merrier."

Laura dabbed at her eyes. "And the baby?"

"Oh, I thought we'd strap her to her crib."

At first, Laura gaped at me, then she burst out in laughter.

"Bring her, silly," I said. "She's family. I'll walk around with her, feed her—"

"Change her diapers?" Laura asked, a gleam back in her eyes.

"Yes, dear sister, I'll change her chubby backside."

Laura sat on the chair beside the bed again. "That sounds perfect. But there's one more thing."

"Yes?"

"How did you figure all of this out?" Laura ignored the third intercom call for her.

"Aren't you needed somewhere?" I motioned to the speaker in the ceiling.

She waved her hand. "That'll keep. This I've got to hear."

"Ah, alright." I raced through all the events, and then it was time to string everything together.

"How did you connect the clues?" Laura asked.

"First, there's Landon Fisher. He ingratiated himself to Mose—"

"Which seemed fishy."

"Yeah, it stunk alright. Dr. Gates's new TA told me he wasn't well liked. Plus, he'd only gotten Mose at the last minute. That alone raised a red flag. This was right before Robert, Dr. Gates's friend and colleague, was attacked."

"I was on call. Horrible injuries. The poor man suffered."

Laura shivered, warding off the terrible memories. Honestly, I didn't know how she kept doing this stuff day in and day out. The constant gunshot victims, stabbings, car crashes… I cringed just thinking about it.

"That was Anice. She'd caught wind of the bones Mose had received, but she confronted Roger because he examined them first."

"I bet Mosewan feels awful about it."

She had no idea. Mose took on guilt from the lunch lady if some jerk poked fun. He's a gentle soul.

"When Anice failed to get the bones there—"

"She went to Plan B," Laura interrupted.

"Enter Landon Fisher. He wasn't a bad guy really. Money lured him in. His job was to copy the bones, send the real ones to Anice, and he'd receive all sorts of money."

Laura frowned. "Good people don't steal ancient bones for money. Those bones walked and talked at one point, and it doesn't matter if it was over a thousand years ago. That's wrong."

She *would* see it from a personal viewpoint. Plus, she's right. Ragnar once talked and walked about this Earth like everyone else.

"The joke's on Anice. Those bones were replicated not once, not twice, but three times."

Laura's jaw dropped open.

"Landon duplicated them the first time under Anice's orders and she paid him handsomely. Then along comes Brian—"

"Who's Brian?"

"He works for Boss Man."

"Isn't Anice Boss Man?"

"That's what I thought, but apparently not. They both work for whoever Boss Man is. Brian's the cleaner. He denied knowing her, but when I mentioned his name to her..." I snickered.

"So who else reproduced the bones?"

"Shane."

Laura gasped. "That little twerp."

"He was also working for Anice, but I heard him arguing with Brian after the explosion at Christof's law office. At first, I assumed they were all in on it together. It was only when Shane denied killing anyone that I started piecing everything together. Brian kept out of sight from Anice, but he'd never let Shane in on why he'd arrived. He's got Shane on a plane right now to somewhere safe. Apparently Boss Man isn't done with him. Why would he be? Shane's got resources and clout in his parents' reputations. He's gotten himself in over his head this time. Poor Shane."

Laura scoffed. "Why? He tried to ruin your career and he almost got you killed. Multiple times."

I sighed. "His parents never paid attention to him. As you've always said, kids learn from their parents."

"Meaning?"

"Look at the fountain outside the anthropology building. Who paid for it?"

Laura grunted. "Shane's parents."

"Yep, and that's not all. He learned to bribe, steal, and cheat to reach the top. Except this time he went too far."

"That doesn't give him a get-out-of-jail-free card. He's a grown man, Didi." She stuffed her hands inside her white coat pockets.

"He'll answer to the authorities. He can run all over the globe, but one day he'll slip up, get tired, or—"

"Get killed. Like the others." Laura's voiced lowered. "Anyone else copy the bones?"

I gulped. "Mose and I did. But it was to lure Anice out of hiding."

Laura slid her palm down her face and inhaled.

"No one got hurt," I hurried on. "She blew up the trashcan before Mose could plant them. That's not the point. Landon had gotten greedy. When Brian showed up on the scene, Landon put two and two together and decided he'd up the ante."

"Ah," Laura tilted her head back. "Greed has killed many a man."

"In his case, yes. Still, there's something odd about Landon's death. I don't think Brian did it."

"Who else would have done it?"

I eyeballed the flowers. "Laura, please bring those blue flowers over here."

When she handed the vase to me, I fingered the flower petals. Where had I seen these before? I searched for a card, but there wasn't one. "Who sent them?"

Laura shook her head. "The others are from Christoff."

I ignored her downturned lips and asked for my phone. Within minutes, I found the trusty flower app I used whenever I was traveling or away on a dig site. It's remarkable what ancient people used flowers for. Medicinal, ceremonial, and simply as adornments. But flowers were also a status symbol.

"WHY THE FROWN?" asked Laura, huddling around my phone. She squinted her pretty hazel eyes at the screen. "The blue lotus? Pretty. Shame there isn't a card. There's no one to thank."

I smacked my palm against my forehead. "Good grief. Of course!" I sat up straighter and asked Laura for a pen and paper.

"What? What did you discover?"

I scribbled vigorously while Laura looked on, perplexed.

"The tattoos." I let out a low whistle. "How could I have been so blind?"

"You've lost me."

I pointed at the image I'd sketched. "What do you see?"

"They all have a snake either curled up or squiggly like, but all of them have different colored flowers."

"Exactly." I tapped the snake entwined with a green vine. "Poison ivy." Then I moved on to the snake coiled up in a bed of red petals. "Poppies." I circled the last tattoo. It was of a snake eating its own tail and surrounded by purple flowers. "These we looked up. They're blue lotus flowers."

"Okay, but it's still not helping. What's their significance?"

I jabbed the first tattoo again. "This was on the man chasing Mose and me through Boston. We escaped at the club. He had this on his forearm. The next tattoo I saw on Brian Smith. He's a cleaner for Boss Man. Then there's this one..." I stared at the last one. "This one was on Olivia."

"Who?"

"Olivia. She's Mosewan's girlfriend, except she's not. Shane said she's an international thief, and ruthless to boot. I saw this flower on her wrist. It's the spitting image of them. What's more? There was one purple flower that matched these in Mosewan's office scattered among some papers beside Landon Fisher's corpse."

Laura's eyes widened. "I thought you said Brian confessed to the murders."

I shook my head. "Not exactly. I assumed he had and questioned him about it, but thinking about it now, he never admitted his guilt. I also believed Roger's clue, the 'S,' meant either Shane or Brian Smith, but it wasn't that at all. It was a symbol. A serpent."

"Why would Brian Smith take the blame for something he didn't do?"

Why indeed? There was only one real reason. "Olivia is Boss Man. Or close to him."

Laura clucked her tongue. "As much as I dislike Shane, he told you about her."

I nodded absentmindedly. "Anice hired her to infiltrate the university. She's been spying on all of us. Me, Shane, Dr. Gates, everyone at the university, including you."

"What?" Laura snapped.

I gulped. The plan was to tell her when she was more rested, more able to handle the invasion of her home and privacy. I'd already alerted Nick, and he'd debugged the place in about an hour. Plus, he'd picked up the phones I paid for. But in ordinary fashion, it flew out without me thinking, so engrossed in solving the case. "She's bugged your phones. She's left though. After Anice's arrest, she'll be long gone."

Laura pinched the bridge of her nose. "Good. But I'm still getting another phone. For Nick too, and I'll pay a tech expert to debug our house."

"Uh, Nick's already done it. He's picked up the new phones I bought for you both. He's great with stuff like that, you know."

Laura held up her palms, closing her eyes. "Don't. I can only take so much at one time. He's been at me since you returned from Scotland about double majoring in cybercrimes and archaeology."

"He's so good at it, Laura. Just hear him—"

"Another time," she cut in. "I promise I'll listen, just not today. Promise me you'll tell Detective Soo about all this."

"Promise." No matter what Detective Soo said, I knew in my heart of hearts that Olivia and Anice were whispers in the wind. They were too cunning to have stayed behind or stay arrested for long. Round three would come. But not today. With that, I'd take some solace.

Laura bent over and gently kissed my brow, patting my hand. "What about Mose? Where's he? How did he take the news about Olivia?"

I felt the prickle of teardrops threatening to spill over. "Uh, he's... gone. No," I raised a hand, warding off her speech. She'd always preferred him to Christof. "He's safe. He needs time to reflect."

"I should think so." Laura cocked her head. "How are you two getting along?"

"Fine." I set the flowers on the bedside table and took the pen, ignoring her piercing stare.

"I'm supposed to believe that?"

"I'm sad he's gone, but we're just friends."

Laura rubbed my feet, moving briskly toward the door after yet another overhead request for her. "You need rest, and I must get to work. I'm sorry to say that Anice has left the country. Detective Soo told me while you were resting. We didn't want to bother you with it, but since you've figured it out..."

I nodded. "A cop outside the door keeps peeking in from time to time. Although, if Anice or Brian wanted me dead, I doubt a local cop would deter them."

Laura shuddered. "Let me keep believing in the sanctity of our police force. Otherwise, I won't sleep. Oh, and one other thing." Her rubber-soled shoes squeaked as she turned at the door. "The DNA results came back. I sent you an email about them. Look at the results. With all your spare time, I believe you'll find them interesting."

Laura opened the door and stepped out, turning back one last time. "We've got quite a lineage from the British Isles. Ireland, Scotland, even Wales. But there's also the Scandinavian line."

My eyelid twitched. "Scandinavia?"

"Yep, we're Vikings." She grinned. "Some small town. Uh, let me think. Oh, it was along the Oslofjord. Shocking, yes, but it's our lineage. Mom and Dad always said it's important to know where we come from."

My throat tightened. "Oslofjord?"

"Yeah, somewhere called Kaupang. Got to run."

Laura breezed out, leaving me searching for my cell. It was on the rolling lunch tray that stood a few centimeters too far. I leaned over, reaching against the stabbing pains shooting through my body. Wiggling my fingers, at long last grasping the blasted tray, I pulled it over, and with shaky hands, I brought up my emails. One by one, the DNA data scrolled by. Page after page of hereditary information, both from my father and mother, popped on screen. While the British Isles information was fascinating, I couldn't take my eyes off the portion that was Northern Europe.

How was this even possible? Eighty percent? That couldn't be.

Over and over again, I studied the numbers. On the global map, Denmark and Southern Norway were lit up like the Fourth of July.

I set down my phone and clutched my hands under my chin, rocking slightly forward and backward. A movement by the foot of the bed caught my eye. Fleeting white, wispy masses danced about. The chilled air swirled with heat, flushing my cheeks and arms. I stared at a glittering solid mass. It was like a billion shining stars condensing into one. A rush of wind whipped my hair about. Scents of cardamom, damp earth, and cool mountain air smacked me full on. I inhaled deeply, transfixed by the second head, and torso that appeared, standing beside the first. A thready strand of white curled its way over to me. Like a hammer splitting me in two, it hit me dead center in the chest. My head jerked back and I grabbed at my throat. A sudden jolt thrust my chest backward. Head flung back, arms wide, I stared upward. Streaming rays of vibrant green streaked where the ceiling once stood. In the instant where two stars collided, my limbs twisted, pulled taut. A fire burned through them from head to toe and an ear-piercing scream ripped from my throat. I was consumed by green fire. As soon as it came, it left, and I dropped to the bed, a wet heap of bones, muscles, and not much else.

"What the...?" I twitched my fingers and toes. No pain? Slowly, I raised myself onto my elbows and craned my head toward the foot of the bed. There, hand in hand, stood Hulda and the other Viking I saw in my apartment only a couple of days ago.

Hulda spoke in a thick Norse accent. "Find him, datter. Bring him home. Bring Ragnar home."

Their appearances shimmered until they faded into nothingness, leaving only the medical cabinets and sink in view.

"Datter?" My voice wavered. "You're my... you're my..." I couldn't continue. Reality had sunk in. There was no doubting it. Hulda was my ancestor. I was her great, great, great, great...

I sucked in an unsteady breath. "That means... No. It can't be."

I rocked in the bed, arms wrapped around my legs, which were tucked under my chin.

They had but one request. Bring Ragnar Lothbrok's bones home. I cupped a hand over my mouth and wept.

They'd both protected me. Of that, I was certain. They'd also healed me. Now, with killers on my tail, it was my turn to help them. But where to start? Who had the bones? My suspicion was that Anice would have stashed them somewhere. However, first things first.

I pushed the nurse button and got dressed. Pulling out my burner phone, I texted the one person who could help.

The white-haired woman with keen eyes sized me up. She'd listened to my pleas and only once I'd agreed to take it easy did she discharge me against her better judgement. I don't know if the bribe worked or not, but soon I was hopping into an Uber.

Ding!

After reading the text, I grinned.

"It would be my pleasure. When you get to the hotel, pack a bag. We're headed somewhere cold. I'll be the one with the Boston Red Sox cap on. See you soon, J."

I would not fail them. I'd retrieve Ragnar's bones and return them with their child or die trying. With Callum bedridden and Mose off to who knew where, Mystery Man J was my only hope.

I tucked my phone back in my jeans pocket and relaxed into the seat as we crept along the jammed city roads. I ogled the pedestrians lost in their ordinary lives on the busy sidewalks. A chubby toddler, bouncing on her mama's hip, bit a chunk of her mother's warm pretzel, but the mother was too busy chatting on her phone to notice. A loud-mouthed vendor selling hot dogs to baseball loving tourists was clad in Yankees and Red Sox paraphernalia. Street musicians bustled for cash-happy patrons to toss a dollar into their velvet-lined instrument cases. Most people either scurried by or trudged on with their heads down, unconcerned with the world around them. Until recently, I'd been among them. However, the last encounter with Hulda and Ragnar had shaken me. Opened my eyes to the life that wandered about. And their baby, those tiny, fragile bones. My ancestor.

I laid my head on the headrest and shut my eyes. For the first time in ages, I thought of my parents. What else had they kept from me? Did they know about our heritage? Had Hulda presented herself to them? While I'd never know, it didn't matter. We were all linked. Hulda, Ragnar, the baby, my mom, and my dad. We all possessed a sequence of DNA that forever bound us together, and it didn't matter how much time passed between us. We would always need each other. So, I remembered them. From my dad's musky cologne to my mother's sweet smile, I drank them in. We were family, and we'd never left each other. Not really. Family always sticks together. No matter what, I'd find Ragnar's bones come Hell or high water. I would not fail them. Never again.

To be continued...

Subscribe to author newsletter here! *Wait for the pop-up to sign-up.*

Don't forget other books by the author here!